INNER C

GARRET SCENARIO No.2

Inked in New Orleans By

BRIGHTDAWN

The Scenarist in The French Market

With Love,
BrightDawn

MADE IN THE ENCLAVE

W A R N I N G

Under no circumstances after recovering from this story should the word *MAYBE* be used to conquer your sex life or workplace. The Scenarist does not endorse the use of Molecular Sacraments, VIP lap dances, haunting brothels, or multidimensional sex. Any and all places, substances, activities and people in *THE MAYBE* are elements that nearly controlled the Scenarist during this Scenario and should not be sought out all at once, as he did, without notifying friends and loved ones that you'll never be the same again; emotional disorders result. Side effects include but are not limited to: tattoos resulting from lucid dreams, misreading clairvoyance, open relationships, broken relationships and breaking the bank. Neurotransmitter serotonin, neuropeptide endorphins, and adrenaline give mix messages and may cause a disruption to interdisciplinary fields creating outrageous mental images while reading. Sometimes eviction notices, institutionalization, and procreation may occur. Certain images and their resulting emotions can be transformative, others trigger mania and cause serotonin depletion. Dizziness may occur when accompanied by wine at book clubs.

SPOLTLIGHTING

The Luscious
BELLA LENIN SPARKS

The Head-Case
BRAZE SCANLAN

The Scenarist
BRIGHTDAWN

And
The Prick-Head
MES

Cover Shot
TODD TAYLOR

"My business is to paint what I see,
Not what I know is there."
J.M.W. Turner

GARRET SCENARIO No.2

This building was a Dance Hall and Bordello on the once notorious Gallatin Street circa 1850. Yet more recently while writing this story I occupied the Loft with the Love of my life Bella Lenin Sparks. Where just beneath that roof, my mind, and the life we were building together disintegrated while living out this Scenario. Though it was a groundbreaking chapter in my life's work, and perhaps worth the final exit of my sanity, it was certainly not worth the demise of us. While chemically researching the depths of the mind my perception of truth consequently fell victim to fantasies. I chased lucid dreams, and let our relationship be eclipsed for the ink I craved on these pages. It appears that finishing this book mattered more to me, than us. I'm grateful for the loving times we shared in the Loft before the darkness surfaced… where moonlight glowed through a lunette, and blessed chemical experiments altered my perception of events! And every now and then just behind those bricks…

…I had multidimensional experiences on molecular sacraments! Now what I'll share with you is fiction, despite how true it feels. I owe it all to my Love, and pray The Family heals. Through it all they stuck together, and managed to move on. While I split in *TWO*, writing more *BRIGHTDAWN*.

Bourbon Street

*"If I paint a wild horse, you might not see the horse…
but surely see the wildness!"*
Picasso

GARRET SCENARIO No.2

Police broke us apart with Mardi Gras war paint on our faces atop the Crescent City Connection Bridge as morning traffic rubbernecked by the scene when she screamed…

"Tell me you love me?"
Just tell me that you love me!"

"I love you."
I said uncertain of everything but that.
"I LOVE YOU LENIN!"
I screamed back while being
handcuffed and led away from her to a
New Orleans Police cruiser.

None of the cops were there to play matchmaker, they were there for me. Most of them probably just thought we were another crazy couple. But at least two of the Cops on the scene where familiar with us. The same two Cops who weeks ago escorted her in the same police cruiser to and from our Loft in the French Quarter. Now, it was my turn to roll in it. When my ass finally hit the patrol car's back seat, I realized that there was a little more in that envelope she handed me on the Bridge than just a letter that Cop was cool enough to let me keep.

Then she started screaming something. I didn't know what. I never saw her like that before. Downright optimistically hysterical! She screamed something on the Bridge that morning that in retrospect, wouldn't have made sense to me even if I got it right. It sounded to me as if she were yelling…

"Uwe-dey-pur! Uwe-dey-pur!"
She cried with joy before nearly begging me,
"Be kind to the mind.
Uwe-dey-pur!"

…or something like that. I initially got the impression it was some kind of new age hippie slang. Whatever it was, it didn't make sense. But I wanted, no-no… needed to figure out what she said! I had to know. Because for all I knew they were the last words that would ever come from her lips to the broken man I'd become; I lost my mind. She had good reason to leave.

By that Ash Wednesday I was too self-abused and confused to decipher anything from her wavelength. Then, it got better when that goddamn overbearing multidimensional presence voiced…

"You should have stolen her back from that Cop
when you had the chance bro."

But I knew better. She was never mine to steal back. She and I didn't think in terms of possessing each other. But him, my lower-self, he got me in these handcuffs! I wouldn't have been there, or here at all if it were not for that side of me. My ass would have been good and gone if that sneak didn't stop my roll. What brought us all here that morning was not the changing seasons of love, but hopelessness.

As the police took me to University Hospital, I turned around to look at her one last time. She looked as hot between flashing police sirens in broad daylight, as those center stage spotlights the night before. She kept venting that same beautiful nonsense through tears and smiles as we cruised away…

"Uwe-day-purr, uwe-day-purr!
Cherish the uwe-day-purr!"

I probably had my mouth open looking back at her mesmerized trying to figure out what she was trying to convey, when my fractured personality on my left side spoke up again…

"I got no clue neither yo.
That hippies out there singing
Zip-a-Deey-do-Dah-dey
for all I know bro."

Or Portuguese for all I knew. I blew him off. I appeared in my worst shape ever because of him. Everything just echoed like techno in my head where dopamine superhighways ran the cerebrospinal fluids dry after months of writers' risk behavior. For those who haven't read me before, my lack of composure can be immensely out of what's thought of as humanly possible.

When she appeared to only pantomime those undecipherable words as she faded in the distance and was eventually out of sight, I turned around and politely murmured softly to the front seats for help clarifying things.

"What-duh-hell she said officers?
Huh? Huh guys?"

But they just ignored me. The one driving called it in…

"Domestic dispute, male, 38,
Scanlan, Braze, in custody, 10-96. Copy?"

I recognized him; I knew that cop for sure. I wasn't crazy, I was broken. Had flying eyeballs nested in my foreheads, but not crazy. I knew that cop driving probably helped break-us-up in the first place. How did a *Love Story* such as ours come to this? There's something in my written words that I live by that brought this on.

"You're so shtoopid yo.
You popped your last brain cell."

My fractured-self had some nerve! Like he's never screwed-up some science? He looked towards the Cops in front seat and had the gall to continue…

"He's just shtoopid."
Then looked back at me and yelled…
"What were you doing on
that bridge!"

Before turning back to the officers again and oh-so calmly continuing with a sympathetic…

"Braze knows he's shtoopid.
And that almost makes him… "

"Shut up!
Just go-away. GO-WAY!"

When your lower-self holds your higher-self accountable, you're in real trouble. I gave up…

"Please go away.
Just let me be. Please *MES*?
Just go back inside with
BRIGHTDAWN."

The cop in the passenger seat turned around and looked down on me like I was a crazy Quarter-rat talking to himself. The other cop looked back at me in the rearview as if I were a brat in the backseat who just wouldn't shut up. That made me boil! Unhinged, anxiety from my out-of-the-box state ignited…

"What? What!
You must think I have Two Heads?
Do you?"
I asked the cops upfront.

Nothing feels worse than being saved by emergency responders sometimes.

S E L L I N G

THE MAYBE

A Red Light District Love Story

An Inner City Outlier

BRIGHTDAWN JAWN

S P R I N G L O V E

I'd been having reoccurring dreams floating over waves of hands on Bourbon Street for weeks. And sometimes they inadvertently drifted into my girlfriend Bella's head too. She finally got fed up and told me so just before we hit the sheets one night…

"Braze,
dream up something better tonight,
or sleep on the couch.
Last night's vibes
were awful."

It's not that we didn't enjoy sharing dreams, we did! We were so in tune to each other that sometimes we did more than fantasize or plan our future. But actually, had conjoined-dreams! And I was having sordid ones at this time. Bella, like I can only assume many of you, just didn't care for big ass beers and the boobs on Bourbon Street; nor did I. We certainly enjoyed living in The French Quarter, yet to stroll that lowbrow beltway… yeah, not so much.

So, when I had another dream flying over Bourbon later that night where in it… I felt completely stoned and wearing nothing but a gold sorcerer's hat with colorful stars sewn on it? Flying high again while cover bands played from bars as I raced by with apples out riding my phallus like a magic broomstick? Dipping below street lamps just beyond the grasps of parading topless people on The Street reaching for that wicked dream stick between my legs? Just low enough for people to tickle my danglers before soaring past a familiar DJ on a rooftop above a flash mob! I knew for certain I would be in trouble if there were any at all psychic leakage from that weird-one.

When I woke up from it in the middle of the night, I held my breath paranoid she got drift of it. I didn't turn my head, but looked over to Bella from the corners of my eyes. And not until I heard her snore, did I breathe again. Why such dreams were surfacing in my sober mind and monogamous life was troubling; for both of us.

I slipped out of bed to splash cold water on my face. Then I burned some incense in the Loft to cleanse the atmosphere of any possible telepathic-particles bouncing off the brick walls. At this season of my life, I was a late blooming adult at best.

After decades of drinking and drugging I was fried, or some might say I had wet brain. But for years since the sudden loss of my Brother by suicide, my head was not home to mayhem, flooded with alcohol, or polluted with chemicals any longer. That chapter of my life was behind me in my last book. By now my cerebral matters made up a sustainably fuel-efficient metropolis I called my City of Lakes. It was surrounded by calm, clean and serene brain fluids powered by organics, meditation, and exercise. I became aware of my personal triggers that empowered the manic episodes of my past. And I'm fortunate to have recovered from a habitual lifestyle that did me great disservices. Since, I've acquired habits that serve me better, such as writing & cycling.

But evidently there was still some dirt spreading in the back alleys of my head that had gone unnoticed till recently. Thinking of my brain as a City onto itself, simply helped me realize that I am not my thoughts, nor my emotions. But merely the complex biosphere in which they inhabit. Detaching myself from thoughts and emotions is a matter of life and death for me. Thus, being the observer of my City of Lakes, and not always the reactive body of it, is how I survive.

Yet that night, still uncertain if my mind was the only one in the room that strolled through the gutter? I crashed on the couch holding my stones in the fetal position just in case the incense didn't work. An hour or so later, coast clear, I hit the sheets again and wrapped my arms around Bella. Some lovers often stick together like gum. We'd usually roll up in the sheets like a big burrito! The moonlight through the lunette made the space feel so euphoric only because there were enough particles of joy between us to make one swoon at times. I've been told by others it's like waking into a dream up here. Moonlit nights like this in our Loft were as breathtaking as the love we made in it. The most common light is full of beautiful things when you're in love. And the light up there would be any artist's dream, it certainly was mine once upon a time.

GARRET SCENARIO No.2

I didn't know where these Bourbon Street dreams were coming from. But reassuring Bella that I wanted her and only her was more important now than when we first met. Since then we experienced some of the highest highs and the lowest lows together. So, I had no reason to think we couldn't handle these new, shallow, subconscious distractions of mine; it was just a phase I thought. The openness of my mind had fed Bella's dreams for years. But at this time, they began to fuel her insecurities. Up to this point, I always thought she was one of the more self-assured people I knew.

Later that morning, just after dawn, I found one of Bella's legs free from our love burrito. An ankle was cast over the edge of the bed, a foot dangled a loose sock that barley clung to her by a toe. A sock that would surely fall off the next time she moved. And if that did happen, and she woke up? And I knew she'd wake if it fell because that's all she needed to sleep in; socks. She could sleep without me, without a pillow, without underwear, but not without her socks. If that sock fell off, she'd wake.

In the faint glow of dawn through the lunette, I gazed at her body that I unwrapped like naked brunch. A moment later she smiled, but didn't open her eyes. Then I wiggled the sock off, giving her a chill. I warmed her foot with my hot breath, before I slowly kissed my way up between her thighs.

"Love me. Love me."
She sighed.

…as I French kissed her insides.

On our balcony I served her coffee, tossed in a tad of coconut sugar, and stirred some cream in before I asked…

"Will there be anything else?"

She turned her nose up…

"My nose itches,
scratch it gently?"
She asked closing her eyes.

I picked up a miniature spoon off the table, licked it, and put it on her beak before I took my seat, before I asked with caution…

"Sleep good?"

When she nodded YES, I went to clear the air further and asked…

"Dreams?"

She shook her head NO. But opened her eyes wide! And in doing so, asked if I had any. I replied not so enthusiastic…

"I did.
Had another weird one."
I confessed.

For all I knew, she had it too. Her eyes remained wide and waiting to hear from me, so I continued…

"You really want to hear it?"

She sat up, and moved to the edge of her seat. I took a deep breath to ready myself.

"OK, alright.
I said eyebrows high,
"I think I dreamed about
dance battles!"

"Hmm… where?"
She asked.

"Here in The Quarter."

"Oh."
She said lips puckered.

I paused with a half-smile. Then she continued…

"Please go on. Dance battle,
bouncing boobs."

"No-no, well… yeah.
But it was more than that!
The whole atmosphere was,
completely in sync."

"Ok then.
What were the dancers,
dancing to?"
She asked as if testing me.

"That's a good question.
Carl Cox, from a rooftop!"

"Carl Cocks? No Tits. Hmm… "
She said shaking her head,
"I guess that could be interpreted
as, progress?"

She didn't let me sort that before she added snarly…

"I think Thorsen was right
about you."

I smiled and just blew that comment off. Her older brother Thorsen never thought I was much more than a graffiti writing train hopper. I summed it up…

"I just got the impression of dancers being
choreographed on Bourbon Street.
That's all."

"I've heard enough thank you."

Bella studied ballet in the bayou and did recitals growing up. I thought mentioning that aspect of my dream would speak to her inner performer, perhaps radiate some mystery as it did in me, but nope.

Love & honesty took priority along with education in Bella's upbringing. She found it quite normal to be home schooled, walk around half naked in the woods, and eat desert before dinner. Whereas I skipped Catholic school classes, didn't even talk about my private parts, and never thought to flip the menu and enjoy my brownie before the TV dinner. To me, her background was odd. But to her, revolutionary!

Her father Harry was a most radical big thinker. Bella and the rest of the family looked up to her Dad like pop culture does to Che. In fact, I gathered if he had his way, Bella would have been the next leader of the communist party. I was told her entrance to the world went down something like this…

Blood splattered on a wall when the umbilical cord was cut during homebirth. Her father Harry immediately took it as a sign! He stood and raised his finger in the air and called out to the family watching…

"The die is cast.
She's a revolutionist. Lenin!
Bella… Lenin!"

What he read in the blood on the wall was that Bella was asserting herself for the first time. Thus, he immediately gave his daughter Bella a middle name on the spot. Only hoping she would be the next leader of the communist party and rebirth of Vladimir Lenin perhaps. Moved by his theatrics and forecast at birth, her family preferred to call her Lenin ever since. Bella was her public name, but she's Lenin to her closest comrades.

Harry preferred to keep his family off the map and always lived on the edge of towns, bayous and what have you. But they loved him for it! He created an alternative lifestyle for his family that was nothing but a fantasy world to his kids, who… swung on ropes from tall trees over big puddles he painted as quick sand! Kids who skinny-dipped as a family in remote ponds he informed them were actually fountains of youth! And drove the kids down old Highway 90 in the back of his pickup truck telling them they could surf in the trunk bed with their mouths open to catch insects in their teeth because…

"Bugs are protein!"
He'd scream.

The kids had more fun with him then a spoiled family on Space Mountain at Disney World. Harry was the truest of outsiders and not just in persona. What he was, was a man of many faces too. And he showed them all to his children… dad, father, husband, friend, equal, revolutionary, businessman, goof, teacher, intellect, son, dreamer, big reader, and most of all… upright and honest. Shockingly honest to me! He spoke to all his kids in their eyes, on their level. As if they were intellectual cohorts not just innocent kids. No child was too young to know what was on his mind. Being the tall man Harry was, he often got down on one knee to talk to his kids in the eyes. Nothing was a lecture from above, but a conversation on the same level. I observed this relationship most often with one of his youngest children, Bella Lenin's stepsister Kireka.

Much later when all his biological children and his wife Denise where a little older, Harry fell in love with a younger woman named Carol. Harry being this intensely honest man kept no secret of his love for the other woman. Carol was an employee of Harry's with a young daughter of her own; that's Kireka. When Harry announced his love for Carol to the family it was of course hard on them all. But they tried to understand. The family was grounded in accepting others. They had to be. Dad was always bringing home strays. Carol was eventually accepted into their family too. But unlike others who drifted through Harry & Denise's open sex life, this one was a home wrecker.

Carol was a Deadhead who lost her way after Jerry died. Instead of going home to Canada at that time, she fell in love with a puppeteer. While following Phish with him, they had a baby; Kireka. When that guy pulling her stings split, she rolled to New Orleans to stay with "Dead Family" who settled down here in the late 90's after cashing out of the scene with "Shakedown Street" doe. They sold tie-die dresses in the parking lot of the French Market. There, while working the tie-die tent, Carol met Harry and his hippie family selling artsy drink coasters. Both the French Market and Harry's family were wide open to rolling stones like Carol, and she rolled right in.

From there, Carol not only fell for Harry, but his whole family's lifestyle. She didn't just want Harry, but the life he created with the Mother of all his children. As Harry tried to bring everyone together, Carol tried to steal it all away from Bella's Mom, Denise. Nonetheless, when Harry was living with two women, he would later tell me…

"That was the best time
of my life."

His dream was to move the whole family high in the Canadian Rockies, as close to the clouds as possible, and off the grid completely; at peace with his tribe, and two wives. He called his grand idea Cloud Nine, but that never materialized. Bella's Mom and older brother Thorsen finally put the brakes on that one. He ended up moving out with Carol & Kireka from the family trailer in the Bayou, and to a dead-end street in New Orleans. But the family stuck it out and stayed together from afar.

When I met Bella long after all that, Harry definitely needed a friend outside the family. And I tried to be that guy. He knew I was in love with his daughter; we talked about it…

"I find you and Leni,
very interesting."
He noted,
"You're separate,
but parallel."

"It's been a while now Harry.
You think she'll ever marry me?"
I asked.

"Braze,"
He responded,
"A feminist is a proud mammal.
You may want to think in terms of just
continuing a partnership
with Lenin."

Although he fathered a small tribe, he always looked like a very lonely person to me. He seemed to carry a grey cloud over his head from the day I met him. A greyness I got the impression he was born into.

Harry was an only child. Mom was a bartender. She was a vibrant woman who lived in the backseat of her car with Harry as much as hotel rooms. They had no fixed address growing up. But like the close family he raised, him and his Mom stuck together. None of them may have had much growing up, but there was no shortage of Love. Everything else, they learned to do without.

GARRET SCENARIO No.2

Contemplating a way to make the marriage I wanted be more a partnership with Bella, I drove Uptown to a not so fancy jeweler on Magazine Street. She would never consider an engagement stone from a world that historically exploited labor and drew blood for it just to raise the social status of a person who's been fooled by its embellished scarcity on the Earth. No, no there was no question about that. And I had to think not so precious metal too.

As I browsed the jewelry cases I wondered… if she said YES, how would a ceremony work? There would be no giving away of the bride. Definitely not that. A banquet hall would be too much of a luxury. A rooftop perhaps? I slowed that traffic down in my head to find a subtle ring, nothing bling. When a most perfect pair surfaced! A molded design that looked like comfortable pieces of fabric wrapped around our fingers. I left with them.

While having dinner on our balcony over the park of the New Orleans Jazz Museum, moonlight began to glistened in our wineglasses filled with pomegranate juice. Across the street a guitarist strummed some jazz while another musician tickled a snare drum with a brush on the corner. I made us her favorite… salmon and brown rice, broccoli, and homegrown herbs with my garlic butter sauce strewn over the dish and dripped delicately towards the edges of the plate. When she took her first bite, I immediately got up and said…

"Oh,
I forgot the napkins."

I ran inside quickly and came out with a couple. Ok, they weren't napkins. But at a glance it appeared so. They were white handkerchiefs. I couldn't fit the regular napkins we used through the ring hole. I nonchalantly handed the "napkin" to Bella with the Ring holding the handkerchief rolled up before sitting back down to start eating. When she noticed the Ring, she paused before saying…

"What-duh-hell?"

I put on a smile to hide my nerves, before I finally got it out. My proposal sounded something like this…

"Will you Bella Lenin,
co-author a life
with me?"

"Have a kid?"
She asked.

"Well, that too."
I said with a smile.

She half smiled. Before she noticed I was serious. Things got silent between us, and only us. Across the street buskers and gutter punks where yelling at each other on the corner, even their dogs where arguing. People were laughing at the tables out front of the pizza place downstairs. A homeless guy was serenading them for loose change. And a passing freight train a block away blew it's horn louder than bombs. All before she asked for clarification…

"What exactly are we talking
about here?"

"Everything?"
I responded in a high pitch.

"What's everything."

"You, Me, forever."
Then I added,
"And some…
free-range parenting?"

I thought that would soften her up there at the end, but nope. As she held the ring in her hand, there was no debating at that moment that my choice of words was not working. But I kept it cool, and stayed on script…

"First, we author a
life together.
Then,
we produce a kid!"

Made sense to me. NOT her.

"So...
you want to give me Writer,
and Producer credits."

She got up and walked inside the Loft. All I was trying to do was be sensitive to her new age hippie millennial needs. I followed her inside where I found her looking for her shoes when I asked...

"Did it really come out all
that wrong?"

She ignored that. I was confused, and just tried to make sense of us by pointing out...

"We may come from different
places, but... "

"Oh, where?
Where do I come from Braze?"

I exhaled. Before answering...

"A place of open relationships.
I want us, to be more solid
than that."

I brought up her family. And shouldn't have done that at this time. She pointed at me letting me know sternly...

"You know how much my family
means to me."

"And that's what I'm talking about, family.
What do you want for us?"

"I don't, know...
what I want.
And I don't know if I want
kids."

I was hurt. She knew it, and shifted gears and got less defensive before continuing...

"I didn't mean, I mean,
what I meant is...
I don't know what I want for me.

Let alone us."

I felt awkward. And feared I'd say something else stupid, or worse, so I clammed up. She continued…

"My family loves you.
But do you love them?"

This was an ongoing convo. One I could never win.

"I care about your family.
And I have given a good deal of time
and support to your father."

"Why do you always bring him up?"

"I'm…
closer to your Dad then the rest.
I've had conversations with him I never had
with my own Dad."

"He loves you.
But you just harp on how we've
had to take him in.
My family took you in too."

Took me in? I should have ended it there. But I must have murmured rather softly…

"I'm not the one sleeping
in my car."

"You think I like seeing my Dad like this?"
She asked.

"Can I ask you something?"

She nodded YES.

"Why is he with Carol?"

She took in a breath, before responding…

"He thinks,"
she took another breath…
"She's the love of
his life."

That was his way. Policy of hard truths. I tried to pull her in for a hug but she resisted, and said…

"I'm going for a walk."

"Where to?"

"To meet Dad for coffee.
He texts me earlier.
He said he had to talk."

I wasn't surprised. She parented her parents often.

"Why don't I go meet him.
And you chill.
Stay home and eat your dinner."
I suggested.

"No, I got to go."
She insisted.

She grabbed her cell phone and must have walked out of the front door barefoot. Moments later as I saved our plates for later, I noticed her shoes under the sofa. And she only had that one pair.

To settle myself I decided to get out of the Loft and go to The Athletic Club for a steam. All I wanted to do was love her forever, not push her away. I think she was as mad at me for not fully embracing her family, as she was reluctant to let me in it permanently. Perhaps she was more comfortable with people coming and going. Let me remind you, the last person they truly let in, was Carol.

Bella walked into the coffee shop on Royal Street a few blocks away, the one we first met at years ago. Her Dad Harry was sitting in a window. Inside she took a seat with him when he asked…

"What happen to your
shoes Lenin?"

She looked down at her feet as if she didn't realize she was barefoot till that moment.

"Oh-Braze asked me to

marry him."

"I see,"
Giving her a puzzled but calm look,
"So, you had to get out of there,
quick?"

I entered the steam room at the Athletic Club where a few others were sitting around chatting it up before one noticed me under the towel on my head…

"Hey Braze,
How's the entertainment business?"

"I… don't know.
I'm just a guy in a flea market."
I said with a smile.

"I caught you're interview on TV."
He said,
"Congrats on the Book.
And I'm sorry to hear of
your loss."

I nodded my head and responded,
"He died before his time."

During that interview he was referring too, I was asked to speak about the mental illness theme of BOOK SAFE GLACIER and how the loss of my brother by suicide led to my first novel. His loss blindsided me, and completely altered my trajectory in life; life's all about trajectories. I wish I could have altered his. The loss of my only brother never healed. But only worsens with loneliness in time.

At the coffee shop Harry was holding his daughter's hand on top of the small table for two. They appeared at the end of a deep conversation when he then asked…

"Do you truly love him?"

Lenin nodded YES. He reminded her…

"True love is rare."

She picked her phone up and text me…

Where r u

I text back…

Leaving gym now

Lenin looked up to Dad, who said…

"Go find him."

"Yeah?"
She asked.

"I would. I love um'."
Harry said without a smile.

"What did you want to talk
about tonight Dad?"

"It can wait."

Lenin wiped some happy tears away and gave her Dad a big hug across the table. His thoughts were gospel to his children. Or, as if they were from the lips of Edgar Casey in his sleep. With his encouragement she dashed out the front door and passed him by the window like a shooting star. With nowhere else to go he resumed a position with his chin in his hands above the worn elbows of an oversized suit jacket with paint splats on it.

As I walked down Royal crossing Toulouse, bright headlights approached me at a STOP sign just before Bella crashed in to me asking…

"Still love me?
Tell me you love me!"

In each other arms in the middle of the street I answered with utmost certainty…

"I'll always love you."

The car with its high beams on went around us at the STOP sign. A horse and carriage passed by on Royal Street. Then, thunder struck! It suddenly began to rain.

Tourist scurried by us as we kissed unaware of nothing more than our feelings for each.

We didn't have much money, but I think we threw ourselves a nice little "celebration of coupling". I connected with a gallery I once ran in an old carriageway on Royal Street and asked them if we could host friends and family there for the shindig, they obliged. Our Moms got together and made some food, and we bought a big cake to smear in each other's faces later. For entertainment, I had some buskers show up and push a piano in the alleyway to perform. And because Bella was a home schooled hippy and I was no more than an award winning criminal at best, we felt no reason to call on a Justice of the Peace or a Priest to make it official. Stumps duh Clown would do just fine! He said clowning but in a most conservative manner before all our guests…

"Do you, Braze Scanlan,
take Bella Lenin Sparks, in your
wildest dreams?"

"I do."

"Promise to house up with her,
and partna with her till
the show is ova?"
Stumps asked me.

"I got this."
I responded.

"Do You Bella Lenin Sparks?
Take Braze, Mr. *MES* Scanlan in your wild heart?
And promise to partna with his shaggy-self
till curtain time?"

"I scooby-doo."
She responded.

"By the power vested in me
by The Know Nothing Circus,"
Stumps declared,
"I pronounce you both together, fo-ever!"
Quickly continuing with…

"I may now kiss the bride."

And, he did so, with a peck on the forehead. Just before Lenin and I kissed. It was time for us to celebrate, and with all who came to join us, we did not hesitate! Following our hearts, we danced in circles palm-to-palm one way. Then palm-to-palm the other way; back and forth happier than ever. With all that we survived in our travels together the past six years, from camping on rooftops to cross country train hops, we had much to appreciate. Then, as if on que, the sky opened up! Everyone quickly took shelter in the carriageway entrance, but us. The band, no strangers to the elements, kept playing and simply stepped back a foot under a balcony around the courtyard where the piano was.

Lenin and I rain-danced body and souls in the sun shower. Mouths open to the sky we filled ourselves with blessings from above. Our spirits departed our bodies and sat down on the fountain wall in the middle of the courtyard to watch us celebrate together. We could not be stopped, only encouraged by nature. I remember hearing guests cheering, angels bowling, band playing... all as our heart beats kept in time as water bounced off everything. Everything was in tune with one another as if orchestrated by an unseen maestro. There just had to be something unseen at work to bring it, us, all together. My arms goose bumped with the indescribable virtuoso I sensed composing it all.

As we danced in the courtyard and got downright soaking wet, our guests conversed in the dry carriageway, taking pictures and eating wedding jambalaya. I just couldn't be happier that such a beautiful fountain was there to seat our souls! As quick as it started, the sun shower stopped. Married and baptized by nature our faces glowed and our lips glossed with fresh rain. I'd not felt such euphoria since hopping trains in the rain with her back in the day to LA.

Yet I was brought back to Earth by Carol who caused some sort of ruckus in the carriageway. I couldn't make out what it was, and I wasn't too concerned. Just assumed she had too much to drink before she arrived and another ugly family debate broke out. Her happiness that day was as important to me as an extra in a movie. Whatever went down, Lenin's brothers took Carol out front to squash the conflict in private. Her Aunt Samantha came up behind us with a tall cold one in each hand, cigarette in her mouth, and insisted that we…

"Cut the cake.
Come'on!"

"You got it aunty,"
Lenin replied.

Then our friend Craig yelled over,
"When do I get to body paint
the newlyweds?"

Early the next morning, awaiting our boarding passes, Lenin was sleeping next to me in the New Orleans airport possibly being troubled by a bad dream. I would often find myself in her fantastic nightmares where she was constantly saving her brothers from apocalyptic scenarios. In those nightmares that often seeped into my head by her telepathic leakage, hurricane winds, floods, and burning inferno's where always impending dangers on her home and family. Just as I noticed symptoms of another bad dream on her face, our names were called out by the gate agent…

"Scanlan. Sparks."

We were flying on discount stand-by tickets compliments of my Mom, a retired airline employee. I closed the comic book I was reading, nudged her, and whispered…

"Wake up. We're on.
We got seats!"

As she woke and I gathered my things, I didn't notice the comic book I dropped in my rush to get to the gate agent waiting on us. Lenin picked it up and followed me.

The gate agent informed us,
"You have the last two seats on the plane.
But of course,
they're not together."

Lenin was tired and looked disappointed we couldn't sit together. But I wasn't surprised, just happy not to get bumped.

GARRET SCENARIO No.2

With our boarding passes in hand I was excited as we walked down the ramp to jet off on our honeymoon. But Lenin, never a morning person, looked tired while we boarded the redeye. And she even got annoyed by my PDA when I put my arm around her too. When she knocked my arm off her shoulder, I inquired…

"What's up?"

"I didn't know you were into
big tit cartoons."

Then she held up the comic book I dropped.

"Whoa.
That's not just a cartoon.
That's Vaughn Bode."

"Who?"

"Cheech Wizard."

"What?"
She asked.

"It's art."

"It's porn!"

"Belly-Bell. Come-on."

She then gave me an intense stare belting out…

"Look!
Nothing but big tits."
She pointed out.

"Jeez Lenin…
It's only a comic book."

She was hurt. And though we had to get on the plane immediately, I had to stop her in her tracks before we got any closer to boarding like this.

"Lenin,
I'm not into porn."

Then she held the little paperback in my face! Which I guess… you could say would make this issue at hand debatable.

But I furthered my defense with,
"I'm really not into that.
You're perfect."

"Lucky for me you prefer perfection,
over size!"

I quickly put my index finger to my mouth trying to signal her to keep it down. Then I whispered with intensity because, we had to board the goddamn flight and said to her…

"I didn't pack the freakin'
comic book.
It just happened to be
in one of the attaché pockets since
before I don't know when."

Then, suddenly holding back tears she suggested…

"If this is what you're into,
then we can look at it together."

Holding up the Cheech Wizard Comic. Then she added…

"I just want to be what
you want."

I had to do everything in my power, to contain myself. We were talking about a comic book here! Not a Victoria Secrets catalog.

"Bella Lenin, I love you.
I don't want to bring no Cheech,
or ANYONE else to bed with us.
Ok. Ok?"

She shook her head OK.

"In fact,
if Craig really wants to body paint us?
I'm wearing a sock on my cock
like a Chili Pepper
the whole time."

She lightened up and laughed at that. Feeling better I rushed us on the plane, we were the very last two passengers boarding.

As we boarded it seemed everyone there had their eyes on us, as often is the case, when the last two stand-by passenger's board a flight. The flight attendant pointed out…

"The last two seats are only
a couple rows apart."

"Thank you."
I responded graciously.

As I lead us up the aisle, I found the first seat and offered it to my wife. I went on to find the last open seat two rows behind her. When she looked back to find me, I blew her a kiss before I sat down.

When I could finally relax, I put my seat belt on and acknowledged the two I was sitting between politely with smiles. They were young, perhaps college students, dressed casually. I apologized for the little hold up…

"Sorry to delay things ladies.
My wife and I… "

…when out of nowhere Lenin suddenly popped her head over the fluffy chest of the girl next to me insisting…

"I want to trade seats
with you."

"Ah, a-oh."
I stuttered.

"NOW!"

Once I was settled in the other seat, I retrieved a notebook from my old attaché. If this was how worked-up she got on a plane about me sitting next to other women. How much are things going to heat up on our trip when I crossed certain storefront windows on our honeymoon, in Amsterdam. Yeah, why an Amsterdam honeymoon? Because I won the coin toss!

Lenin wanted to honeymoon to India without a plan and just hop the first passenger train to anywhere. I wanted more privacy. Hopping any trains was really something I wanted to leave behind me. Now if I knew how to sail, I would have chartered us a sail boat to be alone at sea. But the next best thing to me was renting our own house boat in Amsterdam. So, we flipped for it. Heads India, tails… Netherlands. I let the coin hit the floor, bounce, and rolled to its resting spot that led to our destiny. She screamed in response…

"You always win!"

"Not true."
I said with a snicker and
raised eye brow.

She vented further,
"And,
you always get the good
fortune cookies.
Not fare!"

It was Amsterdam over India with a simple, fare, flip of a coin. Not my fault.

Now if a sober guy wants to stay sober, why is he going to Amsterdam? I suppose my inner child *MES* may have been at work. But *MES* wouldn't be calling the shots over there. You wouldn't catch me tripping on truffles because of him. The last time I let that alter ego have his way was when I let him loose in **CURE** *for the* **CRASH**. And as I just said, that was the last time.

MES reads his favorite book ***A Confederacy of Dunces*** in CURE *for the* CRASH

GARRET SCENARIO No.2

I led a few lives before I met Bella Lenin, and *MES* fully surfaced during certain chapters. The more recent personality to surface, *BRIGHTDAWN*, he was open for anything to write about other than a train ride; we're over trains. And I know how this may sound. But I didn't have a personality disorder. *MES*, *BRIGHTDAWN* & I… we had things quite in order at this time. They just help me departmentalize seasons of my life. I had it under control. I just worked with the personality I needed, at times I needed them.

When we touched down it woke me from another weird-one in my City of Lakes before I could gather myself. We hadn't made eye contact, nor said a word to each other since we took our seats in New Orleans. She wanted space. I gave it to her. Once I deboarded I waited for her in the jetway to catch up. When she emerged, she still looked annoyed. Nonetheless I greeted her with a warm smile.

"I don't want to talk about it."
she said immediately.

And then those two girls passed us. I smiled and nodded goodbye to them. The only thing Lenin said about it was…

"I don't ever,
want to talk about this."

As we surfaced from the Subway across town to search for our place, I felt another sudden air of loneliness. The day we arrived in Amsterdam was my brother's birthday. Since he'd taken his life, every time I got somewhere new in mine, I couldn't stop thinking of him. He'd never see us married. I'd never enjoy his laugh again. We couldn't shoot hoops on a playground anymore. And I'd never watch a Sixers game the same. My Mom would later say that it was he who pulled some strings to get us those last two stand-by seats that morning. I can't prove that was the case, or prove it was not.

When we finally found the houseboat, Lenin was impressed and didn't hide it. That lifted my spirits. With a beautiful kitchen, hidden bedroom, and hot tub with a skylight over it, it all felt perfect. I noticed a supermarket on the way over and told Lenin I'd cook for us later. Simple things like food shopping with her where some of my biggest joys back then. She'd examine all the ingredients before buying, and I'd ignore every price tag just to annoy her. Not that I ever had a lot of money, but I've spent much more on far worse than pricey food in my lifetime.

It felt like the longest day ever, and that was fine with me. The sun really seems to take it's time in that part of the world in May. Later we had a candle lit dinner on deck. Discussing our endless dreams held my heart at full attention. The way we dreamed one lifetime would not be enough for us together! By candle light that night we talked about finding each other in the next life to pick up where we left off.

Afterwards we took a romantic stroll though side streets and over canal bridges while we talked further about personal things, such as fore-play. Inspired, I led us beneath a translucent bell tower beside a church to gently arouse her in the shadows of a sacred doorway by a faint neon glow. Alone in the alley I slowly began to play her passionately. Tickling her opening movement as if she were a grand piano! As I hit the tip of that note for minutes on end, she soon wanted no further intro. The hungry moans under her breath came to a gushing sigh of relief when I came inside her just below a Bell Tower as bats circled overhead. As I looked at the Moon…

She whispered,
"Tell me you love me?"

"I love you."
I whispered back.

"That's enough. That's enough."
She said,
and we zipped back up
our cloths…

…and walked with after-lust back into the neon glow of the nightlife as she bit on my shoulder with the weight of a vampire that was hungry, no more.

The next morning, we woke on the boat and met the sun on the deck energized by Love. I was led to believe that there was an endless supply for us. Over coffee and pastries Lenin asked…

"Did you know
that our boat was so close to the
RedLight District?"

"Not till last night."

Though we didn't actually walk through it yet, we just noticed it from afar; silently. After the Cheech Wiz incident in the New Orleans airport and, the musical chairs we played on the way over, I purposely sidetracked us from the women we'd pass on display in the RedLight District. But by now she loosened up and didn't seemed to be as bothered, and shared but yet another, interesting, family tale…

"You know,
my Mom got hired as a stripper once."

"Do tell Bell."
I encouraged.

"Before Dad, she hiked and camped
The Appalachian trail.
When Mom emerged months later,
she was bald and broke."
My happy as hell Bella Lenin said
with a big laugh.

"Bald?"

"She shaved her head at one point
along the walkabout."

This got my full attention. I could only imagine her Moms hair was once as long and beautiful as Lenin's was at this time. I urged her to…

"Please, continue."

"She walked into a truck stop Strip Club,
bald and broke, auditioned, and got the job!
But on the stipulation
she'd show up for work later
wearing a wig."

Her Mom Denise once gave me directions on how to doctor the registration of an expired year on a license plate. And, how to clear coat it with some dirt so it's weathered properly. In ways like this, I fit right in!

"How'd it go?"
I asked.

"Chickened out last minute.
Couldn't do it."

"Wait.
Didn't she live at a
free sex commune at one time
before she met your Dad?
But… she couldn't strip?"

I thought I remembered hearing some sex commune talk at a family BBQ. Lenin kept laughing. I continued…

"Am I right about this commune thing?"

"She did live in a sex commune
at one time in Germany!
How'd you know that?"

I often found things this bizarre in her family background worth noting, and notes I took. She continued with a smile…

"Mom's so beautiful,
she would have been an amazing stripper."
Before adding for whatever reason,
"My grandma was a nudist."

My face must have read like a blank notebook waiting for more. *BRIGHTDAWN* sat behind my right eye at his desk typing what your reading as she continued…

"Sometimes
when Grandma noticed the mailman making a
delivery to our house,
she would open the door just before
he got to the box,
and answer it nude."

"Dang…

Does she still strip in
the nursing home?"

"No.
I guess she forgot
she's a nudist."

As usual I had a pen in hand writing key words in a Moleskine…

Broke & bald. Wig to strip. Nude G-ma.

BRIGHTDAWN blew me off
from inside with,
"I got this."
from behind my right eye where
he was typing.

Lenin was fully aware that everything that crossed my radar was material. She, must have known where this was going.

Over dinner that night, just like many others for years now, she listened to me go on and on about random ideas. And she reminded me of hers such as traveling without plans; she didn't take losing that coin toss lightly. She also had a pining for South America, specifically Brazil. While that brought Beco de Batman in Sao Paulo to my mind. Graffiti wasn't what attracted her to Brazil. Her Dad spoke of South America often. Growing up he shared books with her by the spiritualist Chico Xavier from Brazil. At the end of our meal she decided that we had to visit Brazil, next. She urged…

"We must go.
Promise!"

"Ok.
I'm open to raise a budget
for that."

She squinted just like her Grandma at that answer.

Upon the urging of *MES*, we made our way to a nightclub much later that night. And for hours into the next morning we traded goose bumps brought on by slick

DJ's, smoke machines, and laser rays. I could simply watch her dance till dawn! She's a heavenly body that attracts satellites; everybody watches. Nothing made her more attractive than when music plays and she just let go! But she didn't realize that. She had no idea how sexy she was, or how the music made her even more so. She just came off as humble because she wasn't aware of herself. Or, seem to notice or want the attention she got when the music took hold of her. Since she was a kid in ballet class, she only thought she got stared at because she towered over other girls; and still did. If Taylor Swift needed a double, look no further.

On the way home she mentioned in the cold, earlier morning damp air while snuggled under my arm that she wished…

"When the music builds
in those songs,
to that point where it brings you
to that high
just before it drops.
…You know what
I mean?

I nodded YES, of course I did.

"I want to learn how to cut loose
right at that moment!"

"Everybody does."
I said without a second thought.

Socially, she was a late bloomer and had some catching up to do. But then again, she showed me how to make friends with cows to find magic mushrooms after it rains when we first met. In her own way, I guess she was very outgoing.

The next morning as Lenin slept in, I picked up my notebook, a jacket, and a pen, then went above deck to journal in the sun to fuel *BRIGHTDAWN*. Journal entries are his jogs in the morning. By the time I was done my notes and found my way below deck once again, Lenin was on the couch wrapped up like a lonely frozen burrito, when she shivered out…

"It's so-so cold."

The slightest drop in temperature affected her like this. I took her hands in mine and began to blow warm breaths on her fingers to melt them. Then rubbed her cold feet through her socks to give her some more relief. All she wanted to do that day was warm up our bodies and creat heat from heartbeats. I never touched such beauty or perfection and was never so healed by it, before her.

We finally left the boat to find skinny pancakes in a 2nd floor restaurant that must have been the tiniest eatery in Amsterdam. As it approached the magic hour, we walked them off hand and hand through crowded sidewalks as the city transitioned into the nightlife. I recall passing a couple of young men standing on a canal bridge, who then greeted a macho friend that walked up high fiving the other two apparently waiting for him. They were speaking German, but their hollers where universal. Proceeding down the street we had to walk around others gazing in windows. I glanced over to see exactly what mesmerized them, and found a woman in the window with an outrageously-curvaceous body on display, up for sale.

Feeling my wife begin to overboil emotionally, I took her hand in mine a bit more firmly and led her down the street a little quicker. But the further we strolled down the brick road, the livelier the windows got! With nowhere to turn I moved us forward not glancing again towards a storefront. But my eyes just couldn't stay straight in their sockets. Not only was I afraid to turn my head towards a window, but I was afraid to look at her too. It was as enjoyable as rolling down Boob Boulevard with my Mom. Lenin was about to have a meltdown on this Machiavellian Highway. When suddenly her hand yanked away from mine. I stopped in my tracks and put my head down for a moment. Before I turned around to see where she'd run off too.

I found myself standing alone in front of a window sectioned off into cubicles filled with women trying to get my attention; but I was somewhere else. After a deep breath, I walked back in the direction we came in to this sector to catch up with my Love. By the time I made it to the edge of the RedLight District where I thought I'd find her waiting for me, she was nowhere to be found. When I noticed a bookstore, I thought I'd check in there for her before heading down the road further.

Inside I looked down every isle. But with no luck. Along the way I accidently noticed a little book by Tim Burton. Inside it was filled with cute sketches and short stories. After paging through enough of it, I bought it. And hoped it to be the first book of our child's. A child we had yet to agree on having; but, I'm a dreamer.

I popped a squat on the curb of a random corner with a slice of Pizza on top of the shopping bag with that little book. Just as I bit into the slice, eyes to the ground, those beat up brand-less shoes of Lenin's appeared next me. When I looked up with my mouth full, she said…

"I know, I know.
I'm acting stupid.
I just can't control it!"

I chewed the crust looking up thinking, yup.

A week later we jetted back to New Orleans First Class. No young women between us on that flight. I didn't even make much eye contact with the flight attendants. As for that little book I bought in Amsterdam, I made sure it went unnoticed.

SUMMER STAGE

Back here in The Quarter I resumed my bookstand in The French Market, caught up on pages, and responded to emails. One message was a reminder from our friend Craig asking us to stop by and get body painted. After the reactions that surfaced most recently, I thought Lenin seeing her body as a work of art would be a great idea so, I had to find a cool sock to wear. While off for the summer from her job as 5th grade teacher, she briefly disappeared into her family upon our return. Her father was in another crisis with Carol and he needed her company. She was always there for him. But there seemed to be no helping Harry at this season of his life. He seemed to always want to open up to me, and would often come out to The French Market on his bicycle just to shoot the breeze. Kireka too, though she usually rolled over on her skateboard with friends. Living on top of the French Market and working there, I was always available. My co-vendor from India, Myra, was always most complimentary…

"Where is your beautiful
wife?"

"Doing yoga up there probably."
I said pointing up at
the Loft.

"Please tell her I said hello.
I am sure her glow is as radiant as ever."

"I'll share your hello and kindest
regards with her Miss Myra."

"Please do!"

Just a couple weeks after getting back Lenin invited the whole family over for dinner as a little going away party for her brother Thorsen who was going to South America. Kireka skated over too, Carol stayed home. Thorsen worked at a catholic school teaching foreign language and created an opportunity to go down to Brazil with some of his students to visit a new school that was being built down there with donations he raised. He also used the trip to record a language on the verge of extinction. A focus that would take him into a favela where a few indigenous peoples who spoke the language of his interests migrated after deforestation cleared their lands.

I cooked my seasoned pork sandwiches marinated for hours on the old gas Chambers Stove served on toasted rolls lightly dipped in the gravy which is basically, my kind of delicious! Afterwards her younger brothers and Kireka sorted through our vinyl collection and some spun records while the others talked up South America. I think Thorsen was napping on the sofa when I excused myself to have some tea on the balcony. I must have dozed off listening to a young lady busk on the corner as the sun was setting, before Lenin woke me up excited…

"Braze. Braze!
My brother invited us to South America!
He said we could go with.
Stay AND eat for free
with The Brothers down there."

I was still waking up…

"Wow.
That's cool.
When?"
I asked.

"This weekend."
She said quickly.

That woke me up. She continued…

"Two students just called him
and backed out."

She was serious. I inquired…

"Ok.
How long of a trip
would this be?"

She took a beat before answering. I shrugged my shoulders, mouth open, waiting.

"Ten days."

"Ten days?"
I asked feeling the pressure.

"What?
Same as Amsterdam.
We don't even have to pay
for food!"

I exhaled. Two plane tickets, rent and expenses here with no income in the meantime? Business is slow enough in the summer. I needed every dollar I could make just to stay in biz. So, I didn't have to do the exact math to know that…

"I'm sorry,
But that's impossible this time
of year."

"I can pay for my end."
She boasted.

"Oh yeah?"
I asked surprised.

"I have a stack of
credit cards I never use."

She was right. She never shopped. But I had to remind her that…

"I'm running a small business
outback. And we don't live
cheap up here."

"I never wanted a car payment.
Or this Loft."

"WE moved in here.
And WE bought the car."

"I want to live cheaper."
She said.

…And apparently decided so at that very moment. I washed my face with my dry hands before continuing…

"Well, we should have

talked about that before we moved into the
French Quarter."

Then Harry stepped out onto the balcony.

"I'm sorry to interrupt,
but I think we're all going
our separate ways now.
Thank you for dinner Braze.
You should think about opening a
sandwich shop sometime.
Just delicious!"

Sometimes I felt like her Dad liked me more than Lenin did. At that moment, he gave me a sorry you're in the outhouse look.

"Thanks Harry.
We'll walk you down."

Lenin stopped me.

"No Braze.
I'll do it."

The next day she charged a plane ticket to South America, and just getting back from Amsterdam, a passport wasn't an issue. She easily found a way to get to Brazil. I was happy for her, but I don't think she really wanted me to be happy at all. She was too disappointed I wasn't traveling with. I'm month to month here. Taking 20 days off in two months would be impossible. But I thought staying home and paying the bills was smart, and doing my part, for us.

A few days later I was dropping her off at the airport to meet her Brother and the High School students he was chaperoning. I really admired how she could pack; one small school bag was all she brought to Brazil. She was still disappointed I wasn't going, but that didn't stop her; nor should it. If I looked at the prices when we food shopped, perhaps I would've had a savings to go with her. I don't recall what exactly we said upon parting ways at the airport, but I fully regretted not going with her by the time I got back to the car. And to add to this mood, as I drove from the airport, *Beethoven's Moonlight Sonata* was playing on New Orleans Classical 104.9FM public radio station.

GARRET SCENARIO No.2

Left alone I knew I had to reaffirm the enthusiasm for my work, my healthy lifestyle, and check back in with my therapist at this time. Without Lenin home I had to channel my energy and update my focus. But what I really needed was a new project to write about. Prior to Book Safe Glacier, I'd been living off my movie laurels for quite a while.

My days usually started at 2am and were filled with tasks till I crash around 7pm. I enjoyed waking up to write some pages as the nightlife in The Quarter burned out, and I liked going to bed when it started up. At those opening hours of the morning, I let *BRIGHTDAWN* surface and sit at our desk undisturbed by *MES* and arbitrary passing clouds in our City of Lakes. Each of my breaths stir the creative winds of information down the streets and around the corners of my mind. Between he and I, pages materialize every morning by way of cerebral fluids that race on the dopamine superhighways inside me. New dimensions seem to appear passing information on to me that stir complex emotions throughout cells in my body. In short, this is mania at work. Everything feels so real inside me that when I recollect basically anything, I have to ask myself… did that really happen, or is this just something I dreamed up? Since I've been sober, this has been much more manageable. But accidents and occasional misreads still happen before I get it right, in rewrites.

My therapist has suggested medications, and I've tried a couple, but I find they disturb my focus rather than add to it. These days I think I'm level enough to know what's best, and, what's best I don't put on billboards. Such as my occasional glimpses of supernatural clarity. Sharing those visions with friends outside of my personal historical fiction, or worse, with doctors, may institutionalize me before my goals are reached. Thus, I feel safer using the experiences as material rather sort out how much truth there is in them. During these… episodes, my nostrils open wider than usual. I get throbs of expectancy. And a slight quiver follows in my bones before the un-nesting happens. In my skull, lives an Eyeball with wings. And in this story, I don't care if others think I'm crazy. Apparently, neither does *MES*. Who said at that moment from behind a green window to my City of Lakes…

"People who are real about it don't talk about it they write about it."

I suppose history and mystics would call it a 3rd Eye. But I call'um Dutch. He's the one who seemingly shares the visions with me over the years. Inside *BRIGHTDAWN* and *MES*, keep Dutch as a pet. But it's all good. I got this. It's copasetic don't call an ambulance. The way I see it, you got to work with what you got. And I got it weird as *Strangelove*. But, just let me be. I know what I don't know.

To keep myself centered and to nurture my visions I have to be mindful of my vital energy to shift the functioning of my ordinary ego, to that of a deeper nature. This type of concentration seems to only be possible when I'm completely alone and writing. Being isolated in the Enclave of the Loft's Garret relinquishes the psychic turbulence and creates an environment for healthier daydreaming. But at this time, outside the Enclave, those daydreams got under my skin and followed me, among other places, to bed.

After our trip to Amsterdam, my City of Lakes began torturing me with unfolding sexual scenes in storefront windows. What I was experiencing upon Lenin's trip to South America was so distracting, it created nearly unbearable anxiety hangovers. If she was home and caught drift of those dreams, it would have certainly been curtains for us. I never thought of myself as an exhibitionist, but there I was doing the bare-assed hokey-pokey in Amsterdam windows on repeat in my box when my lids were closed. Where those wonky drifts came from; no idea. I woke up a couple nights in a row and took a cold shower to settle myself.

One night after I dried off in the bathroom, those Red Light visions must have opened another door. It got multidimensional in the Loft! It was faint, but when I walked out of the bathroom and through the Garret, I found the Loft as it appeared in the 1850's. When at that time it was a brothel. In that antique waking-dream I watched translucent men and women with my eyes open go in and out of curtained off rooms. The vision was almost liquid in texture, as if it were captured in time by a water color camera; a filter over reality. The glimpse of this dimension sparked such curiosity in me that I wanted to chase it once it dissipated, but I wasn't sure how; yet. My clock was soon off due to experimenting with Ibuprofen PM and espresso in search of that ripple in time.

It was a couple nights later that my semiretired self, *MES*, decided he wanted to peruse an impulse for a hot minute. When *MES* surfaces he's a euphoria junky. Once he's on the go he'll do whatever it takes to keep hitting the high notes on our Piano of Emotions. After Googling Best Strip Clubs in New Orleans, our wheels were in motion and I got dressed. I, BRAZE, who usually had the final say about making any such bad moves, was merely hesitant at best that night. *BRIGHTDAWN* had motives too; research. And that was enough to push "us" out the door.

A few blocks from the Loft I turned onto Bourbon Street and was soon bombarded with cover bands, hand grenade drinks, and big ass beers. But none of that was tempting, nor the skinny girls with bad tattoos in so many doorways. Other than meeting my pal Sepher at his old job at Wild Forest for lunch to talk about **CURE** *for the* **CRASH** edits, I'd not visited another local strip club since. But that night, I wasn't thinking straight. If I were, I would have known that the *Communist Daughter* would split quicker than she flipped seats with me traveling *In The Aeroplane Over The Sea*. But this Rising Sun had rave reviews, that's where we were heading; The Rising Sun. One review read as such…

"Where semen stains mountaintops!"

It's a spot I'd not taken notice to before. But when I got there, it seemed mysteriously familiar. Perhaps it's where I saw Carl Cox on the rooftop? The building doesn't look old like most of the architecture in The Quarter, it's bricks are much younger than the others. From its façade it tried to differentiate itself from Bourbon Street. It's a marriage between Corporate America and a Billiard Room; nothing historical. More a club built for the American Manic and not just holding it together like so many others.

When my B-Boys and I stepped inside, I was hit by a sonic force not felt since the dance scene boiled out of the Haçienda in Manchester. It was not the T&A show that Sepher worked at down the street back in the day; no sir. This place, was amaze-balls! I had no idea such a club existed on Bourbon. And it would have been better off I didn't. It was as irresistible as an old school Brooklyn Bomb pill. Today, if you don't know what I'm talking about here. Seek a Rave veteran. Those who survived The Great Personal Chemical Wars of the 1990's usually found in this new millennium shopping at Whole Foods for 5HTP's can clue you in.

From the doormen to the dancers everyone was an ego all their own, but I had one too. When I sat down at a small cocktail table, alone, I went into show mode and spread some cash out on it in front of me. Small bills I make change with in the Market every day, probably no more than 100 bucks. Yet as soon as the table was covered in cash, the seat across from me was filled by a beautiful independent contractor looking work.

"Why do you spread your money
over the table?"
She asked.

"To get your attention."

"What are you going to do now
that you have it?"
She said as she sat down.

A waitress approached.

"Buy you a drink."
I replied.

She had a vodka tonic. I had a cranberry tonic.

"You don't drink?"

"Nope.
I'm allergic to alcohol."
I said with a smile.

"I'm Fiona."
She mentioned with her hand out
to be shaken.

I told her I'm
"Dickie."

She took notice to my ring, but didn't say a thing.

While I spoke with her, *BRIGHTDAWN* was looking around and took notes behind my right eye, as *MES* took her breasts in behind my left green window. From trapeze artists to body building midgets, it was a circus in this joint! There was of course the mahogany, polished brass, and velvet seats everywhere that you might expect in such a place. But the best part, no stripper poles. It was more theatrical than that. The celebration seemed to overpower exploitation. *BRIGHTDAWN* made fragmented mental notes scrawled in graffiti penmanship of the individual personas each entertainer and patron chose to market themselves with. Such as the customers in business suits that contrasted those of the hip staff attire. The shot girls that looked more like cigarette girls with trays hanging from their necks offering roses and five hour energy drinks. The bartenders with as much dental work as some of the dancers augmentations. And swarms of little people who seemed to have more energy and passion than other employees!

There was a glass elevator that appeared to bring VIP's up and down from a 2nd floor lounge area. Higher above were sheer silk fabrics falling from the sky for topless aerialist to spin around and tease patrons. Below a synth grand piano was at work that added a layer to the DJ mixes. The DJ was older, crazy dude in in his 60's. At one point the old guy set the wax on his turntables on fire and looked more like he was having a séance rather than spinning music. He was appropriately creepy, but the little peoples stole the show! So many ripped dwarfs lighting up the scene doing cartwheels, miming games, and super-pop locking around the club. They surfaced in random places unexpectedly like whack-a-moles just to freak you out sometimes.

Up on the 2nd floor overlooking the stage, a guy up there with Gazel 955 looking down got my attention, just before it came to me who the fuck it was; a Jizzy-Mack from way back, Gaten! It was him. I knew immediately. This had to be his club. Gaten was once an underground celebrity, but you wouldn't know who it was unless you frequented the NYC club scene decades ago. I could hardly believe it, but there he was… Piter Gaten in the Russian flesh.

Long ago Pieter Gaten-Thieves was not only a NYC club owner, but founder of a gang of rascals and runners known as BTS, the Brooklyn Terror Squad. My brother, through degrees of separation via the hands of his BTS Boys, had done business with Gaten a lifetime ago. Gaten and his BTS gang were Born to Steal in New York. The Rising Sun had to be his brainchild; it oozed edginess. He must have been hiding out in plain sight down here after he got spring out of jail up in New York.

Suddenly a little person ran by with a plastic glow in the dark bazooka distracting me from those observations before stopping to shoot it towards the stage with an alarming pop! It released yards of streamers and a pound of confetti over the place like fireworks on the 4th. With such theatrics the Rising Sun was nothing like any other club I'd been to before; though some parties came to mind close 2nd's. Intrigued by it all but defiantly not there to cheat on my wife, I tipped my company and ducked out before a lap dance. The Rising Sun appeared to market trouble superbly.

AS I walked down the middle Bourbon Street from the Rising Sun thinking about the overload of atmosphere I just emerged from, *M*ES & BRIGHTDAWN left the green window seats of my head and went back to their compartments in the City of Lakes. I swam in my thoughts for a block or so before I heard…

"Braze!"

…from underneath that familiar old movie-style marquee that Sepher once worked at. *M*ES & BRIGHTDAWN came back to the windows with the quickness thinking the night might not be over after all. I looked down from the bare bulbs of the marquee and in the direction of the voice that called me, to find a friend Rachelle. I hadn't seen her since the Pseudo-Wedding. I smiled and yelled back…

"Sup Rachelle."

She had a stripper on her arm at the front door. The spot with this unique marquee was Wild Forest, a Strip Club that she managed. No facade looks like a small playhouse on Bourbon like her club.

GARRET SCENARIO No.2

"How you been?"
She asked and waved me over.
"Come in for a sec!"

I contemplating if I wanted to prolong the night any further. When I looked at my watch, I realized I still had to write, bike and meditate before I set up at the French Market in a few hours. I waved back at her politely, smiled, and shook my head NO. Laughing her invitation off.

"Come on!"
She urged.
"We remodeled.
Let me give you the tour."

Oh-god! Last time I was in there during an afternoon meeting with Sepher to outline edits I was witness to a Tampax string dangling between a stripper's legs. Not to mention the tasteless DJ spinning a *Pour Some Sugar On Me* dubstep remix. But she kept waving me over. So, I asked timidly while looking around for a way out…

"Same DJ Rachelle?"

"WHAT!"
She laughed hard,
"You're the only guy
whoever asked me about
the music!"

"Oh?"

I stood my ground in the middle of the street. As people passed in between us hooting and hollering. I asked…

"What do they usually
ask you?"

"Ah…
How many girls are
working."

I shrugged shoulders. She wouldn't take a NO.

"Come on Braze!
We'll skip the girls.
I'll introduce you to the new DJ."

I gave in and walked over.

"OK.
My wife would appreciate that."

She fist-bumped me when I reached her
before she asked,
"Where is that wife of yours?
She's hot as fuck."

On our way in I told her…

"She's out of town."

"If she wants a summer job,
I'll hire her in
a heartbeat."

"Don't you dare Rachelle."

As I stepped inside a Dude in a cheap suit opened the door and greeted me with…

"Welcome to Wild Forest!"

I nodded thanks. Looked around at the porn magazine wallpaper, thought of Lenin working there, and mumble…

"She would never."

Inside, the DJ had *Set It Off* spinning as I followed Rachelle. Years ago, it looked like the bedroom of teenage girl with creepy pink and baby blues; mirrors everywhere. But now, laser rays shot across the club and bounced off disco balls while other lights silhouetted the dancers as a steam machine created a few inches of cool mist drifting over the main stage; a disco flashback. The club was crowded, but the energy was far from the Rising Sun. As I looked around, Rachelle gestured me to follow her to the DJ booth.

In there, the DJ had his gut kissing the shelf that the media players rested on. His left hand tweaked some knobs, right hand rocked a clenched fist, head bobbed with puckered lips before he took his headphones off, glanced over at me, and puffed an E-Cig. Rachelle introduced us…

"This is DJ Joey Good-as-Beignets.
Joey… Braze.
He made a movie about… "

"The Art of Train Hoppin!
I bought it off you one night
at the Art Market."

We shook hands.

"Fuckin
work of art that movie.
You really drink that Listerine?
What-a-ya-doin here?
Hanging?"

Jeez, what was I doing out of the Enclave? Then those reoccurring visions surfaced and reminded me what triggered all this. Walking up and down Bourbon Street that night and ending up in Wild Forest? Was like coming full circle on The Boardwalk. It felt as home as 88's Quo Vadis Night Club (Formerly First Methodist Church) at the Jersey Shore. Weird, but I must admit… some of the best times I've ever had on dancefloors have been in old churches turned into new clubs. That in mind, *Lookout Weekends* spinning, and without checking in with me, *BRIGHTDAWN* hijacked my lips…

"Can I have a job Rachelle?"

My eyes darted towards the top of my forehead wondering what-duh-hell only to find *MES* doing The Whop in a window. While I processed this Rachelle belted out…

"Hell-yeah."

I was totally pushed aside and not part of this decision-making process. Next thing I heard…

"You're in my hut now."
When Joey dropped another old track.

God damn *BRIGHTDAWN*! *MES* acting the fool! I should've known better. I didn't get drunk, didn't get high, yet still my mind played tricks on me; fuckin' ghetto!

On the way home through The Quarter they co-signed each other's bullshit. *BRIGHTDAWN* said he just wanted to get closer to those recent scenes unfolding in mind. And *MES* kept saying he knew his way around in the dark and that he could help get us in and out before Lenin got back. My argument… we're going to work in the wrong club!

"The story's up the street
knuckle-heads!"

The next morning, I dragged ass out of bed after a short nap, made some notes, and had some tea. When within the steam from my cup… last night's images of the Circus inside of the Rising Sun seemed to materialize in miniature scale before me. The mental notes *BRIGHTDAWN* made came to life before my eyes! In the evaporating tea I found a physical connection to the projection of unnatural images before me. My nervous system and reproductive part made my adrenalin system flood. Feeling a sudden climax coming from nowhere I slumped in my chair and looked around the Loft to find on every brick, breathing breasts! *MES* and *BRIGHTDAWN* stood behind each one of my windows with their hands pressed against my eyeballs eagerly looking out. Then, I woke up in bed. My mind was no stranger to playing tricks on me, but the Loft never tripped me out like this so much! One night a brothel, the next… a tit padded room.

Completely sober, I really didn't want to believe that these lucid impressions I was getting where perhaps premonitions. Nothing is more misleading to me than thinking I'm smart. And connecting dots between my dreams and my future fuels my mania and boundless fabrications. But that's what I was doing on Bourbon Street, chasing lucid dreams; I knew that. Sensing a story waiting for us on Bourbon, *BRIGHTDAWN* spoke up last night. But I've learned that he's an expression of my mania, and really can't be trusted any more than *MES*. I knew that my mind was just racing. But when a mind like mine is attracted to something, the chase is on. From train hopping to love bombing, my head takes charge. By this time in my sober life I was much keener to my feelings and where my chemical messages were actually coming from in the brain. By labeling everything like I have, things weren't so mystifying.

I would already be getting it from Lenin once I told her about me even going to those clubs. But if I went there for a higher purpose, I'd have more than just wandering in on a whim as my excuse. Looking back on it, I should have cut my losses and just told her I slept walk to Bourbon Street one night when she was gone. But instead, I would later let *BRIGHTDAWN* show up for work that night to research a hunch that a story was still waiting there for us on Bourbon Street.

My first night employed in the shadows of Wild Forest I was of course clean shaven in a suit wearing heavy cologne I hadn't splashed on the face since forever. Rachelle let me float around Wild Forest the first night. I had a little black notebook in hand trying to keep up with the info in front of me like a student in class. Making those notes immediately freaked some women out who assumed I was a narc or something. But my buddy Rachelle ran the place so it seemed whatever I did, was good with her. In fact, she seemed entertained by the reactions of some of the strippers in regards to my notes. She found that a "Spy" in this house of love could be as effective as the "Eye" in the Sky; the surveillance cameras around the joint. She introduced me to everyone that first night as…

"A filmmaker-friend."

That allowed me to note observations with a purpose. I was honest with my new co-workers about researching a project. Some opened up, others clammed up. Yet after one night working in a strip club, I think I'd rather have tea than a lap dance. The dull night ended at 3am.

My alarm to get up went off at six, I didn't let the moonlighting slow my roll too much. In fact, it got me back on track and off the Ibuprofen PM. I went to my turntable, drop a needle on a record and let a soft drum beat start *Morning Phase*. Coffee brewed as I opened the French doors to the balcony and took in the first fresh breath of the day. Then, two home bums started arguing below. A weed-whacker fired up across the street. And a Febreze-truck turned the corner spewing a ton of chemicals on the street. After breakfast and my Morning Pages it was off to lap Crescent Park before I set up the bookstand in French Market.

Once I was opened for business, I was signing Paperbacks and taking questions. Such as…

"Rehabbing from what exactly?"

For me that's far from a one-word answer.

I responded,
"I didn't discriminate."

Rather than… you want a list? I was so looking forward to my ten-minute nap at lunchtime after my first night in Wild Forest. I called my naps, the scenarist-siesta. Often at lunch time that summer I began running into Lenin's little step sister Kireka, practicing tricks on her skateboard in the parking lot between the Loft and The Market. She hung with the Humidity Skateboard crowd at that time. Her and I always it chatted when she caught me on the way to a nap.

I showed up for night two at Wild Forest after working all day in the French Market when Rachelle decided to give me a hospitality position. That allowed me a good perspective of things and let me keep floating. I made it no secret I needed to cram my experience into one work week before Bella returned from Brazil; they thought that was a joke. The strippers just figured me for a closet voyeuristic lurking to writing some erotica while my wife was out of town. But Rachelle was very, very interested in my notes. She said…

"With the staff knowing you're a filmmaker,
They'll tell you things they
never tell me."

Rachelle really wanted to read them because she thought everyone was doing things on the sly in there. I told her I'm open to her looking at them, but to clarify her motives I asked…

"Are you looking for some sort of…
ethical audit?"

"Wow. Yeah! Exactly."

"What exactly do you want to know?"

"Who's fucking me.
And, who's fucking who."

Evidently that was a big NO-NO. No dating between employees was permitted in the club. I had to sign a confidentiality agreement too. Thus, not including here much, or anything about the "Eye in the Sky" office. That was deep back stage, off limits to most employees. But I will say this, it was obvious to me that the coked up main surveillance guy back there under his cowboy hat wasn't just focused on security, but a great deal of self-interests. That info would later be currency.

Into the groove of working all day in The French Market and all night at Wild Forest was actually what I needed to quill the sadness I felt while Lenin was in Brazil. Every other day we'd video chat and she'd share some more Portuguese she learned, or show me a new move she was learning in Capoeira. I was so happy for her! And fully regretted not being there to enjoy it. I was careful not to share the memories of my own inner city breakdance circles in my youth when she was describing the Afro-Brazilian rodas down there. I wanted her discoveries to be hers, and not, just an opportunity for me to relate. As I listened to her talk fast with such excitement about Brazil, I certainly thought it best to keep silent about moonlighting on Bourbon Street. Until she got home that is. After just a couple nights in the Strip Life, I knew it wasn't right for me. And more importantly, what I wanted for the next chapter in my life. I wanted something brighter with Lenin. So, telling her about hitting a dead end on Bourbon Street could wait till she was home from Brazil.

Yet before I made the final decision to completely nix Bourbon Street, I gave *BRIGHTDAWN* just a little more room to see for himself that *MES* would probably be the only one who'd want to keep hanging out in Wild Forest. BRAZE plus *BRIGHTDAWN*, would easily cancel *MES* out. At that time, I felt that my stint on Bourbon was beneficial to clear my thoughts, restart, and perhaps dream bigger dreams again. And just after a couple nights working around the clock, I had a pleasant dream of my brother… He and I sweating it out on the courts of 18th and Wallace with old friend J-Smooth. My brother had such a nice jump shot.

Night three at Wild Forest I stepped off a rose gold elevator and onto the 2nd floor that opened to the VIP lounge where Ballers gained access to Fantasy Rooms. To get in one of those Theme Rooms, you had to get bottle service. That could run anywhere between 500-5,000 dollars. Around the VIP room were mini stages that were anchored by poles and surrounded by cocktail tables and love seats. They appeared to be foreplay stages where High Rollers got drunk before going back to a room of their choice with the stripper of their dreams. Some of the Guys appeared to have ongoing relationships of sorts with these Strippers. It appeared that despite them having to pay for the attention, they had their ego filtered it through a mind warp that told them they were natural players and not merely good paying customers.

I walked through VIP and to a balcony over Bourbon where customers and strippers' teased passerby's with out-of-season Mardi Gras beads. Looking out over the action it appeared like the good life to countless down there. I found a coworker Rasan playing his trumpet over Bourbon as if the Balcony were his stage. Below, good life it was I suppose, in that even some homeless people party on Bourbon with similar smiles as those parading around in upper-class attire. The French Quarter brings people together.

Night Four after another day in The French Market I found myself listening to a dancer tell me her story talking really-really fast. She accelerated with perverse and inhuman animation as I stood there burned out after only a couple hours of rest each night for days. Nothing plays tricks on my mind like lack of sleep. By then I'd totally seen enough. If there was a story worth pursuing in this place, it wasn't coming from these strippers. I gave *BRIGHTDAWN* & *MES* the taste they wanted, but there wasn't enough in there to keep me interested at all. If it doesn't take me to an edge, it's not edgy enough to write about. But hanging out with Joey in the DJ booth and discussing the ancient Rave era was enough to make the whole experience almost noteworthy to me; he was a character.

To switch it up that night I decided to shadow a lap-dance tracker at a kiosk that accounts for how many songs a stripper dances to with a customer. Basically, it's a register that keeps track of the cash that's owed to the club at the end of the night. It was there that I receive an alert in my headset. I looked up to the Eye in the Sky and responded immediately…

"Copy that!"

I rushed into the lap dance area upon urgent directions from the Eye in the Sky and raced by cubicles filled with dancers and customers to where one dancer was passed out. And a customer, was sucking on one of her breasts. I quickly, but gently, remove the thin dancer from on top that customer siting underneath her… just before six foot Rasan pulled the customer from his seat and threw him against the opposite wall!

Rasan asked sternly,
"Do you have an open tab
at the bar?"

"Na-no."
The creep said shaking in
his pants.

As Rasan relayed that info into the mic on his headset, I revived the dancer with a bottle of water. She was ok, but still out of it.

Moments later Rasan and I were in a back room with this guy. A room I'd not had access to prior. In there a picture was taken of this prick with a polaroid camera. Then it was hung on a large cork board with dozens of other headshots. But on the wall behind this asshole, unbeknownst to him yet, were graphic photo's that really got my attention.

Rasan went through his pockets and found some pills. He took a closer look at them, then dropped them in the trash before he turned to me and said…

"That's what he slipped her."

Rasan slowly took a key from his pocket, looked at it, then opened up a locker right next to the customer. Pulling out his trumpet case, he then slowly placed it on a counter, closed. Keeping eyes on the customer, he slammed the locker shut! Both the customer and I got nervous. Rasan was cool. He went to the trumpet case, looked up to me, then to the customer. Building an atmosphere of intensity with every calculated move he made. As I got anxious, the customer got terrified. I watched the large hands of Rasan closely, as he gently, unsnapped the clasp on the trumpet case. Before slowly opening it up with the contents in view. That being a beautiful brass trumpet on one side, and, extra-large shiny ass brass knuckles on the other.

"If I see you in this establishment again.
Ever again.
You'll go from this board…"

Pointing to the creep's polaroid shot on the wall in front of him before continuing…

"…to that one."

Pointing to corkboard behind the customer. The creep finally looked over his shoulder at the wall he stood against, filled, with headshots of men unrecognizably beaten in the face.

One would think this would be an issue in the Ethical Audit, but it was nothing more than how Wild Forest handled predators. It spoke to their balls, of which these guys had little. It was simple. If they clearly got the message the first time, they avoided leaving with a bloody reminder the second. There was a Zero-Tolerance Policy when it came to predatory monsters behind this classic marquee at Wild Forest. Reporting issue to outside authorities at times could put liquor licenses in jeopardy. Thus, managing such problems is often contained in the club. Outside, it's as common to find someone beat up on Bourbon as it is to find a street person overdosing on French Market Place. We escorted the creep out a side door and into the early morning chaos of Bourbon Street with a shove and kick in the ass. That sent him into the gutter and on his hands and knees. Then Rasan took his trumpet from under his arm, and put it gracefully to his lips. And proceeded to gush his soul onto the street and gently towards the rough necks in the crowd with talent and taste I suspect were undetected most. As he continued to blow out the blues, I went for my ink pen and Moleskine to note what just went down. This is not, not how I should have started out our marriage that summer.

GARRET SCENARIO No.2

The next afternoon I eagerly closed my bookstand early to pick up Lenin at the Airport with a hand full of flowers. When she surfaced from a wave of upper-crust travelers in the airport she emerged with that one beat up schoolbag as happy as I'd seen her in years. Absolutely glowing! That while her brother Thorsen looked as if he were sleep walking in the middle of his students on their iPods. When Bella reached me, she gave me wild kisses on my face like she was a love crazed pigeon. I'd play the role of her love pigeon any day; any day-ever again.

On the drive home she was holding on to me around my neck with both hands as she spoke in my ear and went on about how…

"Brazil is such a mystical land.
It's incredible!
You'd love it."

"Mystical?"
I inquired.

"I think most are Catholic.
But even some of them go to
Spirit Mediums for healings.
And most who say they don't believe
in Spiritism,
appeared to fear it."

"How about the graffiti?
Did you ever make it
to Batman Alley?"

"No.
I never got to Sao Paulo.
I was too busy with my
friend I made."

"Who's the new friend?"

"A beautiful, strong girl named Izabelle.
So beautiful.
Such a sad story though."

"How so?"

"She escaped drug dealers who forced
her to have sex with them."

"Was she on drugs?"

"She said she never took them knowingly.
But she knows she was drugged the first time.
After that she woke up with other girls
imprisoned somewhere.
They were only allowed out of confinement to eat,
or have sex."

"She was a sex-slave?"
I asked.

"In the process of becoming one."
Lenin responded.

"There's a process to it?"

"Yup.
And when they break you,
they sell you."

"They put her up for sale?
I asked dumfounded.

"She got away first.
She ran as far as she could from them.
About a thousand miles away to Rio.
To the statue on the mountain with arms open."
She described,
"Christ, the Redeemer?"

"Yeah. I know it."

"She was to ashamed to
return home."

"How old is she?"

"Seventeen.
She's graduating from the
High School this year."

"Good for her!"

"She wants to go to college."
Bella added.

"Cool."

"I'm going to pay for it."
She informed me. Then added,
"And she needed an apartment now.
I got her one down there."

"Why'd she need an apartment?"
I asked.

"She was staying with cousins,
and the family made her do
all the house work."

I guess I gave Lenin a perplexed look. She responded…

"You can't study and be
a fulltime maid."

My expression must have said more.

"What Braze?
There are worse things to do
with my money."

The first thing that came to my mind was, what money? But I just smiled. My wife has a big heart. I'd thought about having a kid since that bookstore in Amsterdam. But my wife seemed to adopt one first. I thought… we were kind of on the same page; maybe.

While incense burned from her Buddha statue and a couple candles burned next to our bed when we got home, we were lovers again; nothing compares to that. With Bella Lenin back the Loft was home again and the multidimensional happenings ceased. It felt like a new beginning.

While she was gone, she got a package in the mail from Australia. When I pointed that out, she said…

"Oh, that took forever.
I forgot all about it."

"What is it?"
I asked.

"Supplements."

The next day I got back on schedule and woke at 2am to journal…

I write to survive.
Ive been doing this since I was a teenager. But I dont think anyone knows this about me. Not even Lenin. When times are good, I usually write in this journal about my days. But when times are bad, a project surfaces to save me from myself. Death has been a hangover away for decades now. Writing is the only tested, tried, and true way to buy me precious, thoughtful time. When I get up early to write there's no time to drink or drug. And when things weigh on me, I always seem to write my way out of it. And perhaps thats why I'm so departmentalized these dayz… to hide from the side that wants to get high, or worse. Im often asked if what I write is truth or fiction. My automatic response is that I release my work as fiction no matter how true it is. I find my work most therapeutic through meta writing. And truth is Im held less accountable for fiction. Though Im a confessional writer, I dont want people to think somethins really wrong with me.
Im often asked…

"How are you doing now?"
Or,
"How are you feeling since?"

Im not a person who can trust his feelings!
Nothing should matter as much as it often feels to me, Not till the last mile. But perhaps thats the problem. The end always feels right down the road. So here I am again. Doing these Artists Way Morning Pages till the next big thing happens.
I really need a project!
One that MES, and BRAZE, can get behind.

Later that morning after two more pages of longhand stream of consciousness writing I went for a bike ride at sunrise by the River. It promotes emotional sensitivity, physical wellbeing, and awareness of Earth passing through nature. The priority's not to let my mind race with arbitrary thoughts out there. But rather to feel the emptiness of mind to a degree of spatial awareness so not to exhaust my City of Lakes. My racing mind mind is sure to exhaust me, if I let it.

On the way home towards The Quarter in Crescent Park, I can't help but take notice to the Bridge where my brother took his life. For a long time, the sight of it would make me numb. But now years after his death I try to look at it more as a huge memorial. Recovery from anything is a process, and grief is complicated. Some take chemicals for it. Others process the emotions naturally; I did both at times. But ultimately, I get through the darkness of losing my brother by reading. The more I learn about what triggers my emotions, and thinking, the more I learn to observe them. And the less I tend to react. And with that, I've become less prone to my own suicidal thoughts. I-duhno… perhaps more bridges could bring awareness to those we lose through death by suicide, and not just what the Crescent City Connection is through my eyes. Letting things go, or pass, or just slip way, often saves my life. Such drastic feelings as mine account for the sounds in my head from the Piano of Emotions in the uppermost chapel in my City of Lakes. And at this chapter in my life, I probably knew enough to play *Mary Had A Little Lamb* on it.

Upon my return to the Loft that morning, something weighed on me; I was nervous. My paranoia of not being truthful loomed. I'd yet to tell my wife that I let my weirdo dreams, not to mention a fractured personality, lead me to work at Wild Forest. To complicate things, I noticed what was inside that package she got in from Australia; breast enhancement supplements. Looking at those pills and thinking about how she'd feel about me working at a topless joint, made it even harder to be truthful. What the hell was I thinking while she was gone! I closed my eyes and covered my face with my hands, when *BRIGHTDAWN* whined inside…

"Damn COME ON man! Relax.
It was research."
Then *MES* added,
"We're sober not saints."

I opened my eyes and shook those two unicorn-farts off, settled down, got my mind right, and took a shower.

I heard some new music coming from the Loft when I got out. And instead of finding Lenin doing yoga, she was moving, grooving, ducking and weaving like a fighter. Kicking and wind-milling her feet and legs like Bruce Lee taking a ballet class. This I gathered, was Capoeira. And the music behind it, the traditional beats of the practice. I was impressed and joined in, but my uprock busted her groove. She stopped and turned off the music.

"Sup girl?"

But she just walked away. I followed her into the kitchen and hugged her from behind, but she was distant. I just assumed she thought I was making fun when I joined in.

"Sorry BL.
It wasn't my intention to
disrespect or… "

"Don't mention it.
It's fine."

I dropped it.

"What do you have going on today?"
I asked.

"Look for a summer job.
I have to pay off this debt now."

"Where you gonna look?"

"I got on the computer to make
resume when I woke up."
she said shaking her head,
"Then I just decided to look for something
in walking distance that I may not
need one for after all."

She walked out of the Loft and into the bathroom, closing the door behind her pretty hard. It wasn't my fault she ran up some bills. And, blew her savings on some girl in Brazil who probably conned her into paying the rent. But I swallowed that. I looked around the Loft thinking we may be broke, but we live damn good. We had a lot to be thankful for. Then I couldn't help but giggle a little. Her underwear was hanging from the ceiling fan. I must have thrown them up there the day before when she first got back.

When I took them down and noticed holes in them, I threw them in the trash rather than the hamper. Then I noticed those beat up shoes of hers with holes in them that had recently trekked through both Amsterdam, and Brazil among everywhere else she walked last few years. My wife was so unmaterialistic that she only had that one single pair of shoes to her name. Well… two. But she never, ever wore the expensive heels I bought for her at Shoe Be Doo on Charters Street back in the day; nope.

Before I left to select my stall in the French Market that morning, I decided to do what I could to help her make a good impression looking for a job and pushed sixty dollars under the bathroom door.

"Hey Bells here's some cash.
You really need shoes."

But I didn't get a response.

"They might have some Fare Trade
ones at Hippie Gypsy."
I suggested.

Then I heard the tub water turn off in there, and noticed the bills I had half tucked under the door, be pulled inside without a word from her. I just thought she was uncomfortable taking the money, but was very relieved she did. Those sneakers of hers where in no condition to go job-hunting.

Later that afternoon I was sitting at my table signing a book when my pal Todd rolled up on his skateboard. Since producing **CURE** *for the* **CRASH** together he'd visit the Bookstand often to check in with me.

"What up B.
How the Strip Life?"
He asked with
grin.

"I don't work there anymore
dude."

"What happen?"
He asked.

"Not today."

I gestured to him to quickly DROP IT as Lenin's lil-sis Kireka was rolling up. I greeted her…

"Sup Kireka!"

"Hi Braze. Sup Todd.
Did you hear the good
news Todd?"

Todd nodded YES, held his palms to the sky, and replied…

"He has risen."

They both had a laugh; skater humor I assumed.

"You guys know each
other."

"Ever-body knows Todd."
Kireka boasted, then asked,
"Is Lenin back!"

"Yup!
But she's not home right now.
She's out looking for
a job."

"OK.
Tell her I miss her."

"I'll remind her to holler
at you Kirek."

Kireka skated off to some other friends waiting for her in the French Market parking lot.

Across town Lenin walked up Bourbon Street when a few tight piano keys stuck me creating an atmosphere of tenseness that I could feel where I stood on the other side of The Quarter. I sensed her drifting along with a calmness in stark contrast to the sudden winds in my City of Lakes where this information stirred. Goose bumps followed with merely a tickle of the nostrils as I breathed in more info. I looked to my forehead for clarity but found adrenaline giving mix messages that caused a disruption to interdisciplinary fields creating not so clear mental images, or in plain English, Dutch was groggy. Then a loud freight train whistle from across the street surprised me. It was a warm 4th of July, but I was suddenly chilled to the bones at my Bookstand.

As Todd was going on about something and Kireka practiced tricks in the background, I had the overwhelming need to see if Lenin was ok. The train whistle blew again nearly putting a fright in me. I had to cut Todd off…

"I gotta make a call my
T-O-double D."

Lenin picked up and just before she answered I heard an electro remix of Marcy Playgrounds *"Sex & Candy"* playing in the background before she said…

"Hi Braze…

…I'm fine…

…totally fine…

…I'm, still looking."

She nodded YES to a sales person somewhere.

I wished her luck on the job hunt.
Told her I loved her.

"I love you too."

She nodded NO to a sales person who was suggesting something else before she added to me…

"I might be late tonight.
I was asked to come back later
for an interview."

In the Market I slapped Todd five as he skated off while I responded to her…

"That's good news.
We'll catch the Fireworks
after dinner."

I breathed a sigh of relief just hearing her voice. She can calm my waters every time. I gave my attention to a few fellas at my Bookstand reading the synopsis on GLACIER before one asked…

"Is that you?"
He asked uncertain while
pointing to my photo on the
BOOK SAFE cover.

"At one time.
I'm, a man of many faces."
I said shrugging my
shoulders.

"Will you sign the book?"
He asked.

"I'd be honored."

That's how chapters of my life story go, one Garret Scenario at a time. But I'm no big success at all…

Everything from t-shirts to gator heads are successfully slung in this Street Market. But what's produced isn't the issue here, what's being bought is. The only reason such disposable wares and cruel trinkets are sold, is because Tourists are buying these souvenirs. The longer I'm in this Market, the more FUGAZI's *BLUEPRINT* is reaffirmed.

After my evening bike ride through Crescent Park the sun began to set and create a warm glow through the lunette of the Loft. If there's a more peaceful, naturally-romantic lit space in The Quarter that time of day… it's unbeknownst to me. I turned a couple Edison Bulbs on to warm the centuries old bricks as I wrapped *"The Melancholy Death of Oyster Boy"* by Tim Burton in some newspaper comics, made some tea, and waited for my

Love to come home. That little book was to be my baby talk icebreaker personally imported from abroad.

Later, I sat in an armchair that once belonged to my great grandparents as I glanced at my radio controlled wrist watch under a light over my shoulder; I was reading a book in each hand. *MES* devoured "The War of the Worlds" behind my left-socket, and *BRIGHTDAWN* read "War of the Worldviews" with my right eyeball, Dutch read the time: 8:59. Concerned why Lenin hadn't returned yet, I put the books down and gave her another call. But again, no answer. Then the fireworks startled me. I got so jumpy that day! I knew how to cope with nervs, but on that 4th of July I felt like a tweaker, or, as if I were being watched before noticing where the danger stood that wasn't there.

I walked to an open widow over the French Market, let out a big breath, and watched the fireworks over the Mississippi River by the Bridge. Taking a seat on the windowsill, I curled up with my chin resting on my knees eyes wide on the 4th of July sky. There, I sat motionless for minutes, before the front door opened. And the hallway shed light on the cozy atmosphere in the Loft where behind me I noticed the fireworks creating a soft blanket through the skylights; as if watercolors evaporated before my eyes. Lenin called my name over THE XX spinning on the antique 1200…

"Braze?"

"Yeeeah."
I said in a high pitch voice before
clearing my throat,
"Come quick, it's show time."
I urged.

She found me in the far window silhouetted by fireworks and gave me a hug and a kiss just… as the show ended.

"Sorry I'm late.
But I have good news."
She said,
"I got a job."

"Great."

But… she held on to the news. And just waited with a smile for me to ask where. So-this had to be good! I was thinking, Insectarium. I shrugged my anxious shoulders in response and urged her further to just…

"Tell me tell me
pleeease."

I looked into her wide eyes above her frozen smile, but got no answer from her; yet. Even more curious I asked again, confused…

"So… where?"

"Bourbon Street."
She said with the quickness.

"No shit?"
I said shocked!

That sucks. But I comforted her…

"You have to go where
the work is."

I knew she didn't want to work there. But who am I to judge? Still unbeknownst to her I worked there last week, I assumed she…

"Got a gig at The Bourbon House
or something?"

But she shook her head NO, and just kept that frozen smile on her face. That's, when I noticed she wasn't blinking. It was then, immediately… I knew where the danger stood. But it was too late the dagger was traveling my way…

"I'm working at the
Rising Sun."
She said bluntly. Smiling,
no more.

And with that… the harsh, unseasonal chill came upon me once again and through the window itself as if Hell's ice rink just opened.

MES said,
"Damn, that's cooold shitz."

"Wait… WHAT?
I said as if there was a
mother-fucker
at the end.

She was nervous. I was confused to the core. *BRIGHTDAWN* tried rationalize the situation…

"Easy-peasy…
she's cocktail waitressing
big-bro."

"You cocktail waitressing?"
I asked her in a high
pitch voice.

Once again she nodded NO just before…

"Nope,"
came from the mouth of the
woman I love. Jus-before she dropped
"I'm stripping,"
dead in my eyes as if I was
expected to just
swallow it.

But keeping this down was like digesting a bar rag!

My stomach revolted first as I dry heaved a bitter cough out the window, watering my eyes. The romantic voices of THE XX in the Loft were suddenly Bombed by The Gap Band from a passing car stereo down French Market Place.

"Damn, hell, what the…"
I said coughing and shaking my head looking
down at the roof below not being able
to finish a thought.

I gathered myself. And stepped down from the windowsill to stand face to face with her. We exchanged anxious, furious, heartbreaking and nearly violent breaths; the latter coming from me. *MES* bit his fist, *BRIGHTDAWN* stood scratching the back of his head with his tongue in his cheek. Before I finally got the fuck out oh-so calmly…

"I, I don't get it.
I thought I knew you.

Why would you do this to us?"
I asked.

"Let's talk later,
I got-to go."

"Go strip."
I said as if making sure I got this
shit-right.

She nodded YES.

"I'm on a break."
She added walking away.

I boiled! And tipping points lead to tipping points. Truth be known I've turned over furniture and have been prone to further indiscretions in our past, when… instantaneously *BRIGTHDAWN* played the victim upstairs as *M*ES broke a wine glass over his head. Bringing such a thought back, keeps me from the act.

In the soft light bouncing off the A-frame she picked up that old school bag of hers off the sofa and put it over a shoulder, when I noticed the high heels dangling from a strap! The same heels I bought her at Shoe Be Do moons ago. She never wore them out with me once, NOT once! I was about to go ape-shit as I imagined her trotting in them tall heels by a pack of Wild Dickheads! Then giving a lap dance to a human size dog whose tongue was dripping on her breast slobbering out…

"Shoe-Be-Doobbie-Do!"

Before she brought me back to reality on her way out the door…

"You don't have to wait up."

But then, as if scripted, on the other side of the Loft she stopped in her tracks. Appearing to ponder something. Just before she went so far as to ask me for some advice…

"What is
a good stage name?

Bewildered by this sudden orbit I found myself thrust in to, I processed this bullshit further before asking…

"Nobody asked your fuckin'
name yet?"

"Nope.
I just had a drink.
I go on stage later.
They need to know my name.
To, you know.
Introduce me to the crowd."

She waited over the for my input, adding…

"Got any cool names,
Mr. Graffiti?"

I stood there just looking at her, blown away! Confused on multiple levels for obvious reasons. I was definitely not on board, nor would I encourage it by contributing a fresh alias. But *BRIGHTDAWN* got to my fat mouth again and pulled a mind-whammy suggesting…

"Chloe."

"Chloe don't know-a goddamn thing."
BRIGHTDAWN remarked.

"Chloe jus-like me."
MES responded.

"What the fuck is going on here!"
I said shake-n-lookin-at
my forehead.

She must have thought I was crazy, but what did she expect? Instead of engaging me, or co-signing *BRIGHTDAWN's* bullshit, she simply spun around to leave with the grace of a ballerina as my perception of events burned up like film on fire. Leaving me in the dark a desperate soul in the Freedom Tunnel of my City of Lakes. All I could hear was water leaking, train wheels choking tracks, and what I think… was a shopping kart being pushed over gravel between my ears.

Forgetting about the book I gift wrapped in the comics, and rather than chase her down to discourage her, or worse. I emerged from the darkness in my City of Lakes to take refuge in The Enclave at my Write-Away

Chest to scribe what just went down. Once inside my safe place, I felt tall grass that grows below the power lines I've strewn through the hillsides of my mind sway with the winds where birds circled in sync around utility poles inside my head; before I breathed out a disappointing…

"Jeez."

It sure seems like I'm in constant reconstruction in my life. And if I don't roll with the progress it will beat down to an earlier grave. That's why I didn't put up a fight. I've learned not to fight my future when it first appears. But rather keep fighting for it! I find anxiety to be and inferno fueled by wanting the present to be different in the future much sooner. Since the loss of my brother I just let *BRIGHTDAWN* be my guiding Sherpa at times like these. I knew whatever I got myself into here, he could write my out, and he did that night.

While making his notes I gradually felt my nerves easing and my heartrate get jacked by the stiffening synthesizer between my thighs; but it's normal at times to get off on my lines. After a few more power points my nose began to tickle, and my nostrils expanded to the size of Quarters. Now before I learned how to let these feeling be neurotransmitters to the Courier Prime before you, these were the psychological events that led me to self-medicate in the past. At this season though I let thoughts flow and my jungle-heart dance with throbs of expectancy! By the time I looked up, my soldier Dutch was opening with the intro of The Neville Brothers *Fly Like an Eagle Bass Like an Eagle* dub. To jam with I stepped out to windy balcony playing the air-bass to unleash my Eyeball-Beast as *MES* & *BRIGHTDAWN* chimed in…

"Do-do-dodo,"
as Dutch soared from the
City of Lakes.

My 3rd Eye with wings found my wife walking through the Hungry Eyes of the Shoeless as her heels dangled from her bag in the 4th of July mayhem, where ten thousand Tourons walked over Homeless dispersing the Riverwalk and on to Bourbon like cattle over Leftover Crack. Above it all… Clouds filtered the Moonlight where Dutch flew through the ancient atmosphere as natures bassline began to roll and thunder. Followed by electro-fast high hats, the unseen maestro created a bridge in the rhythm as the stride of Bella Lenin appeared to acid-trail in her wake. In this firestorm of hot summer electricity her face glowed and The Animals emerged! Fire-starters and Hell-raisers took notice, and those in her way stepped aside as Bella trailblazed forward with the gravity of her heavenly body paving the way. Just as she made it back to the club, the sky opened up with Eric Burdon's voice as loads people poured inside taking shelter in the Beat-Haus of the Rising Sun.

In the meantime, I found my way downstairs to the Italian restaurant on the corner where the bartender asked me…

"Would you like another
O'Doul's?"

"Keep um' coming."
I responded.

Only hoping that my wife wasn't a late blooming swinger I added…

"With a root beer chaser,
please."

I felt sidelined from the scene! When my shot was served, I washed it down with a quick swig. The bartender gave me a cute smirk. I responded to her unwanted attention by informing her…

"Dummy substances relieve
stress too."

I handed her back the empty shot glass when she added…

"One's soft drink,
another's antidote."

"Give me another please.
Make it a double."
I said not so kindly.

As she poured my shooter from the soda gun, I thought… I'm the writer here, I eat drama for breakfast. Why was I placebo drinking over this?

MES murmured behind my eye,
"Don't be insecure."

Unplugged I looked over
and responded,
"Shut up."
Like Cobain to Grohl.

Which got me a different smirk from the bartender.

"No not you."
I tried clarify
before I went on to ask *MES*,
"Can I do this myself?"

"Do it by yourself."
MES responded frustrated.

Dancing on stage is one thing, but lap dancing is quite another. And the thought of someone spending VIP time with my wife disturbed the fuck out me. I'm possessive?

"You're possessive."
BRIGHTDAWN sounded off deep as a
Novoselic bassline.

One minute I was watching fireworks waiting for the Love of my Life. The next, she's walking out the door to peel off her clothes for other guys. Whatever my issues were about all this, the label "chump" fit too. But I knew one thing, I had to put a spin on this so I didn't look like one later. Dutch came back, perched on my shoulder, and flapped his wings dry on the side of my face; it really wasn't my night. Frustrated, I shooed him back out in the rain to further our research. He'd have to weather it just like us.

Inside the Rising Sun, packed as it was after the fireworks, Lenin was standing in the shadows of the club unnoticed. With a tall iced cocktail in hand showing buku skin she found the air conditioning nothing short of freezing as the music tickled her goosebumps. Born with a body that could break hearts, I never imagined her using it to break the bank! A few of the veterans in the joint assessed her in the half-light she stood. She was fresh meat, looked nervous, and was nothing more than a new comer who's presence was not yet solidified.

But she was there for one thing and one thing only that night. She went back to dance on stage.

Hospitality dwarfs skated by her on roller sneakers bringing a smile to her face. By now Dutch was perched above it all in the rafters taking witness while the DJ began to lead her from the darkness. It appeared her only support in the club was the music. The more the music warmed her up, the more she found the club invigorating and not the overload to the senses it could be on such an amateur performer. Her eyes were on the pro on stage the whole time. Like her Mom at her age, she was probably close to chickening out at any moment. But this DJ could not be underestimated. He was older than dust and burned the place up like a forest in a kiln! Dude was the sum of something else yet to be revealed. You just can't be sure about cats like that who are still rather indecipherable to most at this stage of human development. But to me, he seemed to be channeling something on another wavelength. Perhaps he was the conduit between life and death in there. Although I've seen the music have this effect on many in numerous clubs, this guy brought it to a more, cosmic level. Let me further the impression Dutch got…

It appeared that the Rising Sun was an afterhours stop for the spirits who worked the Sidney Smith Hunted History Tours, not to be confused with the fakes. Old Souls hopped through bodies in the Club like hobos on boxcars joy riding bones like amusements at the Boardwalk. The spirits felt human, and the humans felt more soulful. But none this struck Bella Lenin. She was still too nervous and freezing her butt off whiles her attention drifted from the dancer on stage to the trapeze artists above. Even more ecstasy exuded up there from those stars! In such a spotlight those entertainers high above it all swung from sheer fabrics radiating more and more energy in the Rising Sun. She must have had the strongest desire to sparkle like these other admirable women in this Universe; why else would she stick around? Entranced, she let those entertainers shine down on her with her eyes closed and her face to the sky. I guess the energy from those artists above in this sexual soul asylum finally gave her the courage to make her way to the dressing room and ready herself to let'um hang out on stage. Thus, giving birth to this, my Nightmare on Bourbon Street.

Perhaps delusional in the Loft with these thoughts, wearing a classic goalie mask holding a cake knife. Before I slid the Flyers Helmet off my face and stuffed my mouth with beignets. I took notice to the cake plate given to us at our wedding by my Mom. And found that little book I brought back from Amsterdam still gift wrapped next to it! I was disgusted with myself. I should have given her that lil-book at the airport last week. And had that fucking talk about our beautiful future in the goddamn car! As I sipped my tea, I got hot, REAL hot. I pulled at my t-shirt around my neck to get some air. Then, I must have lost control as I ripped off the shirt as if I were the Hulk! Before I resumed sipping my tea, calmly. I knew I was over reacting and this behavior didn't reflect the progress I've made in my adultish life. Nonetheless I devoured the last donut, gulped the liquid gunpowder, and dashed out in my jeans and sneakers.

Shirtless, I probably just looked like another mad man running down the Moonwalk. But I needed to give my heart a better reason to pound. Exercise levels out anxiety. But under the reflection of the Sun I couldn't outrun the darkness inside me. Earbuds in, *Riders* on… The Doors performed in a packed derelict amphitheater that burned down behind my eyes. I imagined I was dashing up a Hollywood Hill, rather than from myself in the French Quarter. As Chloe's curtain was rising, it felt like curtains for me jogging alone half naked by the Mississippi River; don't know what stopped me from…

Time and space in the Rising Sun began to weigh on Lenin. It was hers to be had, but only if she wanted it bad enough. Back in the dressing room she sat in the mirror taking deep breaths and called on more composer. A big-old Lady appeared in the mirror behind Lenin where she sat framed in stage bulbs applying her make-up who put it like this…

"Ok young blood, you on
next song."

"Yes Mam."
Lenin replied.

"Call me Honey Mama baby."

"Yes Momma, Honey.
I mean.
Honey Momma."

Honey Mama knew she had a rookie on her hands here.

"What's your name again?"
Mama asked sympathetically.

"Oh. I'm… damn."

She already embarrassed herself! Lenin covered her face for a moment with her hands trying to remember…

"What?"
Asked Honey Mama,
"You forget your name girl?"

Lenin took in a deep breath, and looked at her heavily made up face in the mirror. Before it came back to her…

"Chloe."
Then adding,
"I'm Chloe, Brazil."

Honey Mama must have thought she was another head case who's gonna fit right in saying into her headset…

"New Blood next! Copy?"
DJ Crowley Copy?
New Blood first name Chloe,
last name Brazil
Copy-dat?"

A second later…

"Hell-yeah I'm serious.
She proper.
Got two names."

Then she covered her headset mic with a hand and said to Chloe sitting there looking up…

"DJ out there think he a Rockstar,
can't even play the guitar.
Piano Man out there the only real musician.
Ya-heard-me?"

Bella Lenin a.k.a. Chloe Brazil at this time smiled and shook her head YES, slightly mesmerized. Then Mama's attention quickly shifted to something that alarmed her in the background…

"Hey, what? What the!
Oh, oh no."

Before walking off to tend to that business screaming…

"You know dare ain't no live
cyber-sexing up-in-chere.
Internet be killin' our hustle!
Keep it live.
Not Memorex my Babies."

When Bella Lenin branded herself Chloe, my wife would never be the same. But then again, it's been sung… no one ever leaves the same after doing what's done in the Rising Sun.

On the main floor in the club the atmosphere's Wild Style rocked with imported beats. Hospitality half-lings loaded bazooka's with confetti, as DJ Crowley welcomed my love on stage to bulging bloodshot eyes…

"Ladies, Fluids, Gents, and Undead.
Please help me baptize the freshest
entertainer on Bourbon Street.
As our RISING SUN shines
for the first time,
On Chloe…
BRAaaZiLlll!

Insync with the Piano on the other side of the stage Crowley dropped his psycho-somatic science behind the audio deck while Chloe exited the dressing room hallway in full stride, before, suddenly coming to a stop at the stage steps next to the piano. The Piano Man leaned over from his bench as she stared at the steps and asked her…

"Second thoughts
Chloe?"

Though he was right next to her she didn't look at him, but answered firmly…

"Absolutely not."
Before she looked over at him
and said,
"I'm just reminding myself
not to trip."

A much taller stripper walked by with a beautiful cosmic afro, blue lipstick, and silver top and bottom looking the utmost-sexy astronaut, glancing down at the newbie there at the foot of the steps. Who said to the Piano Man…

"This lil-thangs trippin'."

When chloe bent over to check the straps on her shoes, she fell down. A couple of hospitality dwarfs came to her aid immediately. One of the dwarfs whispered in her ear quite loud while she got back to her feet…

"If this happens on stage,
stay down. Crawl around!
Make it work."

Once she got back to her feet the other hospitality halfling screamed up to her…

"Work with what you got!
And you got this!"

After a couple deep breaths, she made the leap. Walked forward up the stairs assisted by the hand of a handsome employee and towards the blinding spotlight of the Rising Sun. Her initial step on stage was immediately followed by dwarfs emptying their party bazookas and showering her with countless tiny gold and silver squares. Once she made it in the spotlight, completely alone within the confetti nebula, Chloe Brazil had arrived! And as conflicted as a hung jury I must say, Dutch as my witness, she danced her ass-off for-fuck's sake.

Back in the Loft I was alone on the sofa trying to stay calm amidst my visions, plethora of assumptions and arbitrary thoughts listening to some classical 104.9 before the front door opened. Bringing me to my feet! We just stood there for a beat looking at each other. I with my mouth open, eyes wide. Her… jus-rather stoic.

That is before she cracked a smiled and gestured me with her arms open to…

"Come here."
for a hug.

As if I were just some unhappy child? And…

She furthered it by saying,
"It's ok."

I stood my ground. Didn't let my anger move me. But told her softly…

"It's not ok."

"What are you upset about?"
She asked.

"Right now?
How you're handling me.
Earlier tonight?
How you sprung this on me."

"You don't want me to strip?"
She asked.

I looked at her wondering why she needed to hear my predictable answer. But nonetheless she waited for it, patiently.

"NO. No Lenin.
I DO NOT,
want you to strip."

"Well…
what about what I want?"
She asked.

"Damn."
Said *MES* casually.

BRIGHTDAWN saw her point. But I responded…

"OK Lenin.
Answer that for me.
What do you want?"

For the first time that night when I could see some vulnerability in her eyes; I yelled…

GARRET SCENARIO No.2

"You want to hurt me
for some reason?
Put a spin on things?
Make me insecure?
Done! You… "

She cut me off,
"Let me answer!"

Then she got real.

"I-just…
I just wanted to see if I could
do it."

I calmed down and asked,
"Why?"

As I rubbed my neck. She stared off for a second.

"Confidence."
She said with vacant eyes,
"It takes a lot to bare yourself in front of
people who are only there to admire,
what you don't admire
about yourself."

"B.L. come-on.
Looking for confidence in a strip club,
is like… shopping for cool point
in a tattoo shop."

She suddenly woke from the vacancy behind her eyes with a jolt of bravado and bragged…

"But I danced for two
songs on stage!"

"I know."
I murmured.

But when I could see how happy she was, I surrendered, and exhaled forcing a smile. Before asking…

"How much money did
you make?"

I knew the more she made, the more Men she teased.

"I lost money."

Bewildering! But that sounded great to me. I lightened up…

"You-go-girl!
How you manage-at?"

"You have to pay $40 to work.
And after I tipped out the Piano Man, DJ,
and a couple other supporters…
I left the club with $27 in
ones off the stage."

At that point I realized it wasn't really the stage that bothered me, but the Lap Dances indeed. As if reading my mind, she added…

"I didn't do any lap dances.
I was just so happy I could dance on stage!
That was enough."

What a relief! Before she added…

"Enough for the first night."

The look in my eyes must have spoken volumes of disappointment. I stopped rubbing my neck and began quickly gripping fists full of hair. Pulling on my roots settles my City of Lakes. She went on…

"I'm going to see if I can
do it again."

In the family she was raised in anything seemed to be greenlighted, no matter whom it hurt, as long as you were honest about it. But I wasn't going to hurt for nothing. *BRIGHTDAWN* whispered suggestions. I concurred. And made our wishes clear that…

"If you're going to do this,
I need you to be honest with me.
I'd like details."

She quickly answered,
"Sure. I've been totally

honest with you.
Have you been with me?"

And suddenly, she looked at me like this was all my fault now. *MES* looked over at *BRIGHTDAWN* and mentioned…

"We didn't erase our
search history."

"Bells…"
I responded sympathetically,
"This was motivated by my Google search for
best strip club?"

"If you can go to the
Rising Sun while I'm gone.
Why can't I work there
when you're here?"

That said, it sounded like she didn't know I worked at Wild Forest; yet. But rather than pour gasoline on the whole situation, I tried to put out the first fire. I responded as if I were overly frustrated and completely disappointed with myself when I said…

"It was those hyper-weird
dream states.
They wouldn't let me rest
while you were gone!"
I expressed tensing up my shoulders
holding an invisible basketball.

But that was weak, no chance her buying that. Unmoved, with all seriousness, she asked…

"Tell me something Braze.
How's that dream look now?"

After a restless nap I made some quick notes in the Enclave and went for my usual bike ride by the River after sunrise. I was torn. Deep down I wanted the details rather than relying on my extrasensory perceptions. But further truths could be torturous. Yet if I could have worked there when she was gone, I would have. So, I needed in now! A little later over tea on the balcony I brought it up…

"Are you going to tell
me about it."

She shrugged her shoulders as if, what? I elaborated…

"About the others.
The atmosphere.
The dressing room, the… "

"You want exact details?"

"Yes."

She responded nonchalantly,
"Read my journal."

That surprised me, but I was careful not to look happy about it. I graciously said…

"Thank you."
Then I dug for more,
"How'd you feel in the mix
last night?"

She clinched her lips and looked around,
before responding,
"Nervous. Freezing.
Between butterflies and goose bumps I
nearly walked out."

"What else?"

"I felt so outshined I hid for a while.
The women are all so beautiful. So-hip.
I felt completely out of place.
Then I danced on stage."
She said with a smile
and half-laugh.
She went on to say…

"Think about it.
Last night I danced, in a spotlight,
on one of the most famous streets
in the world."

"Anybody can sing at
the Cats' Meow.

But that doesn't make
them famous."

She blew that off and thought…

"I could use the money for my
friend's housing and education
in Brazil."

But the fact was she lost money last night. But that really wasn't my concern. I expressed and asked…

"Despite how obviously
uncomfortable I am with this.
You're just going to
keep stripping?"

"Your uncomfortable?"
She asked.

I nodded a big YES! She responded…

"Welcome to my world."

Disturbed, I decided to share that…

"I have some news for you.
I didn't just go to the Rising Sun
while you were gone."

That got her curious.

"Full discloser.
I worked at Wild Forest
for a week."

And with that, back the shoe on the other foot! Her face turned red as a crawfish. Then I asked…

"You feel that Lenin?
That's how I've felt since
last night."

Kaput. She deflated. And screamed…

"Why would you work in a
Strip Club!"

"Bella Lenin.
Welcome, to MY world."

We were on the same page again.

By afternoon the chemical tides were calm and the cerebral traffic in my City of Lakes was moving along smoothly once again. It took approximately 15 hours to level out since Lenin dropped a bomb on me. During which time I can't say I thought about drinking or drugging over it. Nothing but hot tea, a run, a ride, and some critical thinking with those voices in my head. By this season of life, I felt like a spiritual endurance artist. With each challenge, I seem to transform. Martial Artists, Monks, Yogi's, and others have been mastering such transformative practices for centuries. With that awareness, I felt stronger than ever and felt potential to grow in this. I moved forward and opened my Bookstand as usual that day.

When I got home early that evening Lenin was at her sowing machine threading paisley handkerchiefs into, something. When she didn't look up at me once I got the message. It appeared night two would be another solo effort and obviously didn't need any support from me. Up till now I really thought she was just a person who wanted to be with family. Believed in higher education for all. And thought if you can afford to send people to war, you should support them when they return. A woman who gazed at the stars. And wanted to travel just as far in her heart. But what was going on with her now? What could explain something so out of character?

A little later she passed the armchair where I was reading a book and began to leave with her bag over her shoulder, heels dangling from the strap, before she stopped and turned saying…

"Braze,
I want you to know it's not because
of you I'm doing this.
But rather,
I couldn't do this without you."

I think when I sat there with my mouth open in response to that, she thought she had to explain further…

"Just knowing you love me…"

"I get it."
I said cutting
her short,
I didn't want to hear it.

Sad, but undeterred, she left for night two.

The Rising Sun's trapeze artist twirled over the audience, lowered up and down by muscular hospitality dwarfs on the ground. The little people employed at the Rising Sun brought energy to the club like only people of such stature can. While the Eye in the Sky could see everything from above and beyond, they made sure there was nothing going on illegally under the tables. There was never a bar with such security! I think that their gang was called the Bourbon Brawlers. I noticed them around town wearing that club sewn on their denim jackets. They didn't clown-around after work! They were Bikers who drove Ducati Style pocket bikes.

That night a couple of muscle bound dwarfs walked on extreme platform sneakers wearing soaked wife-beaters. Playing Stanley's, they called for Stella to those upstairs who were eye level with the aerialist. Where on the 2nd floor players had the women of their choice in VIP luxury. Much more intimate lap dances with slightly less boundaries where available there. While pervs wanted private rooms at Wild Forest, players wanted to be seen with playmates at the Rising Sun. Sometimes these players upstairs who noticed dancers on stage they desired? Made it rain money on them! That would signal to the men holding the ropes that there was a person above with more money than God calling on that entertainer. The body-built dwarfs would then lower an aerialist only to use the trapeze to pick up that highly desired entertainer from the stage. And with the help of more hospitality bodybuilders that would come rushing over, they lifted the irresistible goddess to the force of financial nature who made it rain paper on her from above. Piter Gaten, no doubt the executive producer of all this, was always watching.

Beneath him and within the mayhem looking at this happen with her mouth open, stood Chloe Brazil on her second night. With her breasts barley covered by her flashy patchwork that she stitched earlier with not so matching sexy underwear. She looked put together and mismatched by the likes of an accidental but rather successful stylist. And of course, at the foundation of it all were those dang artsy heels I bought her. But despite how great she looked, she still felt out of place. Not to mention once again covered in goose bumps by the air conditioning and oxygen pumping in the joint as strong as a Vegas casino floor.

While DJ Crowley worked with a dubstep remix of Porno for Pyro's *Tahitian Moon*, Hospitality Dwarfs stood on the cocktail tables rocking out with strap on cocks out. Bartenders juggled liquor bottles, and cocktail waitresses spun trays like Harlem Globetrotters all so in sync produced by Gaten himself. Everyone played his or her part like jazz musician improving on the same dope. Yet the newbie, Chloe, in the thick of it all… just couldn't find her groove. While she was nearly hiding again that night a slick pale executive of sorts approached her from behind. He looked VIP. All business. But he wasn't looking for a lap dance. He spoke to her closely in the ear, before she nodded YES. Together they walked off the main floor, her following him, upstairs.

Way up there on the 4th floor her face was tense and eyes squinted as they adjusted to a brightly lit office; bright at least on her side of the room. She was on full display under a high-hat spotlight. An unpleasant air conditioned breeze blew the scent of a jerk around. In her presence, source of the heavy cologne, Pieter Gaten. He spoke to her with his American Russian accent from behind his gaudy hand-carved wood desk where even his desk lamp shinned her way…

"So…
Miss Chloe Brazil.
It's your second night."

"Yes, it is Sir."

"I can't help but notice you're…
lack of participation
in my club."

"I am excited to dance here.

But, I'm still nervous."

"It's easy Chloe.
You either play your part,
or you don't. When you don't,
you're just a spectator."

She nodded YES,
"I see what you mean."

"If you just want to stand around,
try another Club."

"Ok."
She said.

"You want to work at my Rising Sun.
Develop a character.
And play that role superbly."

"I understand."

"Do you?"
He asked.

"Yes."
She answered nodding her head so
once again.

Gaten continued…
"In my clubs, and I've had many,
it's not just about the entertainment,
it's about the energy.
You have to bring it.
So that customers can feel it.
Am I clear?"

"Yes sir."

"Now go home.
Come back tomorrow."

She paid a $40 house fee to work. Leaving at that moment, she would go home in the hole; again. With that in mind…

"But I need to… "

He cut her off,
"You need to bring IT.
Tomorrow."

Frustrated, she didn't say another word. But turned around with some attitude and started to walk out. Gaten immediately buzzed the door open for her, yet called her back and made it clear what's-what in the Rising Sun.

"One more thing Chloe… "

She kept moving forward.

"Please."
He added to stop her
as if he had something encouraging to add
before she left.

With the office door now half opened she held on to the door knob, but didn't turn around to face him. She just looked over her shoulder as the hallway light shined on half her body. He paused looking at her, just before he said in a friendly manner…

"You know,
in the hospitality business,
there is such a thing as being too proud.
You know?"

Her eyebrows tensed. Before he went so far to add…

"Please, tomorrow…
wear a T-Back for us."

She dignified herself by not getting emotional. And rose above it responding with a rather plesant…

"Maybe."

She was nearly broke, solo, and walking home down Bourbon Street contemplating if dancing at the Rising Sun was going to actually do the trick. She knew it wasn't going to be worth it unless she came out the other side a better person. If there wasn't room to grow, it would be pointless. I have to believe that she felt something empowering ahead! Taking part had to be more than just Shoe Be Do's, underwear, dancing and a little confidence. She was to smart and conscious to just pawn herself off for cash and a spotlight.

Bella Lenin walked into The Clover Grill just before midnight that evening. By that block you just entered the Gayberhood bars; the Pride of Bourbon Street. The boys with Southern Pride affectionately refer to the track they walk from OZ to The Corner Socket as "The Fruit Loop". And the Clover Grill is where she unexpectedly fell into this rabbit hole. Taking a seat at the counter she glanced at a menu as *Animal Nitrate* played from a cassette player just above some frying bacon where a short-stocky man worked with a spatula dripping sugar & salt from his chin. A thinner man with big eyes and tattoos from his neck to his wrists worked the counter. Over his heart, a *HI MY NAME IS SLIM SHADY* sticker next to a lil Elton John pin. He greeted her…

"Hey beautiful
I'm Vinnie.
You know what you want?"

She looked back at the menu murmuring sarcastically…

"Stripper lessons please."

"I got-dat."
Vinnie said like they do down-ear.

Bella looked up to him from her menu with a glance that asked… excuse me?

"You need style?
Want to learn how to parade?
I got you.
I host a drag class."

All about that power this must have blown her away. Lady moves by men? Sign her up! She glanced around the tiny dinner where a couple ate burgers in a booth by three older horn-dogs way past their prime by another tweaking couple sharing a coke but not eating waiting on a connect. Then, she gave her attention back to this middle-aged counter help Vinnie and asked…

"Please.
Tell me more?"

"Need moves? My Hubby got you.
Need style?
I'm your pusher."

With open stage curtains in her eyes, mouth open, and nearly smiling now, she cocked her head before asking…

"Who's your hubby?"

"Edwin… The Saint."
Vinnie deluged as if she should
know who he was.

Bella mentioned,
"Tonight,
was my second night at the Rising Sun.
And I was just sent home.
I'm out of a job soon if I don't
get it together."

"Oh-the-Rising-Sun."
Vinnie swooned,
"I love them bad ass little fuckers driving around
on those screaming crotch rockets!"
Vinnie gasped,
"If I grow up, I wanna-be
just like them."

Despite not knowing exactly what the hell he was talking about, she continued…

"I was sent home tonight
for lack of enthusiasm,
or not fitting in.
No-no.
Not, bringing it?
Was what I was told."

"Girl you're beautiful.
But if you can't bring it,
you're just a bimbo."

Bella shared a delicate, halfhearted smile with Vinnie. Bimbo, would not be the part she was to play; no way. He continued…

"You walked in here on a night
I'm covering for someone.

More than a co-inky-dink I think.
But you know that.
What are you having?"

She shook her head YES and got back to the menu. Vince was a guy who had obviously been through some chaos and survived his share of life experiments. So-he just gave her space to decide for herself.

"Can I have some eggs over easy,
Whole wheat toast, and…
some mentorship
please?"

"Absolutely."
He responded confidently.

And with that order, she breathed her first sigh of relief all day.

Upon Vinnie's direction, after eats she made her way to The Corner Socket to the beat of *Billie Jean* down a littered sidewalk that lit up beneath her feet on the Fruit Loop. The Socket is a bar full of male dancers, gay for pay hustlers, and rumored to be the favorite drinkery of John Waters when he's in town. When she made it over there and stepped inside, she found the atmosphere balls out but very inclusive. And as if on que, *Relax* spun as the front door closed behind her.

Up on the big U-shaped bar in the middle of this cute spot, and cute it is, danced a half a dozen young men in mighty-tighty-whitey T-backs of their own. Around the bend at the head of the bar commanding the space like a disco diva was obviously him… The Saint. Edwin's a six and a half foot black chiseled Goth-God! Bella smiled, and immediately knew why she was sent there. Saint held the attention of all present. The other strippers were no more than alter-boys next to this grand specimen of man. Saint swayed with his hands over his head while his fingers couldn't help but graze the ceiling. And with every graceful move, he let those long strong fingers orchestrate his motions that boldly signaled to all that he could do anything to them. Everyone in the bar wanted to be in those fingertips! Every old man and little boy in the place knew the words to *RELAX* and sang along. But no one interpreted the music like Edwin. There was no repetitiveness in The Saint's style of dance.

While the other boys danced with familiar steps and practiced routines that projected a certain coolness that they were comfortable in, Saint seemed forever… reinventing! You could see the grace and purposefulness that was once a young Goth Kid in him, but he was on a level all his own at this stage. Apparently influenced by the evolutions of Disco, Locking, Popping, Uprocking, D&B steps, C-walk, Tecktonik, Modern and more. Grooves oozed from his body language that never seemed to use the same words twice. Saint had an unusual way of being graceful and purposeful as a Broadway dancer, but with the spontaneous inventiveness of a street magician. And above all, he was effortlessly confident! Witnessed on the street without the music he would be alien, but in a discotheque… simply out of this world.

B.L. got a drink and found a stool as close to Saint as she could. While men reached for him, threw money his way, and tried to cop his sack for a sec, Bella made mental notes of his presence. But his moves where untraceable. There's no way to follow moves that disappear as soon as they surface. Completely mesmerized, she must have known immediately she wanted his kind of grooves; everybody did.

When she moved closer to tip, he dipped to her eye level on one knee to accept the dollar in the black leather strap around his neck. Bella put the bill just beside the white square below his Adam's apple, then kissed his irresistible cheek! To form, he embraced her small hand with his huge fingers and his perfectly manicured nails, and kissed her just below her knuckles like a gentle giant. Then said in her ear privately…

"Vinnie hit me on the hip Bella,"
then he pointed to an antique beeper
on his Cage Thong,
"Let's connect in five."

Between the Clover and The Socket, she must-a caught a Saturday Night Fever on the Fruit Loop.

While meanwhile, I was bouncing between the Loft and the Garret in a grand-funk! Bouncing is what I call one of my ticks; or monomania-dancing. It's when I'm obsessed with getting little things in my space to the right place, or a better place, but actually only getting things to different places. I bounced around the Loft moving chairs, end tables, desks, and rugs to other spots I thought they'd fit better that night. Then, I rehung the walls as if an art opening depended on it. I even steamed the hardwood floors that night while my wife was having a cocktail at that gay bar a few blocks away.

Where at the Socket Bella and Saint were at a table getting to know each other when she asked him…

"What made you become
a stripper?"

"Stripping provides more than money.
It buys me time."
He replied.

"What do you do with your time?"
She asked.

"Study oceanography,
specifically, marine geology."

"Exciting!"
Bella responded.

"There's a job for me
here in New Orleans when
I graduate."

"In the wetlands?"
Bella guessed.

"You know it!
Gulf Restoration."
Saint said high fiving her before continuing,
"In the meantime, I'm here
two nights a week to pay the bills.
The other 5 nights I study,"
He informed her before asking,
"What's your dilly-o?"

"I just started dancing last night."

"Ok.
But what do you want to do?"
He asked.

"Travel, farm,
write a book. But…"

"But what?"

"My partner's such a planner."

"Not much of a dreamer?"

"On the contrary,
his dreams are his plans."

"Oh."
Saint said slightly
impressed.

"But I want to be more,
spontaneous!"

"That's a conversation for you
and, him… ?"

"Yes, him, Braze."

"…you and Braze to have."
Saint completed.

"I know, I know."
She responded,
"I didn't come here to talk about that."

"Why'd you come?"
He asked.

Bella didn't answer before he furthered…

"My husband
Vinnie just said you got the look,
But are looking for some moves.
Dance lessons are my side-hustle.
Drag lessons are his thing.

But we don't really do that for the money.
In fact,
it's not an open-door opportunity.
It's by invitation or
referral only."

"I don't really go in for exclusiveness."
Bella admitted almost bashfully.

"I wouldn't say we're exclusive.
Vinnie would though.
I'd say we're selectively inclusive."

After a soft laugh at that, Bella opened up…

"I don't know if I really have what it takes
to make it in this business."

Saint gently gave her a warm smile.

"Then why are you
here Bella?"

"I'm not giving up on myself.
I want to dazzle people on stage!
But I don't want to be a stripper,
More… a proud Nudist!
Like my Mom,"
She said, before saying quicker,
"and Gran-Ma."

"I, think…
I like the way that sounds."
He said not sure,
but in agreeance nonetheless,
"Have you ever
had dance lessons before?"

"I studied ballet for years
growing up."

"Great.
It's best to know the rules,
before you break them."

Bella came to the edge of her seat as Saint continued…

"After studying for years,
those moves are ingrained in your body language.
You can't forget them if you tried.
We'll use them as the door to your
interpretive creations."

"How?"

"We'll never approach a song
with a routine.
That always looks, premeditated.
Just let the music play
and go out there with nothing in mind, ever.
Don't think!
That's both the secret,
and the discipline."

"That's, kind of scary.
But I follow you."

He continued,
"Your body is mostly water.
Just let the music
flow with it naturally.
Like the Ocean on
the Earth.

"That sounds beautiful.
But will it always look beautiful?"
Bella asked then biting her lip.

"When it's good,
your movements will interact
with the music the same way the sea meets the
shoreline, naturally.
Though sometimes,
natural disasters happen."

"I don't knowwww…
if I believe in myself enough to
let go like that."

"What I teach
has nothing to do with
believing in yourself. But to know, yourself.
Once you have the knowledge, beliefs are
left behind."

GARRET SCENARIO No.2

After this conversation was planted the Rising Sun was there to nurture things. When Gaten nearly discouraged her, Vinnie & Saint where there for encouragement. And as a result, I would dig myself deeper in the Enclave.

A red spotlight pointed at that half pizza shaped window, making me really, really hungry again. I thought about getting out of bed to eat more emotions before I noticed Dutch return and perch on the sill of the lunette. He wobbled up there like a goofball looking out the glass waiting for her to get home. When she was in Brazil I slept better, now with her only a few blocks away, I was crawling in my skin! A moment later at 2am my alarm went off, and Dutch came back to nest. I suppose if nothing else I had something juicy to journal from his observations last night. I brewed coffee - Warmed milk - Stepped out on to the balcony for some air. Outside some knuckleheads screamed at each other over at Check Point Charlie's while a street cleaning vehicle sprayed down the block with gallons of Febreze below on Barracks. And perhaps as finale that night, a busker smashed her guitar to smithereens across the way on Decatur Street. I finished my first cup of coffee and went back inside to start journaling.

After turning off the front door alarm for her in the Garret, I stepped into the Enclave for my stream of consciousness exercise first thing…

Dancing has been a part of my life since I can remember.
I was raised by dance instructors. I watched my Mom choreograph routines in the living room before Bella was born. My Godmother pushed me out on dance recital stages when Bell's Grandma was flashin mailmen. My older friends and I breakdanced in subway concourses of Market Street before we could drive. We sweat it out at house parties, outlaws, and with hundreds and sometimes thousands of others in numerous nightclubs of Philadelphia to raves in caves in the Pocono Mountains. We even danced inside the Brooklyn Bridge till dawn once upon a time. Today, I'd do Hand Spins on pigeon piss in the 69th Street Terminal if it stopped Bella from givin lap dances on Bourbon Street! She does this I'm liable to write her off fly back to Amsterdam. Make grocerys at a smart shop, hop brothels, trip-face till

…Lenin began fumbling at the front door with the locks, the Enclave is directly behind the front door. Not knowing I unlocked the locks she probably locked them trying unlock them; drunk. I stopped journaling and turned around to see how long this would take. I waited, and waited, till she finally got it open. When she stepped in and tried to hang her keys up quietly, I quietly spoke up behind her…

"Boo."

"Oh!"

"Duh."

"Hi Braze."

She turned the light on before asking…

"What are you working on
back there?"

I looked over at my notebook and fountain pen thinking plan B, but responded indirectly…

"My side of things I guess."

She smelled like a bar room, disgusting.

"Your side?"
She reiterated.

"Yup.
And for me to have a deeper
understanding of things,
I need to immerse myself further."

"You want to work at The Corner Socket?"
she asked with a smile.

"Yeah."
I responded with a pleasant
smile of my own,
"No.
I'm going back to work
at Wild Forest."

Come home drunk smelling like that… not without some blowback.

After our separate notes were made dawn began to surface when I laid back down with her. My tensions outside the bed evoked nothing but tenderness for her that morning. Sunlight as our witness, we kept each other on the edge of climax till the Loft was filled with daylight. The anxiety brought on by thoughts of losing her made me a servant to her in bed. I never made it out to The Market, I slept in with her that morning. It felt great, but self-indulgent decisions like that would soon lead to the Good Life to slip through my fingers.

By nightfall with my wife's permission, I caught up and completely read, and reread all of her journal notes from Amsterdam, through Brazil, to the Rising Sun. And I of course found quite a bit in there about me. She despised the fact that I took India away from her with a coin toss. And, was crushed that I didn't accompany her to South America. Though she had already expressed these frustrations to me prior, reading it spoke greater volumes. India, South America… they were her things. She just wanted to share them with me. But I wanted things my way in the Netherlands and didn't make time for her in Brazil. What I was in denial of since we met, was that our individual ideas of what the Good Life is, were indeed, very far apart. Where I come from living large is doing your best. But in her journal, she went on and on about how she wanted to move out of the "stupid penthouse" as she put it. And trade in our nice little Cooper for a jeep towing a creepy camper to live out of. She called it campervanning in here notes. I thought it would be a good idea to start saving some money, while now she had ambitions to finance the education and housing of girls in Brazil who were in need. Yes girl(s)! Izabelle wasn't the only person she was assisting. I found in her notes that there were three other girls living in the apartment down there that Lenin was to cover expenses for this year. Much more debt was building than I was aware of. Her response when I asked about this…

"Izabelle's in charge
down there."

And Izabelle, took in three other girls in since Lenin came back! These other young girls were supposed victims and recent escapees from the same predators Izabelle got away from.

"They got nowhere else to go?"
MES questioned.

It all sounded too far-fetched and perhaps a scam to *BRIGHTDAWN*. I thought my dear Bella Lenin was naïve and being taken advantage of, but perhaps I wrong; I was definitely conflicted. Regardless, it appeared in her notes that taking on stripping was more than personal for her now, she was doing this with others in mind, the girls in Brazil; just not me so much. I wanted Lenin to be the person she desired. And if indeed these Girls were in need, I wanted to be of support too.

By now I knew if I had just gone to Brazil with her, or that we went to India for our Honeymoon, things would have been different. But it was no time to obsess about trajectories now. It was apparent in her journal that she needed this stage in her life on Bourbon Street despite how much it hurt me. And, as her partner, felt I needed to be a part of this life of hers the only way I knew how… I wrote my way in. Believing I could write my way out! But I should have given this more thought before I ventured back to Wild Forest to even the score.

The next day I slept in again and thus would be the start of me temporarily getting behind in my bills; summers are slow. But there would be many doubles ahead working the French Market, the Art Market, and Wild Forest. So, I just thought catching up would be a breeze. But really? I really-really didn't want to go back to Bourbon Street! I just thought I needed to work at the sleazy strip club to get closer to my wife and save our marriage! It… made sense to me at the time. After taking self-inventory and departmentalizing my fractured self I thought we were as ready as we'd ever be.

I went back to the Club that afternoon to try and get rehired. That was humbling. And Rachelle didn't make it too easy…

"Braze after reading
those notes you left me.
I can't imagine why you'd want to come back?"

"What do I mean?"
I asked.

"I thought your Ethical Audit,
was just an attack on people's character.
And not the evaluation
I hoped for."

"Sorry
it wasn't what you expected."

She went on to say,
"I hoped it would shed some light
on the chronic untracked lap dances, who was being
paid off not to track them, and who was selling the
coke in all the little empty purple bags
I find on the floor."

I in fact had the answers she wanted, but I really didn't want to get involved in all that. I went there to just observe people, not bring their hustles down. But I needed the job back now. So, if… I was going to give her the info she wanted? It wasn't going cheap.

"If I give you what you want Rachelle,
you hire me back as a manager."

The thought of barking at people from the sidewalk on Bourbon Street or worse, accounting for dry fucks on that fast food register? Was more than I thought I could handle a second time around. Without hesitation she said…

"Done.
Who's at the center of my
shit storm here?"

"If you cut loose your
fulltime Eye in the Sky,
you're better off."

Her main "Eye in the Sky" employee was always tweaked and working overtime in the surveillance room. He turned a blind eye to everything he delegated under the radar from his coke runners to lazy lap dance trackers. He had his fat grubby fingers in everything. But I just thought that Racheal knew! And was working the tricks in the shade with him. But no, it turned out he was solo. She confirmed it when she screamed…

"That big dumb ex rodeo clown

with a plate in his head is the dirty
jerk off in my place?"

Then she must have thought about it more, and admitted…

"Damn.
I feel stupid."

Me too. I overestimated her.

"You had to at least see him coked up
all the time in there?"
I asked.

"We'll yeah, but…
it kept his eyes glued to the screen.
And he lived to work.
Now I-see-why.
…Fuck me."
She said shaking her head before adding,
"You're hired.
Start tomorrow night."

On the way home the Bourbon Street construction bucket drum circle crews were hard at work. Two for One everything signs blew in the breeze, and I noticed a person pushing her new born in a stroller through the gutter as if it were just another day in the park. I'd seen enough already. And I just signed up for more! When I got homesick for Longwood Gardens at this time, I decided the next best thing was to get tickets to the Orchestra to keep things sophisticated. When I hopped trains, I lost myself out there; purposely. But I didn't want that to happen again in this project. I liked myself now, yet the mania I still lived with was serious. Once I take leaps there's no foreseeing where I land. But not this time I told myself. And these two! *MES* & *BRIGHTDAWN*. They'd have to stay within the boundaries I allowed them. *BRIGHTDAWN* had his ENCLAVE, and *MES* would have my back in the club. Tt appeared… copasetic.

I logged online to look at the layout of the Orpheum Theater and found the best seat I could in the Gallery. I acquired tickets for a couple different concerts that coming season starting mid-September. By then, Lenin would be back teaching, and we, could shake this summer madness off together in style. I just wanted something to look forward to. Somewhere Lenin & I could listen to good music and no one would spill a beer on us! It's not that I don't remember where I came from partying on South Street back home, I just don't want to go back to it. Sobriety comes with new standards. As soon as I made the purchase I felt better about the whole situation. The pleasant attitude I obtained by simply taking steps to elevate us signaled to me that I could make it through the Strip Life as long as I balanced it with the Good Life. No matter how hectic things got, I knew I had to stay committed to better living. Good foods, exercising, mediating, and just as important, a balanced music diet, keeps things manageable in the City of Lakes.

Lenin came home with a little Trashy Diva shopping bag in her hand before she found me in the Enclave at the Jizzy-Mac…

"Buying concert tickets?
Who we seeing?"

"LPO"
I answered with a smile.

Purposely ignoring the little bag in her hand.

"LPO?
Who are they?"
She asked.

"Louisiana Philharmonic Orchestra,
Beethoven's Ninth on September 15th.
Then, Mozart's Jupiter Symphony October…"

"…Symphonies?"
She asked cutting me off.

"Yes."

"OK."
she said rather unenthusiastically.

As if going to such concerts were beneath her?

"What made you do that?"
She asked.

"I want something to look forward to."

Then murmured,
"While we're slummin."

"Said the tramp to the stripper."
She pointed out.

"Hobo to the bimbo."
MES remixed in mind.

"Good-one."
BRIGHTDAWN responded to him.

Then Rachelle me called on my cell…

"Sup Rache?"

She asked me to come back in for that night. Rasan broke his foot running ball that afternoon and was still in the ER; she was short a man.

"Why me?"
I asked surprised.

She said on her end,
"You wanted to be a manager.
You have to do what's
got-to be done."

"Got it."
Then I hung up annoyed.

Lenin overheard and said,
"Cool! We can walk to work together."

And, show-enough, we did.

I could hardly believe that my wife and I were walking down Bourbon Street to work. It just stirred the chemical tides in my mind and nearly turned my stomach. As we walked by a stinky gold statue, he suddenly came alive and screamed at me…

"Congratulations you have won,
a year subscription of bad poems!"
"You won Braze."
Lenin laughed.

Half way down the block another solid gold joker came alive and screamed to some folks in front of us…

"Congratulations!
You're the winner of a
chicken dinner!"

These particular gold statues were tourist profilers. Apparently, I looked like a pathetic rhymer and not a tourist about to overdose on Sysco. But it wasn't time to think about all that. How was this actually going to work? Was I supposed to walk her to the Rising Sun and kiss her at the door? And then after work? Were we to meet up afterwards at The Clover for a burger? I was just a few blocks from home, one block from Wild Forest but suddenly lost in the sauce. I must have turned around! In the blink of an eye I was in the Garret.

I grabbed a military bag and franticly packed two pairs of pants, two shirts, two pairs of underwear, a windbreaker, three pairs of socks, one gallon of water, a notebook and the Crew Change! And before I knew it, I was in the Avondale Yard catching a hot shot anywhere West. There are no wrong trains when you got-a-get the fuck!

"Braze. Braze? Braze!"
Lenin repeated while shaking me.

When I got back in my skin first thing I noticed, was that nasty hell of a smell. That mix of garbage, beer, and horse manure in the atmosphere on Bourbon can simply make the methane expelled from cows asses a pleasant alternative. Lenin was standing there shaking me by the shoulders with both hands…

"What's wrong?"
She asked.

"I don't feel good
about this."

"Go home."
She suggested.

I shook my head NO.

She pulled me by the arm and led me down the street into a blinding police spotlight set up for added protection. The next thing I remember, she was walking down the street by herself, and I was standing under the Wild Forest marquee watching her disappear into a sea of consumers when…

"Braze. Braze? Braze!"
Rachelle called from just inside
the club.

I looked over to her, up at the marque, and then at the entrance where pornography covered the glass like newspaper found on a cokehead's bedroom-windows.

"You're early."
She noted.

I responded,
"Early's on time.
On time you're late.
Late you're fired."

The next morning, I was startled when I found the Loft filled with sunlight. And when I noticed Lenin wasn't there, my heart dropped before I noticed her crashing on the couch curled up in a ball. Outside in the French Market I could hear names being called for morning stall selection, yet once again running down stairs to pick a spot didn't happen.

As I brewed coffee and Bella Lenin continued to sleep peacefully, I noticed her open journal on her desk. I glanced at her, back at the notebook, and just presumed it was OK to read. With a hot cup a joe and her journal I walked out to the balcony and took a seat in the sun. Her notes from the night before were just about some nonsense regarding the freedom she found in nudity.

"Good morning Braze."
She said interrupting this boring
read I had in hand.

She stood there groggy in the balcony doorway rubbing her eyes.

"How long exactly
are we going to do this?

I need a date."

Then she noticed me holding her journal, and blew me off…

"I'm too tired right now."

She walked back inside. I threw the notebook off the balcony and followed her inside. And just as she hit the sheets in our bed, I pulled them out from under her!

"Braze!"
She yelled.

"I'm not telling you what to do.
Just asking how long exactly until
we're out of this."

"I don't know exactly!"

I gathered myself, and debated on whether I was going to stay calm, or… or I don't know what.

"Is this something
you really want on your
Life's Resumé?
I asked.

"Yes!"

"The rest of your life!"

"Do I,
really have to answer
that again?"

"Do you have any big dreams left?"

"Plenty!"

"Such as?"

"Oh, let's see… campervanning.
Contributing to urban farming,
Becoming a Jazz Singer
in Paris. Uh… "

"I'm serious!"

"So am I!
Why is it that you're the only
one to have unique ideas
and mine…"

"I've always respected your thoughts."

"Yeah.
But not my dreams Braze.
You're always way too wrapped
up in yours."

I gave that some thought, she continued…

"We've spent a lot of time
chasing your dreams.
NOW I got-to do. WHAT I got-to do!"

I threw her notebook off the balcony ~ Grabbed a bike hanging from an A-frame beam ~ Went for a ride.

Outside I raced my break-less fix-gear through The Quarter as fast as possible! By all the slow-moving traffic, even slower coach and horses, a minute later by all the tourists standing in line waiting for beignets at Café du Mode. I pressed on like a *Bullet* in Steve McQueen sunglasses switching lanes, drive into oncoming traffic, swerving behind turning cars, skidding occasionally to slow my roll slightly to time myself through surging intersections. But never stopped!

As I approached Canal Street I gambled and raced at top speed like a downhill skier without a care for his bones. Just as I reached those six lanes and two trolley tracks my greenlight turned RED. I made the first three lanes going WEST in a second. But as I crossed the tracks cars going EAST cars blocked my way, but it was too late to stop. I skidded briefly, let a car pass nearly hitting it's back bumper and began peddling through the next two lanes making other cars slam on their breaks before I entered the CBD to continue my work out. I just needed more than a ride in the park that morning.

When I got home and walked in with my bike on my shoulder and her Journal in my hand fresh off the sidewalk across the street. She was in the bathroom blow drying her hair. With the door half open, I wished her…

GARRET SCENARIO No.2

"Good morning.
Here's notebook back."

At just a glance, she looked quite glamourous. Was she doing? An afternoon shift? So-I asked…

"Wa-sup?
Got plans?"

She nodded YES.

"Going out?"
I asked.

She nodded YES again.

Her hair was blown out. Face done, clothes tight, and she had the Shoe-Be-Doo shoes on too. I waited for her to tell me what was going on, but I got nothing. She knew what she was doing, driving me nuts! Since the 4th of July she just kept moving forward to peruse things rather than tell me her plans!

"Did she meet someone last night?"
MES asked *BRIGHTDAWN* jelly.

BRIGHTDAWN wisely kept his trap shut. But I nearly exploded again…

"Where you going dressed
like that?"
I asked her like you're
average jerk.

"I have a class."

I took a seat on the edge of the old bear-claw tub, somewhat relieved that she wasn't going on a date or working a day shift. But how long would I be wondering what she's up to? I somewhat kept my cool and asked…

"What-duh-hell kind a class
you going to today?"

Then she gave me a bright smile and bragged…

"A drag class baby!"

"Oh, this just keeps
getting better and better."
I sighed.

I forgot about her new Gay Bar friends. In retrospect, I wish I could've enjoyed this with her.

"I'm going to learn how
to walk today!"
She boasted.

"Walk right to them other guys."
MES murmured behind
my eyes.

I scratched my face and sat there on the tub with my mouth open looking stupid. But I knew what she was talking about…

"You mean,
your gonna learn how to strut."
I clarified.

"Yes!
Remember when you told me
about how you learned how to walk the streets growing
up in a way that let people know
not to mess with you."

"Yeah.
I was a skinny kid copping drugs.
And writing graffiti
in ghettos."

"But it was vital body
language."

Not proud, I nodded YES gazing at my shoes thinking of the horrible example I was to my little brother back in the day.

"I want to learn how to clearly
communicate with my body."

She fixed herself in the mirror. Kissed me goodbye. And walked out the door pushing her corny blue bike with her wacky graffiti on the fenders. When the door closed, *MES* spoke up again behind my left green window…

"How the hell she gonna ride that
bike in them shoes?"

BRIGHTDAWN added from the other side,
"How's she going to make it
down the steps?"

I answered,
"I hope she sprains an ankle!"

I let her drag that artsy-fartsy bike down three flights her-damn-self and went back in the Enclave to write the anxiety out of me. By now, I really wished I just lost that damn coin toss; trajectories are everything.

Later as I meditated in the center of the Loft with the windows open as the music from the pipe organ of the Natchez River Boat drifted in the breeze, the doorbell rang. Thinking it was just another person who hit the wrong bell coming over to cop off the Grannie pot dealer downstairs, I ignore it. Before a holler came up from the street below…

"Lenin!"

It was Harry.

"Time for another big talk."
Remarked *BRIGHTDAWN.*

I got up, and threw keys to him from the balcony with a smile. He dropped his cigarette and came in downstairs.

Inside I unlocked the front door of the Garret and left it ajar ~ I put a kettle on the stove for tea ~ Put on some Cat Stevens on the 1200 ~ Lit some incense ~ Fluffed pillows. Harry got-a take-is time. Between the COPD and still smoking, he was nearly crippled. By the time he walked in, out of breath, the kettle whistle blew and I was pouring us some herb tea…

"Sup Harry.
How's it going old boy?"
I asked.

"Well,
the nice thing to do…"
he said while trying to catch his breath,
"…would be not to bother you

with my situation.
But that wouldn't be forthright."

I mildly retorted,
"Well then,
let's have it."

"Oh…
He gasped,
"It's the same old thing.
Carol's bat-shit crazy!"
he screamed nearly losing
his voice.

If that be the case, and there was no doubt it was, then just go back to the Bayou. But then again, he had a toddler with Crazy. Thus, I merely responded in character…
"Do tell old'chum."

Conversations were so theatrical with him I could only play my part. He went on to say…

"I've been trying
to reach Lenin for days.
But she doesn't answer
my calls."

That told me that he wasn't "in the know" to her new means of gainful employment, before he asked…

"Has she had any luck
finding work?"

"I don't think she got lucky,"
I hoped aloud.

"Oh,
I suppose it's better she's not here.
Can I take a bath?
I've been sleeping in the
van for days now."

"Sure.
But a cup of tea first?
Help you relax."

"That's kind of you.
Thank you yes."

I pushed the saucer with the steaming cup of tea over to him as Harry spun his head taking in the Loft.

"Well,
I guess if you like a magnificent space
atop an awe-inspiring city to write your books,
you found it here Braze"

We toasted to that. He continued…

"Oh, this is good?
What's in it?"

"Gunpowder,
With fresh Echinacea & Basil flowers
from the balcony."

He sipped it again
then added…
"It goes really good with the
Cat Stevens."

"Your daughter didn't marry no dummy,"
I said with a smirk,
"Now,
what's going on at home?"

"It's the same old thing."
He said as I sipped from my hot cup
before he continued,
"Carol thinks I'm fucking Lenin."

I coughed! *BRIGHTDAWN* scratched his chin with his mouth open. *MES* was just confused and asked me…

"What the fuck-he-say?"

I finally got something out,
"She thinks you're
WHAT man?"

He shook his head YES. I had to clarify…

"Having sex.

With your daughter?"

"Oh…"
He said eyes wide,
"This has been going on for years."
Almost blowing it off.

But it was the first I heard of it!

He divulged,
"That's what was going on
at the wedding."

I recalled Carol causing some sort of a ruckus at the party, but I never knew exactly what. When her brothers escorted her from our wedding, I was simply grateful. Harry continued while sipping his tea…

"She was trying to get to you.
To warn you, about me."

Bewildered, I started shaking my head NO. Found my arms raised, palms up gesturing… WHAT THE FUCK WE TALKING ABOUT HERE?

"But I'm not,"
Harry clarified,
"I'm not!"

I paused and took this in. This is Carol where talking about here, a person I see as homewrecker.

"She must have been just trying to throw
her wrecking ball our way."
Concluded *BRIGHTDAWN*.

I took a breath, calmed down. But Harry was shaken, it was all over his face. He needed a friend once again. I was there…

"That's absurd man.
Carol creates disasters."

"I know. I know."
He said feeling sorry for himself,
then I heard him say it,
"But she's the love
of my life."

GARRET SCENARIO No.2

We stared at each other. Before he asked me with urgency…

"Could you talk to her Braze?
Tell her that your Lenin's first,
one and only."

"Dude?"
MES reacted standing in
my left window.

"Damn Harry,"
I responded,
That's none of her god
damn business."

"Your Lenin's first.
The whole family knows that!
but Carol."

The whole family was in on our sex life? I pondered that scratching the back of my neck. That's a lot of brothers!

"Harry, I don't
have anything to say to Carol.
You're on a dead end street with her.
Honestly, I think you'd be better off if
you returned to
the Bayou."

"I knooooow."
He said. Before he said,
"…I, don't know."

While Bella Lenin attended her drag class that afternoon, her father and I sat in an uncomfortable silence as I pondered this pedo-craziness that Carol insinuated. Harry broke the silence, and casually enquired…

"Do you have any Epson salt
for my bath?"

Bella was on Rampart Street at Vinnie's studio where three Queens attempted to outshine each other on a short runway lit by stained yellow light bulbs screwed directly into the edge of a stage. Vinnie and Bella sat on large pillows just a few yards away not paying much attention to the Glamazons working programs in the background. Vinnie was making sure he understood what she wanted…

"So…
you don't want to look like just another sexy
girl walking around in the club."

"Absolutely not."
Bella answered.

"But a force of nature."
He asserted.

"Correct."
Bella stressed.

Vinnie took a deep breath before answering…

"A solid impression like that,
comes from establishing a reputation.
You'll have to build that on your own.
But I'll get you to the starting line
and show you how to carry yourself
with integrity."

A loud POP rang out in the background startling Bella, but not Vinnie. Evidently one of the light bulbs on the edge of the stage was just kicked out. The clumsy Queen on stage responsible was frozen with embarrassment; the other two held their hearts.

"My darlings,
Vinnie said softly,
"The bulbs are there for a reason.
Beware, of the ledge."

Unable to Sissy her walk the Big Clumsy Queen popped another bulb!

"Miss Chloe Brazil,
will you relay my message please?
My voice is going."

Bella hesitated, but did so.

"Darlings…
The bulbs are placed there for a reason.
beware of them."

"Be very aware."
Vinnie whispered.

"Be very aware!"
Bella screamed with a smile.

"Check yourself before you wreck yourself."
Vinnie whispered.

Then he nodded YES for her to repeat it…

"Check yourself,
before you wreck yourself?"
Bella relayed uncertain
of that one.

"Now let's continue."
Said Vinnie, just before
another POP!

The clumsy student in the background began to complain how small the runway is.

"Please remind them to CONTROL themselves."
Vinnie directed Bella to say.

"Control yourselves darlings!"
Bella relayed.

The heaviest one back there said to Clumsy…

"Control yo-self-bintch!"

The Fishy Queen in the group stood between those two hands up, not taking sides. Vinnie had the last word…

"Beware of the edge darlings.
If you fall, you're not a Queen,
you're stuntman."

Then he gave his attention back to Bella…

"I might add,
your walk home is just as
important as the one
at work."

"OK."
Bella responded

"Walk home
with a sense of urgency.
Have your money in two spots.
One small fold to give up to jackers,
and the larger one to take home.
Do you have an old
cell phone?"

"I think so."

"It can't hurt
to carry one to throw their away.
They like phones too."

"Got it."
Bella responded.

"Don't get drunk on the job,
That's just tacky.
It's the main ingredient in every
shit show.
But you know that."

Bella smirked in agreement.

"Don't talk too much.
The more you listen the more
you learn."

Bella nodded YES. SAINT walked in with a smile wearing sweats and a gym bag around his shoulder.

"Learn who
you're dealing with.
Listen to your clients.
Don't let them know you're smarter!
But if you let them feel smarter,
they'll never suspect
your play."

"My play?"
"Like, a lap dance you mean?"
Bella asked.

The Saint joined the convo…

"That's a job.
Your plays create jobs."
He pointed out.

She had a lot to learn. And apparently, she was in the right hands. These guys were quite thoughtful.

After Classes Bella rode her artsy bike with gold rims covered with block letter graffiti from the fenders to the chain guard sitting on her custom covered fleur-de-lis seat. She cruised through the Fruit Loop, by Skully'z Records, Clover Grill, a coach and mule tour, and continued down Bourbon under an inferno sky of reds and pinks. Eventually she was silhouetted by a full moon floating on the horizon before turning a corner by a tall American Werewolf dressed impeccably under a hairy mask with a long snout and ferocious teeth playing his violin solo. Unlike Movieland and the rest of The States, in New Orleans you have character, if you simply are a character.

Bella pushed her bike into the hallway between the two restaurants downstairs and carried it up to the Loft. Inside our place it was hung from the A-Frame ceiling directly across from mine on the other side of the space. Everything has its right place up here. From the sidewalk to our front door the building is in shambles, but once inside the Loft… it's Shangri-La. And I like to keep it that way. There are no dirty dishes in my sink, and my desk is always polished. Along with the importantly hung art, our bikes just added to the balance. An old Sigur Ros record spun on the 1200 as I was in the kitchen making dinner. Harry was gone by the time she got home. Usually I tried to stay out of her father's endless drama, but not this time. And not just because I was disturbed by the picture he painted, but because I cared about him.

Apparently in a good mood, Lenin hugged and kissed me from behind, before she asked me like a kid with a new move…

"Do you want to see
my walk?"

When I turned around and noticed how excited she was I laughed out a very calm…

"Sure."

As I drained the pasta, she did her thing. Proceeding to canvas the hardwood floor of the Loft like a girl from up-the-way back home. When Bella & I met years ago I felt that I was in on the biggest secret in town, she never flaunted herself. Now, it appeared the Genie was out of the bottle.

"What do you think?"
She asked.

It was a very soliciting walk.

"I think…
you're a fly girl now."

"This is no Bueno."
MES added.

She may have been a late bloomer, but she was in full bloom now. I resumed my place, in the kitchen.

Moments later outside over dinner by oil lamp a solo guitar could be heard from the corner. Before the usual homeless guy evidently "born by the river" serenaded a table below hoping "change" was gonna-come his way before I finally got on with the drama…

"Your Dad stopped by today.
He's been trying to
reach you."

She immediately took to that sour and responded…

"Damn-it.
I've been meaning to call him back.
You didn't tell him anything.
Did you?"

"No.
Nothing."

"I'm going to tell him."
Lenin said in
defense.

Right across the street a tour operator stood talking about the Dance Hall & Brothel our address once was 150 years ago to a small group, watching us eat, and taking pictures of the building. I fluttered my fingers to the tourist ~ They waved back ~ Before I went on to say…

"Carol kicked him out
a few days ago.
He's been sleeping in the
van again."

"What now?"
She asked.

"She's accusing your father of…"
I paused and
scratched the back of my head, nervous,
before I continued…
"…of having a sexual relationship,
…with you."
I said quickly at
the end.

Lenin sat back in her chair.

"Psh…
She's been saying that
since I was a kid."

"What?
I mean… WHAT?"

That floored me. But my wife wasn't moved, not in the least. She went on to explain that…

"In the beginning,
it was really, really hard
for me to accept
Carol in our family."

If my Dad brought another woman into the mix and said let's just be one big happy family and move to Cloud Nine? Hard to accept would be an understatement.

"I just hated her.
It took me a long time to
love Carol."
She said.

Wow. I sat there bewildered with heavy eyebrows and my mouth open like Nicholson in the cold.

"When I was a kid,
I got obviously jealous
of my father being nice to her.
When she noticed that, she'd pull me aside.
More than once!
And said as…

(Lenin changed her voice to a Frenchy Canadian accent)

"What are you jealous of?
Do you want to have sex with
your father?"

Then my dear Bella Lenin came back to her own voice…

"I just froze up, stood there.
I was like 13.
What was I to say?"

"I, I don't know."
I responded.

Lenin just resumed eating. It was as if that chapter of her life was so far behind her that it didn't matter anymore. But her Dad would always mean everything to her; always.

"My Dad's ok?
Why didn't he wait here till I got
home tonight?"

"He did wait.
But Thorsen called when he was in the area.
When your Dad invited him up,
Thorsen said he could only park
near a gas station."

Lenin gave me a perplexing look.

"Something about having slow-leaks

in his tires?"

His hero was Greg Mortenson. And as a result, Thorsen would send his money to students in South America before he was forced to replace a tire here at home.

Standing on a quarter-apple box at the Frenchmen Art Market under clotheslines weaved with electrical wires and lightbulbs, the circuit breaker box behind me smoked. The electrical system may have been wonky sometimes, but the scene was always electrifying. I held in one hand a brown recycled cardboard box with a DVD of **CURE** *for the* **CRASH**, and in the other a **BOOK SAFE GLACIER** paperback as I got my hustle on. My flat screen TV next to me ran the trailer where my table was covered with merch. I felt like a two-bit carny salesman selling tinctures; but it worked. To gain attention I constantly introduced my work…

"Made a movie. Wrote a book.
Take a look!"

"Fill me in,"
Asked a Gent with his Lady friend.

After that nice couple left the oh-so aggravating Frenchman Street Pirate surfaced. Suddenly letting his presence be known from the back of a small group watching a scene from the movie screaming…

"Galesburg?"
at the TV.

It was apparently showing the moment we got out of a Police Car in, Galesburg, Illinois.

"I'm from Galesburg!"
He screamed at me.

"Ah-no.
Here we go."
I murmured.

"What do you know a Galesburg?"
He demanded.

My friend Kate who leased the parking lot hated this guy. She kicked him off the lot more than once. So-I had to handle this…

"I know everyone from Galesburg,
gets a free book tonight."

Shocked, but receptive to my gesture he stepped forward through the crowd to receive it. When he got to me, I said softly…

"Let's talk later.
I got-a-hustle."

"OK.
"I get it. I Got it"
He said.

Then I gave him the book. He was sentenced to the street for life. If you're homeless and just struggling for a while you can rise above it someday. But if you're out there and have a persona that acquires a label like Trash Humper, Rat Fucker, Dog Shit, or in this guy's case… The Frenchmen Pirate, that's the point of no return. The street labeled your as till your final dirt nap.

Across town at the Rising Sun the now Chloe Brazil sat in a loud dressing room in front of a makeup mirror again putting on the finishing touches of her delicate warpainted face. After being there just a few nights no one who worked at the club took much notice of her; but Gaten. Yet far in the background deep in the music on this night her presence was on the verge of a big boom. After tutelage from the experienced duo of Vinnie & Saint, the beats called on her like never before through the wicked fingers of DJ Crowley. He channeled her through 1979's Joy Division *Dead Souls,* and for added hypnotism 1989's Mother Love Bone *Crown of Thorns* was layered and cut respectively…

Chlo-Chlo-Chloe's just like me.
Chlo-Chlo-Chloe's just like me.

DJ Crowley followed with…

Rest-Rest-Rest your soul away.
Rest-Rest-Rest your soul away.

Between the haunting and soulful voices of Ian and Andrew what innocent soul would not fall to the possession of Rock. Crowley, with his firsthand experience in the occult, brokered this fusion between music and spirit as the bubonic music layers enmeshed with Bella Lenin's soul. Later giving birth to an entertainer that would never be confused with any other again. Chloe Brazil would soon outhustle the others once the music snatched her secret self. While the sexual invasion of my wife's vital force took place the standing hairs on her arms tried to alarm her to it, but by then, it was too late. This underworld club séance of hypnotic beats via hi-fi transmissions was taking hold! As Crowley's sound system presence strengthened, Chloe Brazil began to get comfortable in her new skin whiles Dutch circled the scene.

Outside on Bourbon under a full Moon where Joy Division & Mother Love Bone spread in the air like a fog over the Street, some fell to their knee caps once this cloud of bewilderment hit them. Those who walked through this mist unaffected were most disturbed by those who were taken to their hinge-joints. The tourist brought to their knees crawled towards the Rising Sun like pack wolves through gutter juice. The doorman welcomed these hipsters who succumbed to the madness in the music by taking the Red Rope in hand and allowing them to enter on the VIP side. Not since Big Daddy's was home to a pair of boa constrictors in a glass stage, had a club on Bourbon Street allowed such animals in it; yet this could have been my mind playing tricks on me. The City of Lakes was crowded by digital billboards screening glimpses of this scenario via Dutch. Even when I closed my eyes on the other side of town, my eyelids would light-up like a theater screen to these pictures.

As often is the case, the Rising Sun was sardined with more souls than bodies. In her own unique way Chloe Brazil was on a trajectory to brand a high art hustle on this lowbrow street now that she was schooled properly. After Honey Mama got the OK from Chloe, she gave the greenlight to Crowley from the dressing room. In the background Crowley spoke over the tracks…

"Ladies, Gents, Transgenders,
Young and Old Souls…
It is with the utmost respect

I welcome back to the stage
without further ado…
Chloe Brazil!"

Down a hallway lit with red-light bulbs the volume of the music rose with every step she took forward. Chloe walked on down the hall to where a nebula of disco lights and universal matter awaited her at the outlet ahead. At the core of the energy where this erotic nebula existed before her bass-boomed from a tiny black electroacoustic transducer at the center of what appeared to Dutch as a sexual blackhole to the main floor. On the other side of that hole, no bigger than a small subwoofer, awaited the ecstasy of the Rising Sun. Chloe walked down the hallway in a T-Back through electro audio cobwebs formed by the gothic sounds as the erotic nebula around the sexual subwoofer that magnetized her body forward. When she crossed the event horizon and broke on through, she entered the club with a sex stride from the other side! A strut scooped from the Fruit Loop.

In sync with the clubs universe she passed the charming Piano Man, by the bouncing hospitality dwarfs, and many club patrons as she high-fived everybody in reach. When she floated up the grandstand steps and finally reached the spotlight light center stage waves of primal screams elevated her! And she appeared to glide on stage with the grace of a swan before letting go, completely, emerging from her own zone to join the madness. Performing a Capoeira-glam-Ginga every bone pulsed to each block rocking beat creating even more mayhem in the club. With such body business vibrating, throbbing, and nearly convulsing on stage as if undergoing a public sexorcism, she brought the house down and the roof on fire. The dwarfs encouraged her sizzling performance by cheering together…

"Hoo… Hoooo… Hooo!"

While other brought back,
"She don't need know agua
that mommy-fucker burn.
Burn Mommy Fucker!
Burn!"

"Hoo… Hoooo… Hooo!"

She was more than a striptease, she was bombigity. The audience hurt for more, while the other dancers were stone faced. Even the aerialist above stopped twirling to sit up there and stare down at the action. Gaten was in the balcony upstairs looking down on her in the limelight the whole time. He took in the entire exhibition and immediately knew he had a superstar in the house; his mind was surly raced. A chronic opportunist is always thinking more, more, more!

In the circus of the Rising Sun it was nearly impossible to stand out, being outrageous in New Orleans is the norm. To create a way to rise above it all as Chloe Brazil did that night, was no less a happening than finding Trombone Shorty in a local *Parking Lot Symphony;* it just doesn't happen. By the end of her songs it rained paper from VIP and piled on stage. The Piano Man whistled, Gaten golf clapped, And DJ Crowley raved into the mic…

"The God of the bod!
Witch of tits!
French Quarter's
Chloe-eeeeeeeee Braaaazil!"

Hospitality Dwarfs celebrated by cartwheeling and kicking like devil's advocates as if Rosemary just had another baby! They even went so far as to start copy her Capoeira moves as if they were MJ's 1st TV moonwalk.

When she walked off stage with a stack of cash in one hand assisted by the strong hand of a tall club employee with the other, the Piano Man bowed to her before he said…

"Congrats Miss Brazil.
Just fabulous."

"Thanks! Call me Chloe.
Your name?"

"Billy.
But they just call me the Piano Man
around here."

Chloe's face seemed to make a dozen different emotions by the second while she caught her breath in the aftermath of her performance. Another club employee approached Chloe and spoke in her ear, then gestured upstairs to the balcony where Gaten was standing. She nodded OK to him up there, before departing Billy with…

"Nice to meet you Piano Man."
Tipped him and mentioned,
"I look forward to our
next dance."

Bella was always a bombshell, but within the Chloe Brazil persona unleased that night? She made people gasp! In just one night, she might have become as royal as Saint in The Socket. She figured out quick that all she had to do was bring a little something off the beaten path to main street. The Clover Grill encounter with Vinnie was the game changer that got her to the start of things to come; no doubt.

Upstairs she exited the elevator and walked through VIP where strippers intentionally ignored her, but players couldn't take their eyes off her. Everyone seemed to not only acknowledge her there for the first time, but be almost intimidated by her. But of course, not Gaten, he played it cool. When she came up behind him, she paused for a breath. He must have known she was there but just seemed to be staring off at the party below. With the utmost confidence she stepped next to him at the railing of the balcony and looked down at the scene still buzzing. When the presence of Chloe Brazil was sensed above looking down on them all? Were unconsciously magnetized to her eyes. They looked up, and roared for more at her! She smiled, flashed them, then simply asked over the roars for more…

"Sir?"

But Gaten didn't acknowledge her just yet. But rather gazed at the circus below. Confetti falling… girls twirling once again, the turntables literally on fire beneath Crowley's hot finger tips along with and the other amusements *Burning Down The House*, before finally responding to her…

"Pardon me.
I wasn't ignoring you Chloe.
But once in every great while,
I'm completely entranced by the
energy brought in by a
new performer."

Chloe humored him,
"It's an intoxicating club."

"Indeed.
Look at this."
He gestured below.

It was almost as though he was shocked himself. He finally took his eyes off the main floor and over to her, standing there unemotional, in control. When she stated like a minion to a master…

"I'm happy to be of service
to you here."
Said as if that was farthest from
the truth.
He caught wind.

"Happy to be of service."
He repeated.
Then continued,
"That sounds like you're…
a public servant.
Why are you,
so cold with me?"
He asked.

She remained Poker-faced.

"Next time you ask me to
wear a T-Back?
Turn the A/C down.
Good night sir."
She said bluntly before walking off
bare-assed on her own level
far from beneath his.

She played her part incredibly well that night to say the least. And though she wore what he suggested, she was definitely in control and let him know it. But Gaten just looked perplexed rather than disrespected. He must have found her attitude as interesting as her ass.

There's much to know about Gaten that he must have kept secret from those in New Orleans, you can easily bury a past down here; but I know him. In the 90's he was the King of New York. This man turned a house of worship into a nightclub and brought in more money than God. Decades later in the French Quarter, his profile appeared on the rise once again. A Chloe Brazil in his club could only blow things up further.

Frenchmen Street was a zoo by midnight, most can't read a stop sign by this time. None of us got rich at the Art Market, but everyone quit their day jobs and traded in their wine screws for Squares. Earlier that night I sold paperbacks to more literate and coherent mammals during my wife's torturous-tease show across town; Dutch's visions nearly crippled me with anxiety. I had to retreat to the chapel at the center of my head to pray. Inside *BRIGHTDAWN* took notes sitting in a pew behind me and *MES* sniffed holy incense as I begged for relief from my perceptions. Though my head's given me memorable impressions since before I could walk, I've never been in charge of what I see. In general, I could be overemotional growing up because of them, and since, such glimpses from elsewhere have just complicated my wellbeing. Yet there seems to be something outside my City of Lakes that reflects on the City itself. And it's that perspective, I really, really wish had a bigger influence on the metropolitan of my mind. My troubles including euphoric bouts with self-wrestle mania, departmentalization of personalities and extrasensory hybrid perceptions nearly disappeared for years; before we got married. I felt that if my wife set out in this trajectory with such multidimensional assistance from the beats of DJ Crowley, the coaching of Saint and the Stylistic nature of Vinnie, she'd be even more out of reach in weeks to come. Just thoughts of her lap dancing on Bourbon had a sextet in my head interpret the sounds of *Strange Imaginary Animals* adding to the relentless, overpowering, boiling anxiety just beneath my thin skin seeming to petrify my shot nerves.

Around 3AM I walked in after the Art Market closed and not surprisingly Lenin wasn't home. Exhausted from the weekend crowd I took a couple Tylenol PM hoping they would help me sleep heavier and NOT dream. Sinking into the sofa as if it were a lifeboat over my emotions, I dozed off. When I opened my eyes in what felt like seconds the Loft was glowing at dawn and she was just walking in…

"Oh,
I was hoping I

didn't wake you."
She said with a sorry,
but pleasant face.

"Oh-ah, no.
I just woke up."
I said getting off the sofa,
"You want me to run you a bath?"
I asked her.

"Yes!"
She let out exhausted,
"That be wonderful."

I stepped away, but she pulled me back. Kissed me, and gave me an…

"I love you."

"I love you too.
But you really need a bath."
I said with a smiled.

"You need a shave."
She responded.

I put some lavender Epson salt in her warm bath, lit some incense next to the bear claw tub, and didn't say a word about those conjoined-experiences I'd been spying with the added assistance of Dutch. Once she was in the tub, she asked me…

"Are you outback today?"
She asked.

Referring to opening my stand in the French Market.

"Yup."

"You should stay home.
Rest, write."
She suggested.

If a writer doesn't approach each story like an entrepreneur does a startup, they're not courageous enough to read. So, I said…

"I'll take ten at lunch."

"You need more than naps."
She pointed out.

Moments later I left the Loft with my bike over my shoulder. I had to get moving and just get out of there. We must have lived in one of the most comfortable places in The Quarter, but it was getting more and more unbearable outside the Enclave. Once again, I began to occasionally feel like dropping out if it were not for this project. I find exercising is never so crucial than times like these; my kind of quitting is fatal. If I'm not journaling about the drama in my life and don't see potential for producing a story later, it's nearly unbearable for me to just sit around and wish for the next big thing to happen. Thus, walking over to the Rising Sun when Bella was in Brazil. Now the wait was over, the next thing was happening. I should really watch what I wish for more carefully. The more I meta-write, the more I get lost between the notes.

Later when I just finished setting up in The French Market, a customer came back who had started reading BOOK SAFE GLACIER with it in her hand. With its spine broken and dog eared pages, we greeted each other with smiles. She seemed in a hurry, but speechless. I broke the ice…

"Welcome back."

She opened up,
"I leave today, but just wanted to stop back
and say I started your book last night
and couldn't put it down."

"Really.
Seriously?"

"Oh yeah!
I feel like we're family now.
How's your Mom?"

"She's good,
adjusting to retirement."

"And your Dad.
Do you
talk to him much?"

"On holidays."
Then I joked,
"But since my sobriety
I don't call for bail like
I once did."

"Oh-that's-right!
He's a bail bondsman."
She remembered with
a smile.

We shared a laugh. Then…

"And your brother, I like him.
How's he doing?"

I looked at the Paperback she held close to her chest and noticed that there was a book marker in the middle of it. I looked back to her, kept smiling, and responded…

"I haven't spoken to him lately.
I hope he's OK."

"Well… you tell him,
he's my favorite in
your book."

"I'll, do that."

I suddenly felt horrible. Had I reduced my brother to simply a character in my book?

"Don't we do that with
everyone?"
MES asked *BRIGHTDAWN*.

"Can I hug you?
She asked me. Then added,
"I'm a hugger."

After a big hug she said with a few tears…

"I'm just so happy for you.
That you were able to fix your life.
Look at you now.
Your eyes are so bright."

She just kept looking into my eyes not knowing the troubles behind them, nor should she. I was thankful for that. But I had to wrap this up. I prefer not to feel that exposed off the page.

"I appreciate your encouragement.
I really do.
Safe travels ahead."

When she turned to leave and I thought that was it, I took a very big breath. The thought of someone else who might miss my brother overwhelmed me. Then she asked from afar…

"What's your next adventure
about?"

I shrugged my shoulders
before sharing the first thing that came to mind,
"A red light district love story."

That drew a laugh by her, and others in the area.

"I'm sober, not a saint."
I declared out there.

My neighboring vendor greeted me first thing that morning like always…

"Good morning Mr. Director!"
She said with a big grin from her
stall across the aisle.

"Good morning Miss Myra."

I resumed my composure behind my table full of paperbacks by cluing in those walking by…

"Shot a film. Wrote a book.
Take a look."

Perhaps the biggest challenge for writers such as I… is not becoming a victim during our process. Personally, I remind myself to associate discomfort with growing. When I'm in a project with unbearable feelings, I simply label them growing pains; labels can be game changers. The business of perusing this story kept my City of Lakes in business. To stay in business addressing my anxieties was priority. But the risky investments ahead to become friendly with anxiety would come to bankrupt me; bigtime.

Later that night I was doing another double. With just two naps per day rather than one solid sleep, the new norm was exhaustion. After making my initial rounds at Wild Forest I went out for some air on the balcony over Bourbon with Rasan. With his integrity, and recent injury, he became the obvious choice to take the helm behind the Eye in the Sky. He was happy to do so under one condition. That he got as many trumpet breaks, as others got smoke breaks. One story above Bourbon Street we stood over the scene together, he with his instruments, I with my Moleskin. The pages I journal with a cheap disposable fountain pen seemed no different to me than the diary he kept with his horn. I personally had to keep a comfortable distance from the nightlife because *BRIGHTDAWN,* this fucker… he was ready to die for recognition while furthering this name for himself. The more he wrote, the more the danger was in plain sight; meds. Though *MES* is a wingnut and no less his sidekick, he had my back in the club. That made things manageable in the beginning. When things got hectic in my head my and they conversed too much, my safe place in Wild Forest was the DJ booth. My man Joey was always there to change my tune when my Splits or my jealous wavelengths got radioactive. I was often suspicious of what my 3rd Eye couldn't pick up down the street. It got so that I were dammed if I could see it, and dammed if I didn't! I could only dream that my future would once again feel like the songs by the musicians that inspired it, rather than the symphony of a lonely charlatan in a derelict subway waiting on a ride out of it.

"A symphony?"
MES Asked.

A *Bittersweet Symphony* of dilated-dreams.

Once Chloe found a higher state of mind in the Rising Sun, less was in her way; most of all herself. Fear was not an issue any longer. A lot of women have the body and gravitational pull to get what they want in a club, but Chloe Brazil had more in mind… questions. One being… why are all these people here? Just to see topless women? Bella Lenin being raised by her hippie parents, nudist grandmother and of course caring for her younger siblings butt-naked birth made that just seem silly; there must be more to it she told me.

To learn, she found herself in conversations at great lengths with club patrons. After noting in mind who they were and where they were coming from intellectually, she'd finally try and get back on business track by dropping the…

"So,
would you like a dance?"

But at that point it would often catch a customer off guard. After deep conversations with Chloe Brazil they had so much respect for her that some guys just could not do, what they came to do. Evidently her mind got in the way. Initially, the intellectual conversations were bad for business, but later the character evaluations would help. She had the moves on stage, but wasn't into the groove around the tables yet because she couldn't shake learning about customers, and, the club.

She found entertaining on stage and holding on to her dignity in a lap dance a troubling balance. The barrage of boundless sexual dreams that so many customers wanted to include her in elsewhere often had her put the brakes on conversations and just tell them a flat NOWAY. That was bad for business, but more importantly, judgmental. She didn't want to be that person. Rejecting others seemed to not be in her DNA. She needed a way to stay in conversations and close deals, but most of all… not commit like so many others to rendezvous elsewhere, such as across the street. Rather than let herself be pulled by large disposable incomes to the Royal Hotel like the prostitutes, she needed something that didn't open that door. Or in the process, close doors in the club. This was the challenge that would soon enough work itself out organically. Unbeknownst to anyone yet, she was a shark, learning how to walk.

Many entertainers endgame was getting as much cash by dawn as possible, even if meant saying YES to a private champagne dance across the street. Some couldn't say NO to the money, others just couldn't say NO. It was a matter of boundaries and how far one was willing to go that of course dictated the YES and NO's. She noticed quickly how a YES in the club was a greenlight and brought in business. And a NO always put the brakes on everything, at least in club. But across the street in the Royal Hotel, without the security of the attentive Hospitality Dwarfs everywhere, could a…

"NO.
I'm not down with that."

…be heard by anyone who could help? Nope. She noticed a hangover in some women's eyes the next day that she never wanted to find in her own. She knew she'd always have a greater sense of agency in the club.

As soon as she brought a little money home that summer it went back out via Money Grams to South America. The four young women she was supporting in that part of the world who escaped traffickers just wanted an education and needed a place to live and study together. Tragically, girls were not housed at the dorms by the school her brother Thorsen raised financing for. The organization in charge down there only housed boys. Basically, The Brothers in Brazil gave Thorsen a sales pitch to build a school, and he bit. The book *Three Cups of Tea* Changed his life and made him hungry to help, perhaps too hungry.

Once the bricks were laid, Thorsen had no say in managerial matters of the property. Between the priorities of this particular religious organization and a favela that undervalued women's education, these girls were in great, great need. If Lenin could help it The Girls would not go further in need because they'd come too far. She would not let them be excluded from the same education and resources that boys where getting because the "Brothers of the Sacred Scam" as she put it, wouldn't house girls. Nor, would they assist in this Women's Program that she was establishing! They actually did what they could to undermine Lenin's support. But this outrageous lack of inequality did not surface till after the school built. Thorsen had to feel a little duped to say the least. Without Lenin's support where would these women who escaped captivity go next? She planned to raise all the finances with strip club money that was trickling in. And I'm told Izabelle never asked for a dime, not once.

The first time Lenin sent the money to Izabelle it nearly took a week for her to actually get it. Izabelle had to bribe the Money Gram cashier down there with a promise there is more coming if he let her receive it. Once she got the Brazilian reals converted from US dollars, she smuggled it home through the favela and stashed it in the little apartment the money afforded because none of the girls had a bank account. As a precaution not to get robbed of the cash, they spent the money as quickly as possible on supplies that would last a couple weeks.

Back here at home, it was business as usual for Chloe Brazil to afford these girls a roof, education, and basic essentials. What could I do but love a person who would rather house others, rather than buy a new pair of shoes for herself? She was still wearing those grimy worn-out-bobo's. I'd have to be crazy not to follow a person like this in shoes like that to the end.

In the Rising Sun there were men who came to fill basic needs that were not met elsewhere. Her conclusion was that they were those who just really needed to be touched by a woman. These guys weren't aggressive or control freaks, but just looking for a little affection.

One night Chloe was topless and giving one of these guys a lap dance. A handsome man in his late 40's who kept his hands on the couch by his side the whole song. While he kept the posture of a marine, she slithered on top of him like a cobra to the music. Most men of course looked at her breast when she danced on them, but not this guy, he had his eyes closed the whole time. She even fluttered her fingers over his eyes to see if she could get a response, but nothing. At the end of the song she stopped moving for a beat, and waited for him to open his eyes, but he didn't. Then she gently grazed his cheek with the back of her hand. He finally expressed some joy by cracking his lips open in response to her gentle touch. He didn't come here to watch, only to be touched, just like that! Chloe asked…

"Another dance?"

"Ahhh,"
He said with relief,
No. Never more than one.
Thanks."

"Do you come to the
club often?"

"On the regular."
He replied.

"Great.
I'm Chloe Brazil."

He didn't respond, but cordially nodded OK.

Then she pointed out,
"You never asked my name.
Only for a dance."

"I'm Bob.
I don't get too friendly with dancers.
And I never approach the same
dancer twice."

"Oh.
Why not the same dancer
twice, Bob?"
She asked quite interested.

"Job requirement."

She looked confused. Then he added…

"I'm happily married."

And with that, and him sharing that he wasn't looking to be a regular of hers, she took it as an opportunity to dig a little deeper into this kind of person. She gently grabbed his elbow as he went to leave and asked Bob…

"If your happy elsewhere,
why are you here?"

Half taken by her genuine interest, and probably half taken by the beautiful lips posing the question, he paused. Then for whatever reason, he got personal…

"My wife and I don't seem to,
get truly intimate
anymore."

Then he looked away staring at the thought before back to her adding more coldly…

"We fuck.
But haven't made love
in years."

"Oh, that's any easy fix.
Romance her!"
She said gushing enthusiasm.

Bob seemed open, so-she continued…

"What turns her on about you Bob?"

"Wow. Hmm…
In the beginning I thought it was
my endearing nature.
But then, I desired a more…
daring sex life."
He said staring off again,
"I thought she was up for it."
He murmured.

"I think I get it."
Chloe responded nearly blowing
him off now.

"I suppose,
we never made it back,
from objectifying each other
like that."

He shook his head and briefly held his hands up, frustrated with himself. She retreated…

"Listen Bob,
I didn't mean to pry."

"No-no. I-ah…
I guess I needed to hear
myself say that."

"I don't know you Bob,
but I hope you
find a way to turn
things around at home."

He responded to her with a polite smile. Every dancer on the block probably knew who Bob was, but her.

"One more question though…
What's your wife's defining
character trait?"
She asked.

He smiled and glowed for the first time before answering…

"Actually,
she's always been the
dare devil."

"Maybe that's the way back.
Something both daring,
and romantic.
Do whatever it takes.
True love is rare."

Bob shook his head OK; whatever.

Gaten watched his new Chloe Brazil. On stage she was a beast! Off stage she stimulated her mind where she found people more fascinating than the rush of blood she got to the head from dancing. Since acquiring courage from Saint, she nearly created a state of mania in the club when performing. Guys were simply magnetized to her when she walked off. That was easy money, but not entirely what she was there for. Earlier in the night before she'd perform on stage, she'd observe the ebb and flow of the club. During one of such observations, she noticed some out-of-towners in the middle of the week who traveled to perform on stage that coming weekend; but she couldn't get close to them.

That weekend she complained of a pulled muscle and didn't perform on stage, and it just so happened to be a "First Friday" event that night; the biggest party of the month! That's why those imports were in town. The next day, I found a lot more questions in her notes, than answers regarding Gaten's most prized night in the Rising Sun. First Fridays where by far the most heavily promoted night. A night where amateur exotic dancers where flown in from around the globe to dance on the most famous street in the world. And all VIP bar proceeds went to charity that evening.

It appeared that this "opportunity" he was awarding women from abroad didn't sit well with Lenin. She was puzzled, even disturbed by how insulated the visiting women in that spotlight were from all the other employees in the club during their visit. She'd been watching them for days leading up to the event. They were pampered like movie stars and in the process, completely out of reach of most the staff. She was equally disturbed by the VIP's who flew in to bid on the lap dances with these girls. They exuded such royalty and sense of entitlement that made her wonder… what are they doing on Bourbon Street? Her first impression was that this wasn't just a charity event. But a semi-private gathering of ultra-rich perverse minds; bidding on thoroughbreds? "Auctioned off" as Lenin put it in her notebook. The other note she made, was that these jetsetters appeared to all stay in the Royal Hotel across the Street, where the talent stayed. We debated the FIRST FRIDAY ulterior motives back home…

"He's pimping them across the street?"
I assumed.

"He's actioning them off
to VIP's upstairs."
She said heated.

"Same thing."
I responded.

"Is it?"
She asked me.

I wasn't surprise, but she had fresh eyes. Whatever he was doing it was marketed and celebrated in plain sight the same day every month. He seemed to be worry free about it. But then again, Gaten was an O.G. from Brooklyn. He always took to the spotlight as if he were the 2nd coming of Gotti.

With no signs of cooling that summer Bell's kept taking it off and became a full time 5th grade teacher/part time Bourbon Street Stripper. Me, I just had a hard time keeping my lid on, it was supposed to be over by the time school started! But with the added expenses of the three new girls at the apartment in Brazil, Lenin was determined to put aside a nest egg for them. I was sick of the whole thing; just over it!

The only reason I kept my job at Wild Forest was to keep thing balanced between us in my head. If she was going to keep doing it so was I. I obviously I didn't have her motivations. More than once after watching too many lap dances at my club, Joey had to have a sit-down with me to talk me out of going down the street and acting the fool. So-when the tickets I bought to the Orchestra had come time for us to use, it wasn't a moment too soon! Between the French Market, The Art Market and Wild Forest, I was spent.

The Orpheum Theater may only be a block out of The Quarter, but once your inside it feels like you're a world away from Bourbon Street. When Lenin and I put on the appropriate attire for the occasion it felt to me as if we were stepping out for the first time as a married couple since our honeymoon. Not to mention she finally wore her nice shoes out; with me! I suppose I thought the sophisticated music that night could elevate me from the stink of the gutter, the litter on the streets, and the mindless consumption that creates such a mess. Even, if only for a couple hours. I'm often asked how I stay sober living in The Quarter. Just look around before you leave. Is that how you want to look when you get home?

As we walked out of The Quarter in our Best ~ And by heavy traffic across Canal Street ~ Through the Grand Lobby of The Roosevelt Waldorf Astoria ~ And across the Street to The Orpheum Theater for a splendid evening with Carlos Miguel Prieto conducting Beethoven's Ninth. I couldn't be more excited! A Clock Work Orange enthusiast myself, I'd been eager to hear "Ode to Joy" in concert since dressing up as Alex for Halloween when I was a kid and going to the old Limelight of NYC dancing. And most of all, I was just ecstatic to go there with my wife who had never before looked as elegant as she did that evening.

But then I sensed she was disturbed when she noticed the long line at will-call to acquire tickets, I was perplexed. I had our tix in hand. So-I asked…

"What's wrong?"

She responded to me as we walked past that long line as if they couldn't hear her say…

"If everyone
here donated the price of
ONE ticket to educate The Girls.
I could send them to University
tomorrow."

Well, perhaps she was right. But did she have to be so loud about it? The girls weren't even out of High School yet.

As we made our way to our Gallery Seats her observations continued to be just as critical when we reached them. She wasn't happy about the seat either. I had to nearly beg her…

"Please,
let me chillax tonight."

"Here?"
She asked flabbergasted.

"I'm a seat geek."

"If it weren't bad enough you had your friend
lend me this dress from his boutique…"

…Referring to the extravagant dress she was wearing thanks to my buddy Joe at Fleur de Paris.

"But now were on display, front row,
above everyone?"

Apparently, my wife wanted to be dressed more casually that night, and not on display. If only she felt like that all summer! But I kept my cool. And responded calmly…

"Well,
I just didn't want anyone

on our lap tonight
dear."

We ignored each other while. It appeared as though something, or someone, was delaying the concert.

Finally, a gentleman came center stage and made a nervous announcement…

"Hello.
And Good evening.
Welcome music lovers!"
He gathered himself, then continued,
"It appears as though our Conductor
has been delayed and will not make tonight's
performance."

The audience sighed!

"The good news, Carlos is fine.
But he was in a minor traffic accident on
Magazine Street tonight."

The audience sighed once again.

"But I assure you,
he is OK.
But we all know how long a
Police report can take.
Ha-HA!"

The crowd joined in with a laugh.

"They'll pass a hat to fix his car,
but not help my Girls."
Lenin said in my ear.

She was on a roll. He continued…

"So, this evening,
if I seem as though I'm just a bit nervous?
Truth be known…
I am!"

Everyone laughed, but her.

"It's with great excitement,

and much anticipation.
That our eager, more than capable
and might I add… BRAVE,
orchestra will play for us tonight.
Without, the guidance of
a Musical Director."

The audience nearly gasped. Lenin smirked.

"Now,
let's see what's happens?"
Said the Gent in a high
pitch voice.

Applause filled the theater! And people around us began to speculate about the performance ahead. BL asked me…

"What's the big deal?"

"Ever go on stage and strip
without direction?"

"ALL THE TIME."
She said cocky."

"Was it ever a disaster?"
I asked.

She paused.

"Sometimes."
She said quickly.

I looked around at the packed house, and shrugged my shoulders at her. The Orchestra went on to open with Symphony No. 8 by Franz Schubert, and played for all I know, perfectly, with only the spirit of their missing conductor present.

By intermission, Lenin questioned the importance of a director at all. She pointed out…

"I just don't get it.
Why is a conductor needed up there?
It's Beethoven,
or Mozart,
or whoever it is.
It's always the same."

"Is it?"
I asked.

"It's seems
like over kill to me.
Having some guy spaz out and call him
Mr. Director, or
whatever."

I smiled thinking of my friend from India in the French Market who always calls me that. Yet Belly-Bell's didn't stop there; nope. She continued…

"I mean,
it's not as if the guy up there is
directing traffic or something
important like that."

Then, she pointed out something… valid.

"Think about it Braze.
When you stand on any busy street
corner in New Orleans,
traffic always sounds completely different
one moment to the next.
Mozart…
same old thing every time."

"OK.
I hear what you're saying,
but what's your point?"

"My point?
This Conductor, Carlos…
he's going to be directing traffic soon
as someone else besides me
figures this out."

That was funny, but I didn't laugh. Not because she was serious, or because she wasn't. But because this is why I loved her.

After a stretch and once again exploring our general differences, it came time to enjoy Beethoven's 9th. I couldn't help but come to the edge of my seat when the four operatic singers opened up their lungs on stage.

And much later, nearly blown away by the 50 plus choir behind the Orchestra that brought the symphony to climax! What a wonderful evening. Bella Lenin may have experienced this as an unnecessary luxury. But to me, it was therapy.

From the time we left our seats I began playing the opening of the second movement from public announcement speakers on every corner in my City of Lakes. Despite knowing better than to trigger such mania, that is, to engage something endlessly to escape something else. I let it loop. And loop it did! One should call the ambulance for me if they notice me looping. Because, there's prolly-goin' to be an accident. And just as we made it down the steps and to the entrance lobby, smack; it happened! My wife literally bumped into customer. They were both caught off guard. The man, with his wife perhaps, stopped himself from saying Hi, as did his Chloe at the same time. But they were definitely caught in each other headlights. Then, they had the gall to laugh it off together.

"Lap dance loser!"
MES yelled from inside behind the glass.

My fist clenched. My right leg pivoted back. I scanned the room but just before I cocked the hammer…

"Let me formally introduce myself.
I'm Officer Robert Perlinghi… "

I checked my swing. He continued…

"…A.K.A. on the job Bob.
Honey this is… "
Fishing for my wife to clue him in.

"Bella."
She said coming to his aid.

"Bella is an entertainer on my beat."
He pointed out.

"Pleased to meet you Bella."
His wife said cordially.

He continued,
"This is my wife Tara."

"And my husband Braze,"
Bella followed with.

I nodded, and tried to put on a happy face. But when a twitch in the corner of my left eye began to tremor, *MES* glued himself to that widow glass. *BDAWN* stood in the other making these notes. Everyone outside still had a happy face on. But no one had anything else to say. I spoke up…

"Well,
gangs all here."

I said with eyes sick-o-wide before continuing with…

"One small step from
Bourbon Street,
One giant leap from a
lap dance."
I said looking straight
at HIS wife!

Putting an end to the casual pleasantries I put my arm around my wife like a possessive chump to heard her out fast and said politely…

"If you'll excuse us now."

But this guy really wanted to ruin my night.

"Wait,"
He said.

Putting his hand… on, my, chest!

"May I have a second
before you go."

"Not unless you have a warrant Serpico."
I said nose to nose with him.

"Whoa, wait.
What's wrong with you?"
Asked, what felt like my soon to be EX!

The Cop continued,
"I know how this looks,

to both of you."
He said looking at his wife and I,
"But I'd just like to
thank Bella."

"Me?"
She asked him perplexed.

"You suggested
that I go as far as it takes
to romance my wife.
And, well… here we are!"
He said squeezing his wife next to him
with one arm.

"Is this the one who told you
to finger me during the
fourth movement?"
His wife asked him annoyed.

About time she got the picture! But then he spoiled it…

"No,
that was my idea honey."

"Oh…"
She said with relief,
as if she just had a pleasant flashback
of the orgasm.

And with that, my classical music therapy session, went to shit.

F A L L I N G A P A R T

It was far beyond a summer job once Lenin prolonged the club experience further to fulfill her self-imposed obligations to The Girls in Brazil. Halloween was approaching, and that holiday would mark our extended little stint on Bourbon Street to an overdue celebratory end. These double shifts and double lives really weighed on us. Other than not telling her family yet, Bella seemed to be very honest and open about the experience with me. And the trade-off for my personal discomfort through it all was that she seemed to be more confident and poised as ever.

After only four months of lap dance profits, The Girls in Brazil who boldly escaped their perils could be housed safely until they finished High School before going on to college. The college funds were yet to be sought, but that would certainly be a priority in the future. Thanks to my wife's open heart I had no doubt that sending the money down to The Girls was the best thing to do. Such support would create a new chapter in their lives otherwise not possible thanks to my wife. I think what made Lenin happiest, and most thankful was the friend she made in Izabelle. She'd go on and on about her strength, beauty, and character quite often. It came as natural to Lenin to be of service to others, as it did to her brother Thorsen. They'd apparently been brought up to do so.

Things began to leveled out. By mid-October, I gave my two weeks at Wild Forest just 15 days before Halloween. I had plans to take Bella to a party where The Bingo Show was playing at a mansion in The Quarter. I hoped we could celebrate together again like old times. Once some of my anxiety finally settled after the summer stage, I found a higher purpose in Lenin's stripping. The support she gave to The Girls had me thinking I could look back at this time on Bourbon Street and be very proud of this endeavor of hers. And I must add that I met other strippers doing good things with their money such as raising children, opening restaurants, passion projects, etc. It's worth noting what one Exotic Dancer at Wild Forest mentioned to me…

"I don't save money,
I spend it on investments."

It was a cool and breezy night, the air almost glistened with moisture whiles I had a jacket on while eating dinner on our Balcony. In one of my inside pockets, I had that gift-wrapped copy of *"The Melancholy Death of Oyster Boy"*. Lenin sat across from me bundled up and wearing an oversized winter cap, her long hair covered her neck like a scarf. And my small portable Bookstand heater was aimed at her feet to keep her more comfortable; this would be our last meal outdoors that year. *After discussing* Halloween costume ideas over dinner as the Sun went down, Lenin asked…

"How's your red light district love story
coming along?"

"I'm almost afraid to say it,
but it needs more drama."

"Dig deeper."

"It's not my scene.
I'm still embarrassed walking in and
out of the club."

"I'm not embarrassed."

I pondered that.

"Just a little?"

She shook her head NO. I finally called her out, it was almost over.

"Do your colleagues at school know?
Told your Family?
Do… The Girls know?"

"I'll tell them, one day."

"Great. Why wait?
Let's have everyone
over for dinner this weekend."

This was overdue, I continued…

"In between discussions about
the refugee crises at our Southern Boarder
and the extinction of tribal languages in South
America, you, can bring up how
liberating and empowering it is for
independent contractors on Bourbon Street
to make such a good living
baring all."

She'd been so quick to judge so many for perhaps not doing their part, but couldn't even be honest with her own friends & family about how she was doing hers? Not to mention… is this the kind of example she wanted to set for the girls in her 5th Grade classrooms? But I took a deep breath, who am I to stick it to her? With only a couple weeks to go before it was all over, perhaps now was not the time. I put my head down, and fingers through my hair. Then, I finally looked back up and said…

"I'm sorry."

"No, I'm sorry."
She said.

"You don't have to be.
You've been open with me from go."
I said graciously, and continued,
"You didn't have to share your journals with me.
Thank you for doing so."

"I've nothing to hide in the Rising Sun.
I'm not sorry for that."

She was calm, very calm. Too calm. She was holding something back. I could see a calculation in her eyes.

"What then? …Do tell."

"Let me start by saying I'm not sorry for
anything I've done on Bourbon Street.
Or, who I didn't tell I work there, yet.
Nor am I sorry
for what I still have to do.
But I am sorry…
that it may hurt you."

My mind raced as my eyes probed her erratically as they do when I'm squaring someone up.

"I've decided to extended my experience
at the club."

"Till?"
I asked.

"Mardi Gras."

"Another four months!"
MES yelled inside
But I didn't know if he was happy,
or just shocked about it.

I didn't say a fucking word. It didn't matter why to me. Any radical justification she could fabricate could be of no surprise. I just took another deep breath and thought, damn… Stumps duh Clown may have to be summoned for an annulment.

After dinner I finally threw the damn Oyster Boy in the trash and did the dishes. She never did dishes! Just let them stack up like Jenga. I even kept a goddamn sign over the sink to try and inspire her for years now…

It's COOL to be CLEAN !

…but nope. Her hands never touch the dish soap. Cause her Grandma told her grease added flavor. When I was done the dishes, I walked to Electric Ladyland and got a Cheech Wizard tattoo on my ass to cover her name up.

Later, I combed her notes for something I missed. Why didn't I see this coming? I found at the end of every daily entry, that they usually ended the same way. With her having a drink after work at the Entrance Bar that's outside the main club. It was there in fact where she was making some of her notes. Every night at close she observed many Strippers say goodbye to doormen, and walk directly across the street into the Hotel on the other side of Bourbon. She always concluded her notes with a bunch of Maybe's. Maybe they are, maybe they aren't. Maybe they should, maybe this, maybe that, maybe, maybe-maybe! A bunch of thoughts that made it clear, that possibly, along the way she'd became more open to prostitution. With that assumption, anxiety flooded my City of Lakes once again! I've been victim to brain fluids my entire life. I mindlessly paced the apartment with these ruminating thoughts. The Loft is just enough to house a large living room, bedroom, kitchen, and a little more space near a quarter-moon window where Bella's desk sat. But I must say, it's always a little quitter & peaceful back in the Garret where I write in The Enclave. NOTE: Within there, I'm separate from all else; it's the most soundproof area in all The Quarter. My Write-Away Chest is parked in there. I must have pushed that old desk over every 1,800 square foot up here looking for the sweet spot, before it landed in that smallest area four feet deep. With a slanted ceiling that only gets to about 6 feet at its high side. On the other side, 3 feet away, it's probably only 4 feet high. But it's in this human book safe, perhaps where most would think is the undesirable spot in the whole Loft, is where I've been writing this story.

When I finally pulled myself away from the troubling connections I made between the lines in her Journal, and rushed out of the Building to get to my shift at Wild Forest, I stepped smack into a phycological flood! Ankle deep in my own cerebral water, I felt horribly disturbed on a multidimensional level. But continued on through the liveliness of the evening towards Bourbon Street flooded within my emotions. Flooding sux! By the time I passed musicians busking on the corner who kicked and splashed my brain juice like rowdy boxcar kids bathing in a creek, I was knee deep in it. Further up Barracks as I sloshed forward then chest deep in brain juice, each historic building appeared to sink. By the time I made it back to Bourbon that night, the Enclave would be my only spillway. I was over my head in the real world.

Halloween was my favorite holiday in New Orleans. The weather's wonderful, costumes outrageous, and the vibe is closer to a good outlaw party and not the glam rock show of Mardi Gras. As Lenin and I walked The Quarter and I gazed upon her under street lamps she doted a proper hat with a white net veil over a long pale blue dress that met her ankles. She looked nearly royally to me in her Beatrix Potter attire. And was obviously fond of herself that night. She simply glowed once again! I too felt royal myself in a literary way, but not of her era. I was blank-faced, wearing a conservative grey suit, black tie and shoes. Carrying an antique fire extinguisher like an insecticide container dressed as the Exterminator William Lee of the science fiction novel *Naked Lunch*? Deep down, I still identified as a Junky.

After an upper-crust night in The Quarter with some friends at a neighborhood mansion hosting the Bingo Show, we headed over to Frenchmen where I was clued in that a camp of Brazilian DJ's were hosting an Outlaw. Frenchman Street is so crowded during certain holidays (such as the 31st) that cops couldn't get down the street to break something up if they had to. These South American DJ's were hip to that. Lenin was excited all night at just the mention of Brazil! I bumped into these DJ's in town earlier that day. We'd crossed paths when they came up here on such an occasion years before.

Frenchmen Street was the predictable chaos with nearly 10,000 people on two blocks. A number like that may not sound biblical, but condensed on two streets in a residential neighborhood, it's anarchy. Bella Lenin, out of character, carried a drink in each hand like everyone else around here.

Grooving on the edge of the party, she suddenly grabbed me by the hand when she finished her drinks and barreled our way through the crowd. She pulled me through the mass of 24 Hour Party People in a frenzy! Pissing many people off along the way for being so pushy. I finally pulled her back and gestured her to stop bum-rushing through the crowd and asked her at the top of my lungs through the epic atmosphere…

"Where are you going?"

"Towards the music I don't know!"
She yelled back.

It wasn't till then that I realized how smashed she was. I smiled, and informed her…

"We're here!"

But she looked lost. I took the opportunity to trip her out and reiterated with a sarcastic *Black Hole Sun* smile…

GARRET SCENARIO No.2

"We're here!"

…Standing there looking at each other in the middle of thousands dancing together, everyone was shit-faced but me. As the music filled me up, so did nostalgia. I'd been within this many block rocking hooligans time and time again. Sweating it out till the break of dawn living for nothing but this; what I once called the good life. But her? Bella looked as if she needed a stage to watch someone perform to find her place in the crowd. But in the world of good dance music not to be confused with show business, all the dancefloor is a stage.

"What do you want to do?"
She yelled.

I spoke in her ear as warmly as I could and suggested the obvious. That we…

"Dance."

Some of my biggest joys in life have been dancing unabashed in BPM epidemics. Such energy is even more contagious to those sailing the high seas of frequencies on booze, dopes, and hotdogs like true Americans. Stewards, gone contagions, we further trash the planet while celebrating the miracle of life as we know it in its last mile. Where landfills are the new graveyard, and plastics the new seaweed, we danced like skin cancer on the Earth. And as my attention drifted from her, up to the stars… I find the cycle of life never more present than within this river called the Milky Way. Where asteroids spew life dust ~ Mother stars nurse baby planets ~ And black holes recycle endlessly. Admiring creation, is how creation admires itself. Yet despite such clear observations, I managed to lose my dance partner Beatrix Potter in these drifts of awareness.

Evidently suffering with multiple contact highs, I roamed ankle deep in garbage looking for her. Or at my cell phone for a message from her, before bumping into a guy who read my plight suggesting…

"Dude, work smart.Not hard."

I climbed on top of his parked van he called home in hopes Beatrix, Bella, Lenin, Chloe, WHATEVER she might calling herself to somebody else at that moment? Would hopefully see me up there. With campervan man, and come my way. But, that was a failure too. I slid my-dude some skin, gave up, and walked home alone; worried.

I'd seen BL stoned on Mushrooms before, but never really saw her trashed till that Halloween. Evidently, Tanqueray and grapefruit became her drink of choice at the Club. I felt rather guilty for not slowing her roll down earlier. What was I going to do if she wasn't home? And if she wasn't home, where was she! The balance between being possessive and caring for her was a fine line. I'd be lying if I said I wasn't feeling some anger too. And *MES* was no help asking…

"She's giving someone a dance
in a doorway?"

BRIGHTDAWN squashed that,
"No.
Not her."

But nonetheless, I glanced in every doorway on the way home.

As I walked down Decatur Street between Elysian Fields and Barracks next to the Jazz Museum, I didn't see the lights on in our Loft and assumed she wasn't home yet. I doubled back to go look for her on Frenchmen again. Then a few steps later it occurred to me she might just be home sleeping.

"Check the Loft before you go
any further."
BRIGHTDAWN suggested.

She had me coming and going! I rushed home.

Upon my skidding around the corner of Barracks and Decatur I noticed an Italian Barrel employee power washing kitchen equipment. Before I found Lenin sitting on the pavement against our door with her head between her legs. I called out to the kitchen employee with the power sprayer…

"Yo my bro!
Please, that's my wife right-dare.
Careful wit-the chemicals."

"Oh!"
He said surprised,
"My bad Bigs."

She was locked out, and passed out. I was just relieved.

Standing over top of her looking down, I must have looked like that so many times myself. Mischievously, I snapped snap a picture. Regretfully, it was the only shot I took that night. She looked so prim, proper and ravishing that night, that even the gutter I found her next to couldn't unbeauty her. But only reducer her to a hot mess. I bent down brushed her hair behind her ears to try and wake her, but she was out of it. At a closer look I noticed her shoes were gone, her feet black, and thought… YES! She'd finally have to part with some money to buy some new Toms.

Without saying a word… I opened the front door ~ Carried her upstairs ~ Ran her a bath ~ Made some tea ~ Lit a candle above the tub ~ Put THE XX on low. And let the muck soak off her feet in a warm bath. While I made notes in the Enclave, she began to cry. Instead of going in to check on her, I let her have some alone time with her feelings. She didn't need me now. If it's one thing that didn't make sense to me when I was wasted, was a straight person talking sense.

The next morning as those in the town who got to sleep slept-in, I went for a bike ride on the nearly traffic-less streets before I got around to making waffles for us later. I threw everything in the mix from chia, flax & rolled oats to milk and caramel toffee tea with cinnamon on top. Turkey bacon fried as I steamed milk for cappuccino's, before Lenin let out a moan that morning. She called out politely from bed…

"Can you please,
please bring me more water?"

I handed her a glass of water, put her coffee on the bed-stand, and sat on the edge of the bed just admiring her. After months of her stripping motives being airtight and her nerves practically bombproof, I was happy to be sober when she finally showed some vulnerability that morning. And, I don't think I missed a thing on Frenchmen not partaking in the high life with the sheeple.

"Sorry
I lost you last night.
I got caught up dancing in the stars.
And when I came back,
you were gone."

"I just remember dancing with you,
and then you took my hand and walked
us through the crowd.
Next thing I know I was by the DJ having another
drink and talking to you,
before I realized… wait, what?
This isn't Braze."

I kept cool and refrained from any kind of reaction to that. She shrugged her shoulders. I told'er…

"Gin does the same thing
to Stumps."

She smiled.

"You're a goddamn clown now."
I added.

She laughed, and that aggravated her headache. I went back to the kitchen ~ Ripped open some Alka-Seltzer Cold & Flue tablets ~ Dropped them in a glass of spring water ~ Grabbed a breakfast plate to share ~ And climbed back into bed with her! It felt great to really be needed again. Though sometimes she began to feel like my enemy, I think I continued to grow in our relationship.

With Bella dancing till Mardi Gras, Racheal was happy at Wild Forest to keep someone on who didn't take smoke breaks. At this time in my life my personality was solid and my communication skills where pretty sharp. Despite the insecurities I had at home I was on rather solid ground in public. Selling books all day came with ease and being friendly in The Club at night was a breeze; as long as I wasn't tracking lap dances. When my emotions stirred at work, 5 minute meditations on the Club Balcony over Bourbon kept those feelings from making emotion soup out of me. I had to stay in control, because there was no finishing this scenario of course, if I didn't survive it. I really thought I could handle, MY selves, as it were. To stay in, HER world; yeah.

Often, you'd find me hanging out in the DJ Booth with Joey. The vibe in that little corner of his made for precious flashbacks. And I really needed temporary escape now and then like those. I never ask Joey about the time he did, or how he got Ten down to Two; I didn't care. When he told me he NEVER cared to see an old face again, that was enough for me.

But I did ask,
"You never bump into anyone
down here?"

"Just one.
Down at the Rising Sun."

"Gaten?"
I responded.

"Yeah.
I was looking for work down there
before I got this gig.
You fuckin' know him?"

Joey looked at me suspect for a moment.

"I don't really know him,
just of him.
My brother was in the mix
back in the day."

"Oh yeah?
Who's your brother?"

"Richy."

An ordinary name, but it did speak volumes. Truth be known my brother was dealers dealer in the 90's when the dance scene was still rather big underground business.

"Cool-Richy?"
Joey asked surprised with
a smile.

I nodded YES. Joey commented…

"Richy's a Mack from
way back."

I miss my brother so much I often change the subject when he comes up, and asked…

"You afraid Gaten might notice you
down here on the duck?"

"I'm nobody to him.
But really, he nor I should be
in these clubs no more."
Joey said.

Joey and I struck a bond during conversations in the DJ booth not so much about our gigs on Bourbon Street, but rather where we came from. And from that, we had a certain level of trust in each other automatically. He sensed it in me and I in him long before we had longer conversations. That's what opened the door to them initially. Which… kind-a reminded me of an old interview with Billy Wilder I once caught on the Dick Cavett Show.

Billy said he never trusted a writer with a tan. That he'd take a skinny pale writer who was shaking with nervousness and suffered when socializing then any person who spends his time by the pool rather than a hunched over writing all day. I think the same of DJ's. I don't trust DJ's with tans. Give me an enthusiastic pimp geek turntablist with a vitamin D deficiency over a showbiz DJ any day. My man Joey Beignets here, he's a pale dude.

Down the street Bella went on to create a larger presence at the Rising Sun with the persona of the evolving Chloe Brazil. The sometimes delicate other times wild interpretive dance style inspired by coaches Vinnie and Saint continued to work wonders. Those guys became her fulltime friends, not I. For years we talked about everything, now, I was merely an observer. It got harder to read her notes and keep watching what Dutch shared, but I needed the material.

When Lenin entered the club months ago, she wasn't sure if she could make it through a song on stage. Chole

Brazil lost money the first week. Now she was strutting around as if she was a trust fund gypsy that didn't need the cash and perhaps that was part of the draw. Then Chloe B. even began turning down lap dances occasionally so as not to be just another girl to be picked up. She trotted around The Sun not to be chosen, but making choices. Marketing herself like an artist whose edgy work is more in demand because it's not given away to just anyone who can afford it. She didn't make many friends with the competitive talent there, but the staff loved her. She nonchalantly tipped everyone immediately for their assistance in thoughtful amounts.

Often when waitress came with drinks for her and a guest, she'd pay the bill to establishing that…

"I'm not
letting ANYONE get
ME drunk."

Evidently what Vinnie said about drinking on the job fell on deaf ears. As Chloe came into her own that Fall, Dutch worked overtime for me. And that led to more restless nights for me making notes or tossing around in bed with his projections on my eyelids. While I was up late in the Enclave reading the subtitles from Dutch's lip reads, it appeared then that she started to have more and more of a following by chance of wit. One witty, pixyish word began to set her apart and get her ahead.

When an interesting customer tried to tempt her with something outside her boundaries, she began simply saying…

"Maybe,"
and continue with the
conversation.

As they hung on her every word after a MAYBE she found the responses on their faces telling. THE MAYBE instantly changed the dynamic of the situation in positive ways. Whereas to say NO to dinner, a weekend in the Bahamas, or worse; buzz kill.

But to say YES, even to a cup of coffee, would lead outside the safe zone of the Rising Sun. So, to duck the NO's that rejected them on the spot, and the YES's to future commitments elsewhere, entered THE MAYBE. A rapid advance in the sexual nature of things.

THE MAYBE's power wasn't invented as much as it was discovered. It was merely a side effect of her desire to keep the conversation moving forward to VIP. When she delivered the magic word from her ultra-glossy lips at opportune times it began to drive her regulars nutty! Once people were hooked on a MAYBE, they kept coming back to buy more time, and try to sell themselves to her; jackpot. *BRIGHTDAWN* was shocked by the side effect of the word MAYBE. And *MES* couldn't be happier for her hustle. But it just made me wonder why I was trying so hard to find these words. I mean come on, MAYBE? Chloe, she kept just shooting for the side effects of the word.

According to some accounts she was becoming one of the most sought out entertainers in the club. From her unpredictable moves on stage, to her nothing short of therapeutic sensual lap dances, along with the elite management of Vinnie and Saint… she was growing into the fame that DJ Crowley hyped! Chloe Brazil had such natural talent that she probably cashed in as much as those across the street in the Royal Hotel. The nice humble hippie I married certainly became a pro at stripping, but not hooking, NOT at any price. You'd think that would've been a relief to me. But it made me feel that this would never end. I wanted us out since the end of last summer. Anxiety created hurricanes that had my City of Lakes crumbling during kamikaze panic attacks leaving much of my infostructure in ruins.

Morning rituals such as cycling and mediating began to suffer. Once daily exercise and focus were taken out of my soup, depression surfaced. I should have known then what I was ducking would eventually find me. But instead of slowing my roll and perhaps talking to my therapist, I just went into overdrive! Work ~ Nap ~ Write ~ Rush. I stacked bills, Uber at fast foods, drank Coffee 24/7, blew off friends, didn't return emails, put my gym membership hiatus, let my desk go to smithereens. I was completely out of sorts! But I did my best not to worry Mom when she called. She always thought I chose a tough profession. And often sensed danger ahead…

"We don't need you racking up
more frequent flyer miles

in another ambulance."

"The perceptions not the
reality Mom."

"I think writing about these
Hobos and Bimbos
does nothing but increase your
risk profile Braze.
End of story."

My poor composure must have been apparent at the Frenchman Art Market too. Person after person came up giving me advice. Strangers, other venders, even the Goddamn Frenchmen Pirate…

"You're not yourself asshole."
He said shaking his head.

"Thanks, dude."

"Want a swig?"
He offered from his bottle.

"Nah."

He went into a pocket in his camo cargo pants. Took out a little sheer blue bag with tiny gold stars on it, and tossed it on my table. It looked like it was from Dollar General.

"You'll thank me later."
He said.

Then he walked away. When I picked it up and felt that there were strips of packaged pills inside, I told him…

"Take this back man."

"You need um'!"
He yelled.

"What are they?"

"Organic!"
He screamed, then added,

"A gift from my Guru."

I peeked inside the little bag and found two strips of pills professionally packaged. Along with it was a folded pamphlet with a great deal of information on it. The top of it read like this:

Twenty (20) Tablets EASEtm MOLECULAR SACRAMENT
Church of Neuroscience L3C K&B Organics.

The rest of the information was laid out like a Dr. Bronner's Soap Bottle. Just assuming they were 5HTP supplements of some sort I wasn't interested in reading more, threw them in my leather attaché, and resumed my hustle rather unenthusiastically…

"Made a movie, wrote a book.
Take a look."

"Sure."
Said a young lady with her friends.

Nearly disappointed, I got back on script.

The next morning, I found a note on the pillow next to me that read…

Went to Capoeira class.
Love Lenin

Then the doorbell rang, I ignored it ~ My cellphone vibrated, I checked it ~ Harry was downstairs ~ I grabbed my keys ~ Tossed them off the balcony.

Nearly ten minutes later, coffee brewed and a hot cup in my hand. Harry came in looking unusually horrible and not just completely out of breath as usual.

"Some water Harry?"

He shook his head YES.

"Where's Lenin?"
He asked out of breath.

"Capoeira class."

"She's really difficult to reach
these days."
He said quite worried.

I shrugged my shoulders with nothing more to share. He sipped some water, shoe gazed, and continued...

"I have news."

Thinking it was something "Big" between he and Carol, I responded with a smile and a hint of sarcasm...

"Do tell old timer."

"It's my health."
He said.

"Oh.
What's up?"

"Cancer."
He said bluntly.

I knew where it was. He was holding his chest.

He went on to say,
"I don't think I'm up for
the treatments."

The first thing that came to mind was that,
"Believing you can heal can
work miracles man."

"Yeah, well,
I'm short on positive thoughts.
And I think I'm just
I'm more open to accept this
stage of life."

I took breath, and breathed out thoughts of how hard Lenin would take that kind of attituded. Then I noticed a dusty bottle of whiskey on a bottom shelf. Went over, picked it up, and offered him some...

"Yes please.
Neat."
He responded.

He didn't want to talk about his health, just about movies. It was a long talk. He polished off what was left of that little bottle of Jack as I finished a French Press of Mardi Gras King Cake coffee; good life. When Lenin walked in some time later and found us laughing with an empty bottle of whiskey between us, she stopped in her tracks. He smiled and waved her in to have a seat.

A little drunk, he delivered it as fondly as the actor he resembled in Easy Rider…

"The inevitable is knocking
my dear."

She prepared herself. He continued…

"Time is the
most precious resource.
And my clock's winding down."
He said with his
head up.

The room went silent, the noise from the streets outside ceased, all that could be heard were our hearts in a drum circle.

After just a short talk, she made it crystal clear that she would not, NOT let him just give up so easy. During this meeting of the minds they took on the situation as an opportunity to take a holistic approach into consideration. Thinking outside the box like this came natural to the whole family.

Much later I showed up for my shift at the club to find a bachelor party happening. I called on some girls from VIP and had them work down here because this wasn't a crowd worth sending to the 2nd floor; they were drinking cheap beers. Socially, they appeared comfortable just horsing around in their university colors. And not tipping the dancers much at all who quickly had enough of this polite, polished and obnoxious gang. With nothing further to note, I closed my Moleskine and began making my way to the back of the house to stash it. As I began to walk away someone in that party got curious; about me…

GARRET SCENARIO No.2

"Who'd you say you were?
What were you writing down?"

Hoping they'd move on because cheapness is infectious, I told him that…

"I'm a P.I.
I work for his fiancé."

While in my attaché at my locker I came across that little sheer bag of pills with the tiny gold stars the Pirate threw me, and took a closer look at the soapy literature included on the pamphlet…

Treating You Kind and Keeping You Bright;
K&B Organics.

As I shoved them back into a ripped leather pocket a few of the stars on the bag fell off and seemed to dissipated in the air. It was a creepy moment that brought the hairs on my arms to attention. I paused, then pulled the bag back out for another look. For whatever reason, I shook it up. The pills of course rattled. I waved it quickly back & forth in front of my eyes to see if any stars would fall off again, but nope. After kicking the tires, I took a gander at more of the literature…

EASEtm MOLECECULAR SACRAMENT
TeRM of OFFERING: Blah Blah
SACRAMENT RIGHTS OF BENEFICE: Blah Blah
Foster Love, Respect, Forgiveness & Kindness; Promote Awareness of Intrinsic Beauty & Immeasurable Worth of Ourselves & Others, Cultivate Greater Awareness of The Divine Creator(s), The Grand Architect(s) Who Make This World & Our Miraculous Existence Possible.

NOT FDA APPROVED
WORLD HEALTH ORGANIZATION APPROVED
K & B ORGANICS

By now I was open to organic energy of any kind. Assuming they were indeed Organic, I popped a couple. But actually, unbeknownst to me just yet… what in fact I was avoiding for years now, had just found me that night.

Moments later I was on the Main Floor, Joey was rocking perfect beats, and the girls were bored. Then, I noticed a barback arguing with a Dancer just before he smashed an empty beer bottle against a wall. Before storming out of the club leaving the girl there stunned. When I made it over to her, she tried to explain what happened. But what I gathered between the lines was that they were fucking and got into a personal disagreement on the job. The staff is prohibited from dating the dancers; period. I just told her I understood (her bullshit) and it's OK. But when she kept trying to explain, I cut her off…

"Listen,
I really don't care.
I can do his job tonight, but I can't do yours.
I'm just glad he left and not you.
You understand me?"

"Yes."
She nodded.

"As far as I'm concerned…
you just trying to tell me that
you don't even know what
that guy's name is."

She nodded her head YES, a little confused.

"The Eye in the Sky is on us.
And he's got a job to do.
So-smile,
and just walk away,
now."

She graced my chin with the touch of her fingertips and went to put her curvy body back to work on stage. I went into my headset and told Rasan…

"All good."

"Copy that."
He answered back from
upstairs.

Sweeping up the broken glass I noticed our DJ Joey Good-as-Beignets make a transition from *Perfect Beat* into Donna Summer's *I Feel Love* instantly, bringing a bob to my head, before I dumped the broken glass in a trashcan.

I took a breath ~ And then another ~ I put a handful of fingers through my hair ~ Then I combed my other hand through my hair ~ Suddenly I found myself gripping two fists full of hair pulling at my roots as if fore playing myself ~ Consequently I began rocking my hips to the feelings of love expressed by the purveyor of discotheque synth Giorgio Moroder. All, before I realized what the fuck was going down and acknowledging the happening with a heartfelt, goose bumped, deep ass…

"G-g-God-D-d-Damn."

Suddenly, I felt 100% better! So much so that it reminded me what 100% actually was. I could feel it from my hair to my veins from my body to my brain. The partial blackout in the City of Lakes, no more, power shortage, over, lights got brighter insid, and out!

The boys upstairs came straight to the windows in space suits. *MR. MES* looked over to *B.DAWN* and radioed from inside his astronaut's helmet…

"Ground control this your
inner Mac Miller.
The eagle has lift off.
Copy *BRIGHTDAWN*?"

"Copy that Mac.
The pills are potent.
We are now cruising at a
euphoric altitude.
Copy?"

"Ditto-Dat."

I suddenly had no worries, no insecurities, no sadness, no pressures or fears of any sort. Now I still had my stripper wife, my dying father-in-law, a struggling small business, this lousy moonlight gig on Bourbon and only a half a book done here. But the more Donna Summers sung about feeling love, the more I was loving it; LOVING IT! It was certifiable. Whatever was in those organic pills, was not Certified Organic. *BRIGHTDAWN* declared…

"Such a treasure
could only come from a Pirate."

When the serotonin highways in the City of Lakes got so busy that helicopters began trafficking dopamine above them, *MES* declared…

"We're back
in the feel good business!"

After my shift I took my time coming home. The crisp fall air, glow of the residential gas lamps, and laughs of others walking back to their hotel rooms drunk, hadn't felt this damn-good in half a decade.

Once home and throbbing with raw lust I pulsed with rapid sexergy between my thighs. When I found Lenin resting to the sounds of HEADSPACE sleep radio, I snuggled up next to her. Waking her gently with some kisses, licks, and slight bites before she said…

"Tell me you love me.
Tell me you love me Braze."

She followed me wherever my mind went that night. She needed the escape herself. I didn't taste like alcohol. It didn't occur to her that I was stoned.

Following a nap, I woke up fuzzy; I love-dat! When I remembered why, some remorse crept in. Next to me Lenin was snoring. I rolled out of bed ~ Drank some OJ ~ And addressed the remorse by crushing a couple more pills to snort. After bumping up I jumped back into bed to jam. But I didn't get the greenlight this time.

"What's gotten into you?"
She asked.

At dawn it would be harder tp hide the shade of shit I was on. *MES* pointed out like a jerk we can easily be…

"She didn't complain
last night."

At a loss for words I repeated,
"You didn't complain
last night."

Her mouth opened. Eyes widened. And her heart probably cracked before she said…

GARRET SCENARIO No.2

"I thought you wanted me
last night."

I rolled over, looked out the window. Before responding…

"I do."

"No, you don't.
You can't even look at me.
What are you on?"

"Nothing illegal.
Organic supplements!"

I got up to grabbed them out of my attaché' and tossed the K&B Organics Molecular Sacrament pamphlet on the bed. Perhaps the branding would fool her as it did me. She read some of it aloud…

"Ease?
Church of Neuroscience?
This is a crock.
Look at you!"

"What?"

"Go look at yourself
in the mirror.
Then tell me again how organic
these are!"

"Weeds organic.
Mushrooms are organic.
I probably just took too
many of'um."

"How many did you
take?"

"Two,
this morning."

"And last night?
Before you came home?"
"Four. Five?"

"So,

none of your passion for me was real,"
she said,
"It was for these."

I didn't know what to say. But she did. And tried to ruin my high…

"I should have known,"
She laughed,
"You could've never gone that
long otherwise."

MES was playing basketball in my skull with a pair of custom Air Jordan's on as *BRIGHTDAWN* observed dropping science from the sideline…

"If a player
wants to improve his game,
studies show name brand high-tops
yield better results."

I said defensively,
"Pills like these help me feel
like a winner."

"But it's not real Charlie Sheen.
What your feeling,
isn't real."

"What makes your disappointment,
realer than my joy!"

"This!"
She screamed holding up the K&B pamphlet
before asking,
"Where did you get this
crap from?"

I really didn't want to answer that question.

But, I did,
"Someone noticed I was down and out
and tossed them my way."

"Who?"
"An acquaintance."
I murmured.

"I want to know who!"
She demanded.

I scratched my chin. Then, the back of my head. Before tellin-her flat out…

"A pirate,
on Frenchman Street,
got them from his
Guru."

In response, her face contorted; like a cartoon.

I shut up and walked away, I'd already said too much. She was done talking to me too. After a phone call with her Father, she jetted. Apparently, Carol was on a bender again and stayed out all night. I really should have followed her over to be of service, but I wanted to keep rolling. Thus, the binge began.

After half assed set up of my Bookstand in the French Market I threw a blanket over it. Placed a "Be Back Soon" sign under a train spike. And ran around the block to find the Frenchmen Pirate in hopes to put off my hangover till later. I busted a left at the Louisiana Music Factory when I heard him screaming. At who? Not a clue. Frenchmen Street's dead this time of morning. When I laid eyes on him down the block, he appeared to be curating his finger paintings on the sidewalk and ranting about wanting another chance to kick Russel Crowe's ass off a sail boat; or something like that.

When I reached him, I ignored the state he was in and said…

"Sup dog."

"I'm no maird!"

How would I know what that means?

I asked him,
"Bad day?"

"Just got out of
O.P.P.!"

"Then,
it's a good day.

Any day out of jail's
a good day."

He whipped out some documents from his back pocket and began ranting in French again. But as I said, I don't speak French. And I suspect he didn't either. So, within these Frenchy words of his he kept dropping "court house" and a judge's name who evidently was a…

"Butt-fucker
Va-teh fair foo-trah!"
Or something.

"You want to tell me
what happened?"
I asked.

"It took six cops to hold
me down!"

"Six cops?"
I asked as if I were
proud of him.

This guy actually wasn't that crazy. But he was defiantly a fulltime drunk who lost his teeth to his decadent days of meth use. More recently, on his best bender, two cops wouldn't have a problem cuffing him. So, I had ask…

"What were you on?"

"MXE.
Never again!
Brool-ohn-lawnfet
first!"

"MXE?"
I wondered aloud.

That sounded heavy enough to me. I felt it was then time to connect with him and spoke his language…

"Me-I's-partake?"

He went into one of his many old brown grocery bags laying on the sidewalk next to his paintings. Rummaged through a couple. Then, found what he was looking for, and screamed at the top of his lungs with the strength of a drunk sailor rejected by a nasty whore on Gallatin Street…

"Auhhh!
Ohn-cool-ay!"

Before throwing exactly what-I came there for at my head like a Chinese star where it came to a quick stop in my unwashed hair. I went in my crop to retrieve it. And sure enough… found one of those starry bags filled with pills. Mostly intact! The Pirate kept ranting and setting up his art on the sidewalk as I looked in the bag. The fine print read…

"GLIDE. Treating You Kind
12mg MXE."

There was about 15 of them left. I let the Pirate carry on. I don't even think he notice me leave. Or, ever cared to remember I was even there.

When I got back to The Loft, I opened the GLIDE sack and quickly par-oozed the Molecular Sacrament literature included with my bag of thrills. It was all so official! I'd copped a lot in life, but nothing like this. With instructions, list of ingredients, branding, warnings, barcodes, Rites of Benefice, Preamble, Phone Number, Address, Website, WTF. Was this legal? It certainly appeared so. But the names of the two different kinds of pills I had acquired, the first EASE, and now GLIDE? That clued me in to something close to a street nature was at work beneath all this official jargon. As I sped-read the literature once again, I found a sacred word this time…

"KETAMINE!"

According to the literature I had in one hand, the pills I held in the other contained Methoxetamine (MXE). An "enlightened 21st century evolution" of Special K. I'd gone to great length to acquire K in the past; from BK to TJ. I'd acquired it in many different brands and bottles over the years. But never, ever, had I'd seen it in pill form till now. I crushed two, popped two. Then went back to the Bookstand to sell my book about rehabbing. Yeah… I know, I… know.

Lenin immediately put her Father on a raw food diet, and no sugar. She bought him oxygen tanks, aromatherapy massages, a gadget to help him up our steps, and more supplements than I thought one person could ever swallow and insisted… he wash them down with a dash of food grade hydrogen peroxide in the water. But he was pretty far along, his cough got worse, and he appeared to get thinner overnight on that new diet.

Being against western medicine kept them out of doctor's offices in general. So-after being informed of the severity of his condition at a hospital, they just thought working together on this rather than turning the situation over to surgery was best for him. Together they read ferociously looking for physical and spiritual cures on the fringe of modern medicines. I thought if nothing else, it was brave approach. But I got the impression from his condition that these steps should have been taken much sooner to be effective. His bad health was in plain sight to me since we met.

Days later I was shocked when he showed up at my Bookstand on an electric trike.

"Nice wheels!"
I cheered.

"Lenin believes
that the wind in my face will clear my head."
He said through heaving.

I wanted to share some of these pills I was on to EASE his anxiety, and perhaps let him GLIDE a few hours. But Lenin didn't know I was still on because on the surface I looked fine. As long as I was on the "Molecular Sacraments" everything was manageable like never before. All I had to do was read the extensive labeling to anticipate intended effects.

But I bought so many starry bags in a week that my Pirate's Guru cut me off! The Guru gave my Pirate some official paperwork to forward to me at the Frenchman Art Market. I asked…

"What duh-hell is
all this?"

"The leader our church

wants you to become a parishioner.
If you want to keep partaking,
you got-to pass
the test!"

And with the test, there was an affidavit for me to get notarized. Essentially, I had to join a pill cult.

"OK.
No problem."

Sign me up! Yet as I stood there glancing at the legal documents in my hand, I done-got even more dumfounded…

"This is some pastor man."
I said in awe.

"Joshua's not just some pastor.
The High Priest."
The Pirate said with a smile,
dripping maggots.

And why not I thought? Weed and acid had their churches at one time, why shouldn't pharmaceuticals today? I was in full support to this molecular sacrament movement.

"Where's Joshua's church?"
I asked.

"On line."

But of course.

And with that, these documents from the Frenchman Street Pirate on behalf of the Neuroscience Church High Priest now needed my utmost attention. That is if I were to continue speeding through the dopamine highways in my City of Lakes. I'd been on the pills for over a week straight by then, coming down wasn't going to be without its recovery time. And with what I had going on in the Enclave, I had no time for a recoup chapter. The Pirate and the Guru would seem so outrageous to anyone reading this who doesn't live in this area! So, I felt the money and energy I spent in this direction was simply research for your added enjoyment.

The chemicals in my brain were gushing much too fast for me to install a dam by now. With no more pills that night, I had to start drinking again so not to get the shakes. It would be Gin and grapefruit at the Cane and Table till I hopped the turnstile onto the Pill Express engineered by the High Priest I'd yet to meet. At this point, I couldn't tell how careful or crazy this guy Joshua really was, but he was certainly no dummy.

Back home and liquored up I logged onto the Church of Neuroscience and proceeded to learn more. It was all so out in the open. The language was long, superior, and New Age like. Offering a spiritual connection through its Molecular Sacraments. Breaking bread and having wine has been around for ages. Yet in today's world folks went to church to be good people, and to the drugstores to solve problems. This church seemed to be taking the power from the drugstores, FDA, and others that made such substances out of reach and costly, available at Mass. The church accepted checks, credit cards, and crypto currency. If I got into this church it appeared that Etizolam, Prolintane, 5-MAPB HCI Methylamino-ropy, Benzofuran and an arrangement of atoms creating elements that I knew would have the most dazzling effects on my brain, such as Methoxetamine, would be mine; ALL MINE! After passing The Church of Neuroscience entry exam that night, all I had to do was get my DL notarized the next day before the tabernacle of the Church would be open to me once again. *MES* rejoiced in a suit and top hat behind my watery eyes…

"Hallelujah, Hallelujah, Hallelujah,
Halleluuuu-uuuu-jah."

While I was busy with my research, my Bella Lenin got more distant. But rather than really noticing her drifting from me, I just enjoyed the space to stay high. Although we lived in one big room, we began to only connect in the shower. On these Sacraments I wanted flesh more than ever. Every time she came home from work late at night, I was stoned. And pretended I was asleep. That is before I "woke" and stepped into the steaming shower with her. It was game. While I was high, her lap-dancing didn't disturb me like it had before. My focus was to keep rolling; rollin' like a rolo on the low-low.

GARRET SCENARIO No.2

Long ago I learned of mania's optimistic nature and seemingly boundless powers compounded by certain drugs. Not to mention the incredibly infectious draw it has on certain people close to me while I'm in this state. But I've also learned the price of such energy. It's depressive, self-destructive, and even violent crashes once the hot air escapes the balloon over the Lakes and I collapse. I had to stay high to avoid that low! But a crash was inevitable, it was just a question of time, so, I kept buying more slap-happy pills; come-on! Because by dis-season a-my life I was only one hangover away from suicidal thoughts. One morning as I pondered this on the balcony looking down, alone, with a hot cup of tea in the chill, my co-worker Myra yelled up…

"Mr. Director!
Not set up in the Market today?"
She said with her accent
from the East.

"No Dear.
I'm working the night market these days."

"NIGHT market? Carry a gun.
And tell your lovely wife I say hello!"
She urged with a big smile.

"Uh… OK."

At Wild Forest my composure went a tad super-freak. I'd make myself at home at tables ~ Introduce one table to another to party ~ Set dancers up with shy guys ~ Pick out music to be spun in the DJ booth ~ Even customers began to ask at the door…

"Is Braze working tonight?"

And no. I wasn't sharing pills. Just good vides!

That was my job. It just took some strange sacraments from a church and some experimental sex in the shower at home to make me feel comfortable on Bourbon Street. I'd finally rose to the occasion! When DJ Joey asked what I was on, I didn't want to come clean. And just told him…

"Macca powder."

He was skeptical. But admitted to me later that he bought a quarter pound at Trader Joe's. When he said it wasn't having an effect, *MES* surfaced and asked via me

"Are you snorting it."

He shook his head NO. I shrugged my shoulders. He called out sick the next day. I'd have to make that up to him somehow later.

At this time Chloe Brazil was still dedicated to doing it her way, but with the added expenses of her father, and the girls, she began really chasing money for the first time. She was the outlier in the club that did everything different simply because she thought differently. For her, it wasn't turn and burn like many if not most service industry independent contractors. Her Maybe's had customers coming back by design. Rather than customers just scoring one or two experiences, she developed stronger relationships. And in that process, quite a reputation with regulars and locals. If you were just passing through, she really wasn't as interested in you. Again, it wasn't a master plan, but more a side effect of thoughtfulness. In time the comfort zone she found in the spotlight center stage, evolved in VIP with her regulars. Everything eventually gelled with her in the club, but Fist Fridays. But I thought if women wanted to prostitute across the street, that was their business, with their bodies. Especially if they came overseas to do so. But Lenin had The Girls from Brazil in mind. And, the human trafficking horror they escaped. The more she thought about them, the more she gave deeper thought to the Rising Sun's First Friday events.

She thought the hype was a smokescreen. She didn't buy the "Gallery" of "Global Talent" gimmick. The "Talent" was never seen or heard from after each First Friday; in and out in three days. That concerned her. And I'll admit that the high rollers coming in from around the globe for a lap dance, didn't even make sense to me. Or, probably anyone else who cared to give it any thought. But no one seems to care, everyone visits New Orleans to meet their own needs. She mentioned that she shared her observations with On the Job Bob, and that he listened. But that was it.

Though she did take notice immediately after that talk with Bob, that he very briefly conversed with the Piano Man while dropping a tip in his jar. It gave her the impression that she might not be the only one in the Club who cared to question the First Fridays. But caring and being careful go hand in hand. Without further words, those three apparently exchanged glances that night.

After performing her erotic interpretation of the music, guys boxed each other out for the new crowned Queen on the Scene. Chloe would find one of her regulars, or two, and sit with them for a drink after her performance. When unwanted guys tried to creep in, they were cock blocked by a Dwarf. And sometimes physically with an "accidental" pop lock move. She tipped the hospitality dwarfs the heaviest. They swarmed around her like handlers to theatric royalty. She even paid one to throw rose pedals on the floor in front of her when she came off stage to carve through the crowd. Another to rub sweet almond oil on the side of her thighs when having a drink with a man. And, yet another Dwarf to keep fresh ice in their drinks as the regulars tried to outshine each other and sometimes out bid one another to take her upstairs to the VIP floor. Chloe Brazil no longer did table dances. It was a VIP hour, or you're out. She did Five or Six VIP hours every shift, and two dances on stage per night. If you weren't noticed by her and just wanted to sit down and have a drink with Chloe Brazil, you had to be recommended by one of her now regulars. Or, be referred by a hospitality dwarf. She trusted no one else but the Dwarfs. More than one dancer followed her like scavengers and preyed on her rejects.

She developed a knack for knowing just how much of her body and mind to share within each relationship; only to the point they wanted more. Each time that edge was reached and they pined for more than she was willing to give she'd drop THE MAYBE. Those who bought into it must have known it was always right around the corner. It appeared almost a climax for some! Her crowd were a smart, collectors of experiences. But, it's hard to get smart people to part with their money sometimes. Yet it's dam near impossible to find a dumb one with a disposable income to keep coming back.

When people supported her Maybe's, those who could afford to make sustainable invests into such luxuries at

The Rising Sun? They were in turn were supporting her Girls in Brazil. Though Chloe never brought them up. Lenin never put the suffering of others on a billboard to gain support. It was no one else's business but hers. In her mind, she was just shaking down that Orchestra will-call line.

The brand Chloe Brazil became green money for the Rising Sun. And the man watching behind his signature Gazel 955 tortoise shades was ready to further cash in on her rise to fame. At the end of one night when she was closing out, Gaten approached…

"I'd like
a few minutes from you in
my office before
you go home Miss Brazil."

Moments later, once they were up there were alone, the chronic opportunist made his move.

"Thanks Chloe,
I know it's late.
I'll get right to it.
I want you to share your
ways and means with others
in the club."

"I'm not sure what
you mean."
She said
slightly interested.

"I want more
who are as unpredictable
on stage as you.
And, more women who bring as many
guests up to VIP,
as you do."

She stonewalled him. He continued…

"Will you organize a
group of entertainers for me
to further this exclusive clientele
of yours?"

After a beat, she played her part and cracked a smile.

Before responding,
"I never thought of myself
as exclusive,
but selectively inclusive."

He smiled back,
"Are you interested?"

"Possibly-maybe."

"What can I do to help you
make a decision?"
He asked. And, waited.

She took her time. Before he added…

"I'm not going to push you
into this Chloe.

"Mr. Gaten,
I now know what you want.
But I don't know what offering."

"I'm open to negotiate."
He said with his
palms up.

She opened with,
"It's my way carte-blanche with
the ladies."

"Done."

She appeared obviously unprepared to negotiate further. He led her through the process and got to the bottom line…

"Can I afford this
Miss Brazil?"

But maybe she wasn't as green as she looked to Dutch…

"I think…
one nights gross will
cover it."

"One night's net."
He countered.

She took a moment. Then proposed…

"Ok.
Any night of my choosing."

"Any night…
but a weekend."
He countered.

And without further thought she agreed and put her hand out to shake his…
"Deal,"
She said before
adding as their hands met,
"Fat Tuesday it is."

That made Dutch bulge!

Later the next morning with nothing but sunlight between us she told me about last night's meeting with Gaten. Note: At this time, by day she was bringing home a couple hundred a week from her teaching gig. And, over a grand a night moonlighting at The Rising Sun. When suddenly, she negotiated a deal for over a hundred-grand last night?

"So, let me get this straight.
You teach some girls your game,
and he gives you the Mardi Grass profits?"

She nodded YES with clinched lips. I shrugged her off, and tried not to laugh.

"You'll never see that much
money from him."

"Why not?
I can even track the numbers that night
with help from staff."
She pointed out.

I reiterated,
"Never gonna happen."

"Why?"

"You're from the Bayou,
He's from Brooklyn."

Need I say more I thought? This guy was born to bait and switch!

"What makes you think you know
him so well?"

I just walked away to make us coffee where I had pills crushed. If she really knew me, she would have known what I knew.

"How do I you know more
about this guy
than I do?"

"Lenin,
if took the time to read
the man you love,
you'd know."

She was tongue tied. She never, NEVER read my first book. But sure-as-hell relieved when I finished writing it.

"I'm sorry Braze, but…
since your brother died,
watching you write is enough for me.
It's almost like you're at… "
She took a deep breath before continuing,
"…like you're at war with yourself
back there in that corner.
…Talking to yourself,
telling yourself to shut-up,
get out of your head,
leave you alone?
Who?
What's bothering you
back there in the Enclave when
you're all alone with
yourself?"

As she stood there trying to figure me out. I was pissed that she was listening in for years and never asked what's wrong prior to this! But it comes out wash. Though she already said she probably couldn't read this book either. I was so fed up I just changed the subject…

"How's your Dad?"

That appeared to exhaust her. She took a breath, before…

"He reads, and writes
all the time."

"Who's he reading?"
I asked.

"Rereading lots of Chico Xavier.
And,
writing personalized messages
to each of us.
So,
when they surface when
he's gone, we'll know it's him,
from the other side."

Wow. OK. Later I'd send Dutch over to see this for himself.

"What do his doctors say about
your outsiders approach to
healing him."

"They don't even know his name
without looking at his chart."

"Take him somewhere else."

"I want too."

"Do it."
I encouraged her.

"I want to take him to
South America!"

I meant another hospital, but I didn't say that. I just breathed on it. She took one too, before acknowledging…

"It's just a matter
of time.
I'd love to take him to a place of

his dreams before then."

"Take him.
Let's try and swing it."
"I'd have to take the whole family.
I don't have that much
saved yet."

Siblings, grandparents, wives oh my! That would be a very big budget to raise.

"But if I get that money
on Mardi Gras,
We could take them all
down there!"

And with that, we were back to Gaten.

"What do I need to know
about this guy?
Just give me the cliff notes."

"I think…"
I gave it some thought,
"…there's only one way to get the
money from him."

"How?"

"Corner him.
So, he has to buy his way out."

"How do I do that?"

I pondered that briefly. But had to admit…

"I have no fuckin'
idea."

At Wild Forest DJ Joey was my boy and Rasan was my main man, us three could talk music & movies for days. I hadn't been a part of such "bar talk" since sitting on stools with Stumps duh Clown at The Country Club, St. Roch Tavern, and The Abbey Bar. But Stumps on the other hand isn't much into films, or anything popular for that matter.

The more comfortable I got at Wild Forest, the more pills it took to keep me there. But there was not an unlimited supply. According to church laws, I could only be mailed a certain amount a month. This was a great attempt by Pastor Joshua to avoid abuse and resales. I had to find a work-a-around; quickly. I was running out by this Thanksgiving. A holiday I'd come to skip that year with the Family to work at the Club and keep my high rolling. I couldn't fake the funk around that whole group of intellects in her family that weekend.

After continuing to be way too self-indulgent on the bionic biscuits following the holiday, I nearly found myself out of was getting me by; on a Monday morning! After ordering my last allowance of Sacraments for the month a week ago, this had me in a scramble at the month's end. I couldn't go a day without my meds. Let alone a day, or two! Cause-when I woke, I'd take EASE. After my coffee I popped some GLIDE. Soon after that to get moving on some writing I'd snort some FOCUS. I'd balance out with more EASE after my pages. At the club I CANDY FLIPPED. If I were in The Art Market, I'd juggle BRIGHT and FLOAT till I jumped in one of those hot showers with Bella. By then on that my cock was a bat.

Pastor Joshua named each Molecular Sacrament according to their powerful effects on the brain and nervous system. It appeared to me that he was a thoughtful guy. Though I understand that would be hard for some to fathom. That is, he being a drug-dealing spiritual leader. But if the church was just a cover and he was only out to make a buck… then why did I have to sign the "Rights of Benefice" contract in regards to "Parishioner's Pill Allowances" agreeing to the quantity cap on pills per month?

Later I set up my Bookstand in a fog that morning. It was the end of the month and after missing three weeks of work out there I had to show up a couple more time by December to hold my tenure, and my load weighed in! Like anybody else would be without their regular prescriptions, I must have looked haggard without the proper Moleculars in me. Even as much as I abused of them lately, I thought I was pseudo-sober if I didn't get drunk, do dope, or coke. On Sacraments, I was after all, in full compliance of the law. But without the proper dose, my energy wasn't sustainable that morning. And my drastic crash must have been painfully obvious by noon…

"Mr. Director!"
Myra called out to me from across the aisle,
"You are not getting enough rest
at home?"

"I suppose not."

"Do you still do night
market too much?"
she asked.

"Just until Mardi Gras."
I answered.

"Then you take long vacation."
She said with her
beautiful smile.

I nodded YES and agreed with her, it sounded good to me.

Perhaps we would take the whole family to Brazil. But in the meantime, unbeknownst to anyone, I was falling behind in the bills. Things got paid, but late. Lenin threw in every month, and I was supposed to cover the rest. But… I jus-don't know where the money went. I got lost in my head drilling tunnels in my brain to smuggle more dopamine. By this time in my binge I felt electrical currents from everything. Electricity radiate from my body to that of other bodies, and not just human bodies. But trees, pigeons and even personal solar connections were apparent with stars at night. Desperate like cybersex addict who lost his wi-fi at the office, I went searching for the Pirate on the street to re-up.

Just around the corner by old Café Brazil I found him arguing with himself, again. When I got closer, he appeared off balanced and was stumbling around drunker than usual. I kept some distance this time…

"Yo! Um… "

"Va-the fair foo-trah!"
He screamed at me.

"I hear you man.
But I need you to talk to
Pastor Joshua."

"Brool-ohn-lawnfer!"
He screamed louder.

"I need to see him,
in person.

"Ohn cool-ay!"
He said kicking, swinging
and screaming at me.

But I couldn't give up, just back up! I knew he was more bark than bite and in a fight with himself just ready to bring me in it. So, I regrouped, let him stop swinging, and watched him fall to the ground still barking at me. Standing over top of him, I proposed…

"If you get me in touch with the High Priest
I'll get you the best lap dance
on Bourbon Street."

He immediately stopped barking like a French Bulldog, and began waging his tale down there! And-dare was never such a smile captured on a meth billboard I thought, as, I asked him…

"Can you do me this solid?"

"Fuck yeah!
I'm security for Joshua!
I live in his garage! I'm the yard dog man!"
He said with
that toxic smile a-his.

"Bow-wow-wow yippie-yo yippie-yay."
MES rapped in response.

"Merci beaucoup."
I responded.

I got a phone number from the Pirate and made the call. But the Priest didn't answer. So, I left blah, blah, blah as cordial and composed as any other business message I'd ever left.

And as soon as I got back to my Bookstand, my call was returned!

"Hello Joshua?
…Yes. …Thank you.
It's about a recent order.
It was denied."

He went into why.

"But Pastor Joshua,
it would be such an inconvenience to wait
till next month."

It was only in a couple days he reminded me. He asked why I did all my Sacraments?

"I didn't do them
all myself.
I shared some with friends
over Thanksgiving."

And then I listened, and listened…

"So… I see,
What you're saying is you want,
THEM, to join the church.
I understand Pastor Joshua.
My friends could surely do so.
But we would be grateful if you
granted us my order today.
That is, while they
test and go through the process
of becoming official
parishioners."

He enquired about these friends of mine.

"They're co-workers
at Wild Forest.
Have you been to my Gentlemen's
Club before?"

He liked the sound of that!

"Sure.
I can certainly introduce you around.
That's my job.

I'll put you on the VIP list.
All access.
No cover of course."

He was quite grateful.

"It's my pleasure.
I'm happy to.
Can you meet me at Café Envie
in 20 minutes?
…You're there now?
On my way."

I put the BE BACK SOON sign under the train spike and raced a half block over while I still had him on the line. When I found him at a table on the sidewalk with his dog laying under his chair, he didn't look like the mind I envisioned who birthed the website and soapy literature I'd been reading, but perhaps he was just into Guns & Roses, or Korn.

"Joshua?"

"Yes-indeed kind sir,
you must be Braze."

I noticed the headline he was reading on his iPad…

Man suffered from depression and anxiety
before jumping from Crescent City Connection.

…about my brothers' suicide in the local news years ago. That slowed my roll. I was stunned. He was doing a background check. He noticed I noticed. His dog got up to comfort me. I pet the dog, got lost in visions of the sky raining bodies, the sounds of skin and bones on concrete after impact, after impact, after impact in my City of Lakes before Joshua distracted me from such delusions…

"That's my buddy, his
names Buster."

I pet the mutt, then took a seat at the table for two.

"I am so sorry for your
loss Braze.
Do you believe in God?

Or, a Grand Architect?"

I had to compose myself for the first time that day. I smiled at him. And his dog looking at me. Pastor Joshua looked empathetic, but not disturbed.

"I believe in paths, and
trajectories."

"Is your path created by God?"

"I think the independent powers
of the human body are
more at work in our lives on Earth
than any invisible strings being
pulled from above."

At this point I wasn't going to tell this guy what I thought he wanted to hear just to get the pills after bringing my brother into this.

"We are in a perfect place in this
solar system where life is able to exist.
It must be no accident, and his plan."
He said. Then continued trying to
find common ground,
"Our path,
as you just said."

I gave him a moment with his own smile. Before I answered without an ounce of emotion…

"I think we
humanize God too much.
And in doing so,
some up creation and eternity with
extraordinary stories."
I paused, then added,
"Extraordinary claims,
call for extraordinary
proof."

He sat up straight sipped his tea, then continued…

"Would you say this world is that of an
architect's creation?"

He dropped God in an attempt to connect. But we were after all talking about two sides of the same coin here. So, I brought God back in the fold.

"Beliefs shape perceptions.
What I think, is
different chemicals in my brain
can not only change the quality of perceptions,
but lead to impressions of GOD in
my experiences."

"Yes, yes indeed!
There is a path to God
in our Brains."

OK, whatever. I didn't care to take it any further. I exited this conversation with an…

"Amen."

"It's a pleasure to meet you Braze.
It's an honor to have you in
our church Kind Sir."

"The pleasures mine."

We shook hands.

"…kind sir."
He added, holding on to my hand.

"Pardon?"

"We refer to everyone as,
Kind Sir."

And then he let my hand go. I smiled and wondered how woman felt about this? But I assumed Kind Madam was the answer.

"Understood, Kind Sir.
Can we talk Sacraments now?"

"Sure."

At which point Joshua grabbed a black currier bag at his feet and plopped it on the table. I could hear all the pills jingle inside like Santa's special bag for Junkies at Christmas. Truth be known, it made me fart. Just thinking about all those pills rolling down the serotonin super highways in my head like colorful supersonic driverless tires got me gassed up! I had to clench my checks so my ass didn't start singing the Stars Spangled Banner. Pastor Joshua didn't seem to notice, he pulled handfuls of packaged pills out in broad daylight and tossing them on the table at me saying…

"The monthly limits
to how much Sacraments a parishioner
can acquire are there
to benefit them.
But occasionally exceptions
are made."

"Thank you for understating, Kind Sir.
My friends will be very,
very grateful."

And then, the High Priest proceeded to expose his lower self as many priests have done for ages…

"I have the MXE.
I just need someone to have sex
with for days."

That sudden openness made me feel a little uncomfortable. I mean, he was wearing a kilt. I shyly responded…

"Kind Sir…
I'm, married, I… "

"No. No.
You mentioned that your
place of employment,
is a strip club?"

"Oh Yeah!
Fuckin-right."

Pastor Joshua shrugged his shoulders, like, well?

"Well yeah,
you know how it is.
It's not a bathhouse,
or wishy wash.

But it's the next
best thing!"
"I'm a tit Man."
Joshua confided while handing
over the pills.

"Oh?
Well, me too."
I confessed.

After all he's my pastor now. Then I added…

"I'll put you on the permanent
Guest List Kind Sir."

When he gave me the pills gratis, I felt reborn.

Rising Sun's Chloe Brazil kept getting more desirable and sought after. It was in certain peoples vulnerabilities, neediness, and somewhat hurting for affection that she found the opportunity to be of a higher service than just a stripper, but that of an "Erotic Reiki Therapist" as she put it. She'd use her thighs and fingertips to awaken the Life Force that slowed in those burning to be touched. She opened chakra pathways to revitalize extremely vital functions of the organs and cells of the body, and in doing so, healed the affected parts of her customer's energy fields that where suffering. She charged them with positive energy while they meditated in the world on her perfect nipples and full breasts. It wasn't a magic, but more along the lines most have yet to grasp.

Overall, it wasn't just about getting a customer upstairs in VIP, but about how enthusiastic they were to go with her. For her to give people VIP status, they would have to be excited for her like a puppy. She nearly demonstrated how she wanted them to follow her on stage once. One special night she invited dwarfs up to interpret *I Wanna Be Your Dog* with her; and they did so superbly. DJ Crowley spun a remix of Iggy Pop's classic while the stage was crawling with topless dwarfs on all fours elevating Chloe Brazil to the weirdest sexual beast in the Rising Sun.

As for me, my days quickly began starting at noon. I didn't seem to dream as much these days after blacking out. I sweat like crazy in bed until my skin got itchy and my bones got soar. Hiding under the covers from all the natural light in the Loft became the norm. The moment I got up. I'd have to crush pills. But by that time, the coast was clear; she'd be at her day job. So I could stumble out bed whenever and blast some *Stone Roses* before I crushed, mixed, and snorted my pills openly. I found that the mix of GLIDE & FLOAT was better than any K-HOLE I'd experienced in the past. That became my new twist! My get up and go that took off the edge first thing. Just weeks ago, I was crawling in my skin for months with relationship anxieties. Now, I could almost careless, as long as I was high. My highs disguised that lack of thoughtfulness, as progress. It was all about finishing this story now no matter where it led or what it did to me; as usual.

I'd felt all this before on C,K & MDMA in the Rave days. Now the MXE and these other Sacramental ABC's hit that same parts of the brain. They simply brought heaven to my head! Getting in touch with the Divineness with the pop of a Pill is nothing like the Path of a Prayer. The results of a prayer and the power of those intentions within them can often keep you waiting. Pop a Pill that contains this Molecular Sacrament MXE… and your prayers race through the dopamine highways in your head and get to GOD with euphoric speed! It's FEDEX for better feelings. MXE pumped more optimism in my head than ever before. And we're not talking cocaine here, this stuff was more user friendly. Though, I still got disconnected sometimes; I'm not gonna-lie to me.

Getting "disconnected" is when your brain seems to disassociate with your body. It's not a dope "nod", that would be closer to a "K-hole". Getting disconnected can lead to more bizarre behavior than just appearing passed out or frozen. While disconnected, one can find themselves as the dissociate wears off… with strangers, suddenly south of the border, or worse on the edge of a bridge. Predators use disassociates to rape, kidnap, and even steal bodily organs to be sold on the black market. But to the creative mind such as mine, they're just candy. While in my head and roaming the streets on these substances I've dreamed up many ideas before I woke up and produce them. The EASE pills grounded me from such disconnections and got me back to Earth when I needed to be. Without the EASE, shit… I'd have probably stayed in my head till the grass grew over me. I love it in there on that shit! But most of what I experienced during these episodes would ultimately find their way to the floor and not glued to this spin. There are always hundreds of pages worth of failed experiments while disconnected and masturbating my mind and body.

In the French Market I had to be more transparent than ever. I was ON again OFF again all the time. My burst of energy in between bumps and drips MUST have looked erratic. My stand always seemed disorganized ~ I'd never stop rearranging it ~ This here ~ No there ~ Put the books here ~ No-no there ~ I probably looked as frazzled as my hair. Some customers found my manic energy irresistible, while other began to buy just to shut me up…

"Ok, Ok!"
"One movie,
one book already."

I was wholeheartedly recommitted to a habit once again and my impulsive nature made me an untamed wildfire. The moments that blood rushed to my head at times weeks ago, I now lived in almost fulltime daily. My appetite for these pills, hell, it got completely insatiable! An-dey jus-kept workin! …Can't explain it.

At Wild Forest that weekend as those highways in my head ran dopamine and serotonin, I glided around the club like Jamiroquai. While Joey Beignet spun beats that lifted *MES* & *BRIGHTDAWN*'s game to a rooftop party by a *SuRoC* burner at the magic hour, my pastor Joshua unexpectedly made his grand entrance early that Saturday Night.

His royal highness rolled in solo wearing a faux fur coat, punk kilt, and shiny combat boots like a trailblazer ready for chemical warfare. Everyone without a cheap beer in their hand knew someone cosmic walked in. Pastor Joshua exuded such magnetism that night he must have bottled Molecular Sacraments and wore it as aftershave. I was sure his fur coat was filled with pills. As I quickly dropped my notebook off in the DJ booth Joey asked…

"Who's the guy from
Scotland?"
"My Priest.
Get ready to be
blessed."

I glided over and greeted Joshua with my hand out…

"Good evening Kind Sir."

"The pleasure is mine
Parishioner Braze.
Your very kind for leaving
my name at the door."

I immediately escorted him to the VIP elevator, and gestured two girls to jump in and ride up with us. When the elevator doors closed, Joshua wasted no time. Before I even introduced him to the girls, he began some sort of affirmation ritual with his eyes closed…

"I'm grateful that we
Earthlings are children of God's sprit.
Grateful for the abundant blessings
I've received in life. And grateful for the abundance
of blessings that are on their way."
Then he opened his eye,
"I am here to promote Beneficence and expand civil
liberties and religious
freedom to all."

I gestured to the girls not laugh. He smiled at us.

"Parishioner Braze,
thank you again for your hospitality.
Ladies,
I'm Pastor Joshua."

They looked at me to see if he was for real. I nodded YES, and mentioned…

"Ladies, it gets better.
Much better."

The doors opened and Joshua walked out with a girl under each arm like it was a homecoming party. He didn't need ME anymore. Once he dropped his molecular science on those two hotties… other than Rache and Rasan who kept things in order, the rest of the staff would join his church with the enthusiasm of young Al Pacino's in Needle Park. And *MES*, he could hardly wait to see these girls dance on MXE that night! While *BRIGHTDAWN* wrote the mental notes with the discipline of a monk, he prophesized…

"God's plan is for me to become the
Basquiat of Books."

He does write messy.

My head swam through oil pastels on boxcar steel, 16mm filters on SD video, and ultra-flat black Courier font through off-white pages during my shift that night. I couldn't get any higher, nor could I ever come down; EVER. I lived floating in space. But as soon as Joshua sat on the sofa and squeezed in between the girls, he nearly grounded that high! By openly rooting through his stash of sacraments in his messenger bag that he must have brought in under his coat. I darted over immediately, and gently, helped him up to his feet as *Ful Stop* by RADIOHEAD was opening in the background…

"Excuse us ladies.
I need to speak to Pastor
Joshua outside on the balcony."

Just above the madness on Bourbon I clued him in…

"Dude… Kind Dude.
What are you doing?"

"Parishioner Braze,
I'm here on Earth to spread goodwill
and share with everyone
who wants to partake in the sacraments of… "

I know. I, KNOW!
But here in the club?
We got surveillance called
Eyes in the Sky.
Higher powers watch."

"Everything I do, I do in the open.
God as my witness."

"Kind bro, listen man…
if they video you passing out pills,
you could get thrown out, or worse.
And, AND…
the girls will lose their jobs.
Do you want that to happen?"

"Of course not.
But I'm not breaking any laws Parishioner Braze.
The molecular substances may not be
approved by the FDA,
but nor are they… "

"Pastor Joshua, chill.
Save that shit to present
an argument elsewhere.
In here,
they are considered illicit."

He looked almost insulted, but I didn't care asking…

"Do you want to hang out
in this club?"

He looked inside, and then back at me with the loneliest eyes I'd seen since, I'd rather not say. I knew that fucking look.

"Yes, kind sir."
He responded graciously,
"I'd like to have a positive presence
in this establishment."

"Then,
you need to take my directions.
OK?"

"Yes, Parishioner Braze.
I trust you."

"First off,
you need to be more covert."

"Sneaky?"

"No. Well… yeah.
I can show you.
I'm very good at it."

"I refuse to be sneaky Kind Sir.
I believe that the beauty of what I do
should be out in the open."

As smart as he was, he seemed naive on multiple levels. Or perhaps just arrogant. I'm not sure. But when I breathed on it, I realized the stubborn asshole was just playing dumb.

Then he suggested,
"Perhaps we could
find a private place, like,
a fantasy room?
Where I could share the sacraments in
an orderly fashion."

"Kind buddy,
Don't try and play me."
I said frustrated.

"Parishionerrrrr Braze."
He said aghast looking at me from
the corner of his eyes.

Grabbing at my chin with my mouth wide as a Mickey's, I chuckled once. If this smart guy wanted to get smart, it was time to bring up brought up church policies.

"When you
meet people in here and you
introduce them to your thing,
just get their emails.
Because technically,
they have to take the test before they
can purchase any
sacraments."

"Yes, purchase them.
But tonight, I'm here
to, share them,
parishioner Braze."

"That's, very generous of you.
And, a problem for me!"
I said even more frustrated with
my High Priest.

GARRET SCENARIO No.2

I had to solve this problem before it became a problem. And did so by taking things into my experienced hands Only to duck trouble.

"Ok.
Here we go…
Tonight, give me the pills
you want to share.
And when you connect with anyone
who wants to enjoy them?
I'll pass them on discretely,
upon your signal."

"What's the signal?"
He asked.

"Wiggle
your tongue in your cheek,
towards them.
Like this Y'know?"

I demonstrated ~ He practiced ~there we stood above Bourbon, tongues in cheeks before dropping bombs on it.

"Oh-this is lovely."
He said with a smile, then continued,
"But how will you know what
Sacrament to give them?"

"They're all in here?"

I held up the bag. He nodded YES.

"If we're going to introduce newbies
to such a blessing, which one would they
be most enlighten by?"

We both answered at the same time…

"MXE"

I gave him his bag back ~ He removed a dozen sheets of the proper pills ~ I popped them all out of their packaging so I could pass them on easier.

I never thought this day would come-round again. But there I was sure as Spin Sugar in Jazz Saucony's a Pill Pimp once again.

"Give me a couple FOCUS Kind sir
so-I can stay focused."

I'd still swim, but take care of business too.

Within an hour, Pastor Joshua made so many tongue wiggles that newbies started their own tongue in cheek maneuvers turning others on. He must have shared the goddamn signal! It was a tongue in cheek convention up in the piece. No one got left behind. All the girls got it, every bartender, most customers. I was so busy keeping eyes on Joshua that I forgot to clue in my DJ. When I finally made it to the DJ booth to chill for a minute, he quickly mentioned how oddly alive things got…

"Whas-goin-on around here?
Everybody's in cuddle puddles
all-a-sudden.

*M*ES & BRIGHTDAWN as my witnesses behind the organic glass, Joey was right. And he got hyped when he noticed my own soft gaze over the scene…

"Now I know sumpin's up!"

"Damn, psh…
My bad Joey B.
I forgot you."
I said as I tried to wipe the shade
of shit off my face.

"Forgot me?
Who's the skirt you led
upstairs.

"I told you,
he's my Pastor."

"Mother-fuka's really priest?"

"Pastor of a pill cult."

"BAPTISE ME BINCH!"
He screamed like a devil.

"You want the red pill,

or the blue pill."

He laughed that off with the quickness…

"Shtoop-shucka.
Both."

And so was the birth of the first and only club on Bourbon Street to be turned into a Molecular Sacrament playground. Wild Forest would never be the same after these profound pills. That night, we all danced with our mouths open to the sky on these gushing geysers of galactic glycerol new to human consumption. Nothing magnifies love, like group love.

In a week or so every talking monkey in the Wild Forest elevated themselves to new heights on Joshua's Molecular Sacraments and became Parishioners in the Church of Neuroscience. It was one big pill-party with naked women running around and occasionally men who couldn't keep on their pants. And because of that, I had to unofficially insist to all the lap dance trackers and VIP hospitality that they only take the RED PILLS. They contained Prolintane which elevates one's sense of drive and creates a heighten sense of awareness similar to Adderall, thus branding them FOCUS. Prolintane HCI is a central nervous system stimulant and was among a favorite of Parishioners who partook in the Sacrament. FOCUS enhanced the composure of the Wild Forest staff who protected our boundaries in the club and most importantly the protection of the Entertainers. Rasan of course did not to partake in Joshua's Sacraments, but he knew the deal.

Outside, he and I were standing in the front door on Bourbon during one of his breaks when he elaborated…

"I prefer to smoke my drugs.
It's the process of breathing that really
gets me high."

Then he demonstrated the power and beauty of his breath with hints of his heart and soul through the horn in his hands. Like my old friend Stumps at one time, Rasan, was just as inseparable from his instrument.

While at my wife's club, she was more naturally focused more than ever where she was covertly casting a cast of rookies that would become her squad. You might think she would approach the most attractive entertainers in the Club, or the ones with obviously more talent than others. Rising Sun was home to some of the most gorgeous women on the block. Everyone who was anyone in the know knew that. The Rising Sun "First Fridays" were nothing short of internationally known underground, some locals called it the "Make a Wish to Strip Night." Others considered it a "Charity Ass Auction". Regardless of the label, one could only get away these days with such operations in New Orleans. First Fridays were as out in the open as Joshua's Church of Neuroscience. New Orleans is just off the map enough to get over in such grey areas. You'll never find a Russian roulette gambling hall in The Quarter, but the French Quarter is still (in part) what Old Dirty New York City used to be.

What was also in the open as a Lucky Dog cart was the Grand Hotel right across the street from the Rising Sun. Where as I've said before, the greater majority of strippers prostituted after hours. They used the club to showcase their bodies on stage and then would make arrangements with customers in VIP to meet them across the street at the hotel later. Many of these women who were selling sex could not wrap their heads around selling less. They were just too far down the road of no return. The prostitutes had regulars who would come in from all over to enjoy the nightlife in The Sun with them and spend big money in the club on drinks and lap dances for their Cohorts and CEO circle of jerks. Before these entertainers rendezvoused across the street with big shots after hours where they could make another grand before dawn. Before closing time, the entertainers ran up large bar tabs with their disposable income clientele to satisfy the interests of the Rising Sun. When it was time for doormen to walk the strippers to their cars at the end of the night, it was understood and accepted that many entertainers chose to sleep across the street after a long night in the club because Gaten insisted, conveniently, that…

"No entertainer drive
home drunk."

Or take UBER evidently. Doormen were tipped heavily to simply walk them a few yards across the street to the Hotel, and sleep it off. The club was happy that no sex was being sold on their side of the street, the Hotel's there to fill expensive rooms, and what prostitute wouldn't be happy to be off the track. With that much money and traffic between that Hotel and this Club, it was even more so survival of the fittest in the Rising Sun than others clubs on Bourbon. Yet the veterans weren't too disturbed by the attention Chloe attracted in the club. Because she wasn't intruding on their territory across the street. The vets actually appeared entertained by her at times, as if she was just a rookie on the court with new moves. But not a player who could take their contracts away. In their minds, they were the superstars. But it appeared Gaten certainly wanted more Chloe Brazil(s) in the house.

He must have known if his club was recognized more as a place to connect with sex rather than to get the Best Lap Dance, that he would be perceived as a pimp. And it wasn't long ago that he was brought down in New York City for activities around his club outside of his control. Let me finally tell you more about this man Gaten.

Gaten, born Piter Gaten-Thieves, grew up in Brooklyn in the 1970's. Long before he was born, his family was marked by the mafia in his neighborhood. As soon as his roots somehow came through Ellis Island from Russia, they began doing all they could to steal the American Dream. Though a good thief in certain circles is respected and protected by his own, Gaten's roots had no ethics what so ever. And soon, the Mafia enforced its power and banished this Russian family from all solid underworld connections. They had the whole family branded in the 1930's by having city officials change their last name from Gaten, to Gaten-Thieves. We're talking mail, birth certificates, finger pointing, everything surfaced Thieves. Piter Gaten-Thieves was a Russian kid with the gift to lift, or, *born to steal* as he would come better known to be.

As a youth Gaten stole bicycles from one side of the neighborhood and sold them on the other. Then it was cars, even motorcycles. Till one day, he stole the wrong bike! When the Harley of a Hells Angel was lifted, Gaten had the wrath of those outlaws on his thieving ass. When they caught up with him, he never looked the same again. They completely caved in the left side of his head leaving him blind in that eye. And since then he's worn tortoise color 955 Gazel sunglasses, and or, an Eyepatch to mask the permanent damage done by The Angles. But with thieving in his DNA, the art of the steal was nothing he could ever walk away from. But he did elevate himself from the act of doing so.

He recruited a group of young, hungry and ruthless robbers who would later become BTS; Born to Steal. These kids where monsters. They robbed homes to banks, pawnshops to Jewelry stores, drug dealers to Bar Owners and, were on the forefront of identity theft. He had teams of kids go around and just steal trash to gather personal information. But evidently, what he was best at, was saving money.

By the early 1990's when his ego was running on all cylinders, he diversified his interests and began having KB delivered to the homes of Manhattan residents like pizza. The he went public and opened a couple ego projects in the city that would rival the legend of Studio 57. Once he was in the club scene, he'd found his true passion… Underground Celebrity!

For a man who was cursed and practically tattooed a thief at birth, being admired by every little club kid and hustling-douchebag in New York was vindication that he had been coming to where he got as King of New York since the get-go. Even, if it were only for a brief stage in his life. City politicians would eventually sink him. With money flowing in from the birth of the internet, the ruthlessness of Wall Street, and people investing that money into real-estate, there seem to be no tolerance for good old fashion hippies reborn as ravers in New York. And soon, Gaten's world collapsed. His liquor licenses where revoked, and he ended up doing Time for his ties to that Underworld of his.

Over 20 years later he surfaced in New Orleans inside another ego project called the Rising Sun. With his history, it's no mystery to me that he'd be hiding down here on Bourbon Street just to have a taste of the old action. Being a felon by now I could only assume that his presence in the club was that of a silent partner. But then again this is New Orleans, who knows. I'd seen him down here in the company of Russian businessmen who probably made their bones in the home mortgage game before the Great Recession. Those in "The Know" might call my knowledge of Piter Gaten-Thieves heresy, but, you can bank on it.

With all this in my mind you might see why I didn't think Lenin had a glacier's chance on Earth of getting over on Gaten. If he actually did give her the Fat Tuesday chicken, it would only be done so to make himself look good. He'd definitely have a plan to quickly steal it back. His BTS boys did this to my little brother once upon a time. They were bait and switch pros! The only thing that could stop this guy in his tracks would be cuffing him with another federal indictment; period.

Back to Chloe's Squad and where she casted her prospect talent. She approached them in the same shadows of the club she emerged from. She wasn't interested in trying to flip prostitutes game, but rather, farmed-fresh for strippers. She went to the wait staff. She knew from conversations with the cocktail waitress that many of them wanted to strip but where just a little too nervous or insecure to take the leap. She understood this all too well. My wife believed if such an experience as this could empower her. Then the waitresses who were secretly enthusiastic to take the leap into the strip life could gain too.

After work at the Clover Grill, Bella spoke to six-woman, prospect stripper, who were then still cocktail waitresses. Five of these women were trying very hard to be noticed with scintillating punk hair colors. While the brown young woman with gorgeous long hair the same color seemed to be most comfortable in her flawless appearance. It was there in that diner that these lovely women gathered in the middle of the night with my wife… Daughter of Hippies, Grandchild of Nudists, and by now certified Pipe Dream in New Orleans to hear what she had to say. These women would be the minds to further launch the power of that one tiny word. At the end of breakfast, they fist bumped and appeared to solidify things.

Dutch hovered outside by the Diner Sign when they emerged from the Clover Grill. And as they turned and walked down Bourbon in slow motion, a busker across the street banged a tambourine, another plucked an upright bass, and a 3rd kicked a suitcase drum as she sung *Little Green Bag* by George Baker in real time. But I didn't make even the connection yet because I was so faded.

The next morning as I was trying to pull myself back together, Lenin was more excited than I'd seen her in forever. I was lamping; out of it on the sofa with a cup of tea groggy on the wrong-shit. When she went on to say…

"They understood
the concept of selling the maybe
immediately."

That woke me up.

"Selling, the maybe?"
I asked looking up at her.

Lenin stood over me with the lunette window behind her, looking as if it were in fact a halo. My morning fog over the City of Lakes vanished. My tongue was tied. I'd never heard those three words together before. I just murmured shaking my head in response to her "selling the maybe" comment, as being…

"Wicked."

"Indeed Mr. Graffiti."

While I'd been jerking off getting stoned, she single-handedly formulated the E=MC2 of the known nightlife. While I ruminated in her genius she did a little jig.

Then I asked…
"Do your girls have stage
names yet?"

"They do!
They chose to name
themselves after
the colors of their hair."

"Waaaait.
Ya-got six girls,
right?"

She nodded YES.

"That
just so happen to have,
six different shades
a hair."

"Yup."
She said with a big-ol grin.

I laughed, once.

"Okay. Don't.
Don't tell me… "

I put both my index fingers to the sides of my head like a gypsy looking into the future, recalling, George Baker buskers the night before…

"It's coming to me…"
I said before pulling these names
from not so thin air,
"Miss Pink, Miss Blonde, Miss Blue,
Miss Brown, Miss Orange and…
Miss White."

"You-been followin' me?"
She asked.
Then she yelled at me,
"Your spying on
ME!"

Rather than ever think of informing her or any sane person of Dutch outside a paperback, I simply acknowledged the blinding coincidence quickly…

"You never seen Reservoir Dogs?"
I asked dumfounded.

She looked at me puzzled before she answered, slowly…

"Well,
I've heard of it."

"Whoa."
I said sternly. BREATHED.
Then continued…

"This is solid grounds for
the annulment.
I gotta-find Stumps."

She smirked.

"Let's do-dis."
Urged *MES*.

I stormed out like an opportunist to get higher on the spot! Damn if I'm stuck in the middle on the wrong-shit with a Tarantino-less YouTube millennial.

A little later that afternoon I walked back in sure as Spin Sugar and noticed her at her desk on a laptop. I went over to give her a kiss on the cheek to see what she was up to; buying digital hand counters or something. I didn't think much of it. Other than she watched Reservoir Dogs when I was out, and decided to have her new Tit Tribe keep track of Pink dicks who don't tip.

After Lenin went to work that night, Joshua came over to the Loft for the first time with his usual currier bag of drugs over his shoulder. With tea in hands and Valgeir Sigurdsson in the air, I gave him the tour from the Garret to the Loft and clued him in on the art collection. Intrigued, we sat by the fireplace to finish our conversation when he shared his admirations…

"It's a very a tasteful space,
everything seems to have its special place.
I can't imagine what it costs
to live here."

"I don't like thinking
about my bills."

"I get the impression it's
the home of genius."
He added.

"My wife's the educated one."
I responded.

"And beautiful.
That painting of you and her
is stunning."

Above the fireplace hung the painting where she and I were body painted per our wedding gift.

"What does she do?"
He asked.

"She's a Grade School teacher."
I said,
before confessing,
"And works at Rising Sun."

But I don't think that registered with him. He just stared at the painting, mouth open, for moments on end. I guess he couldn't stop. In the realms of science and spirituality he was well versed. But with women it seemed he was just like me, not so keen.

"I notice you stay
very profession around women.
Why is that?"
I asked.

He was closed lipped about it. I suggested…

"Loosen up."

"I don't like to cross lines
in casual conversation."

Then I shut up, before he furthered…

"But,
you're right I suppose."

I waited for him to continue.

"I am, overly self-conscious
around potential female
companions."

That was the weirdness I was referring to. But just smiled.

"Why is that?"
I asked.

He opened up,

"I often get the impression
I'm the most interesting guy in the room.
But I always feel the
least attractive."

I really didn't know where to start with that one, because I saw his point. I wanted to tell him to trade in his hippy hat for a Goorin Bros. Shave the Magnum P.I. stash and perhaps lose the kilt he always wore, but I didn't, I let him continue…

"I just can't seem to sustain
a relationship with a
lady friend."

"You're not alone man."
I reassured him thinking of the scene
at the club.

"Usually, we just have sex.
And then, it's over."

He sipped his tea.

I pointed out,
"You have to get to know each
other man."

"We'll, we do."

As if the sex was getting to know each other? Then, once again he said, and I believed he meant what he said…

"I have the MXE.
I just love having sex
for days."

And with that, there was no music in his heart.

When he couldn't stop glancing at the body painting over the fireplace. I suggested we go out to the balcony and enjoy some music from the corner. Outside, he hung his K&B Organics courier bag over the back of a barstool and took a seat with me as he shared shocking accounts of sexual relationships gone wrong, and even suing another strip club for throwing him out once. He was just a lonely guy showing more of his cards that night.

We went on to talk about the grand architects of creation, evidence that is in conflict to Darwinism, and where his Molecular Sacraments originated; China.

He set up church offices in Germany and England where he had mailing services receive packages from China, then address and ship out to the United States, only to cover the trail and receive the drugs here, from those countries less suspect elsewhere. Joshua really believed in his brand, and, that his drugs were good for people. He was an educated person with a degree in LAW and had very keen knowledge of the pharmaceutical industry and those substances unregulated; not illegal. He even said at one time that he filed a law suit against the DEA for confiscating his Sacraments that were technically not illegal, but simply unregulated.

"Did you get the drugs back?"
I asked.

"No.
But that wasn't
the point."

The point was, no matter how grey and renegade his church business appeared to be, he did not conduct his business in the shadows, but openly; everywhere. To the point where it was embarrassing, at least for me. I refused to meet him in public because he spoke way too loud about everything, including drugs. And, whenever you received the Molecular Sacraments from him in public, he was never discrete about it. He'd toss the little silver and gold star sparkly magic bags on the table next to my cup at any given coffee shop in town. And I was a guy selling a book about how the rails became his rehab! I just told myself that I had to get this story. And then I'd get back on track.

Thus, I had him over to the Loft that night and planned to never meet him elsewhere again. That is, other than where he became a card caring VIP member at Wild Forest. But there, I was surly not to run into any of my readers in any sort of proactive recovery while I was undercover in this story. Outside on the balcony I listened to him and threw an occasional log on the fire of his chosen topics of conversation for hours. By the end of our long talk, I also learned that he was a suicide survivor who believed he was going to die I violent death one day. By the time he left that night, I got the impression he was in a constant state of contemplating why he was here. And, if he should stick around.

In my clouded head, I was simply immersed in the persona on this Paperback to acquire the Scenarios. Consequently, precious time once spent living good and being thoughtful would be further eclipsed by ongoing chemical research in the Enclave with "The Boys" behind the aviator shades. Soon after Chloe Brazil organized an accidental Reservoir of Bin…

"Let's not got there."
I said to interrupted *BRIGHTWAWN*.
And simply suggested,
"Her selling the maybe's
further bit me us
the ass?"

Whiles these tempest of nonstop voices and boundless emotions in my City of Lakes kept me from noticing much more than myself, someone rather close had been a victim all the while.

A WINTER BLOW

Lenin was meeting her Maybe Ladies for sessions with Vinnie & Saint when her Dad unexpectedly took an Uber to the Loft. It must have taken us 20 minutes to inch his way up the stairs with his walker and oxygen tank. No sooner did I sit him at the kitchen table did he gasp for…

"Water!"

"Sure-thing Harry."

In between small sips he wheezed endlessly. He seemed to be searching for air in his lungs even with his little tank. I can't imagine how it felt. Then he said in a weak voice…

"My world is ending."

And sadly, it was painfully obvious. I felt guilty breathing so easily watching him suffer like this. I could only ask…

"How can I help?"

Exhausted,
he continued in a horsed voice,
"You're going to find out
something about me
Braze."

I nodded OK. And encouraged him to continue. The fact was that there was always a life changing realization occurring in him. "Something big" he'd usually say. But not this time. This time it was…

"Something bad."
He said, then continued to say…
"I've, been molesting
Kireka."

My heart pounded in my ears. The City of Lakes began to quake. *MES* & BRIGHTDAWN came to the windows. Harry continued…

"There's uh. Ah-haaa…"
He wheezed,
"A warrant for my arrest.
I'm turning myself in
today."

"Does Lenin know?"
I asked.

"I don't, think so. It
just happened."

"Just happened?"
Asked *BRIGHTDAWN*.

"Sounds more like,
he just got caught."
Answered *MES*.

"How long you been doing this
to Kireka?"
I asked Harry.

"Years."
He admitted.

All I could hear in my head was her skateboarding, practicing tricks, and laughing with her brothers as Harry continued…

"She broke down in school today.
And told a teacher."

MES recanted,
"I noticed he couldn't hide the reaction of
his eyebrows around her when she passed by him in a
scoop neck last summer."

"I should have called bullshit!"
BRIGHTDAWN said feeling
guilty.

"I'm ready…"
Harry said shaking his head YES,
"…to turn myself in.
And confess to it all."

"Confess?
Now that you're cornered? Hmm."
I paused.
Before asking,
"What are you doing here then?"

"I need to see Lenin?"

"Why?"

With a vacant stare
he babbled out…
"I'd like her to hear it from me."
He said in a high pitch.

He needed to tell his daughter who is stripping on Bourbon Street, about his other step daughter who he's been molesting. Perhaps I just thought the worst. And asked…

"Have you ever molested
anyone else?"

He looked bewildered.

Before answering,
"Not, that I remember."

Then I heard Bella coming in the front door. Seconds later when she made it to the kitchen where we were, the cold silence in the air hit her immediately. She froze up, and asked us…

"What?"

I went out to the balcony for some air and just closed the doors behind me, closed my eyes too, and stood there; against it. A busker played the violin on the corner, gutter punk dogs barked at each other across the street, and the organ on the Natchez Steam Boat played by the River in the distance. Before, inside the Loft, Bella joined that symphony around me, briefly. Like that of a percussionist who chimed in for just a moment. I waited outside for more crying, dishes to break, profanity to surface, primal screams breaking windows, but nothing more reached my ears from inside there.

I was angry as Hell at him of course. Yet I certainly didn't want to pick a fight with her Dad. But I also didn't see how I could avoid it if I went back inside. I was a junky addict in a panic and needed off that balcony immediately! I've had a fight or flight attitude most of my life. I couldn't go bring myself to go through the Loft where I'd have to look both of them in the eyes. Not whiles my mind was having its way with me. It was turning on itself. Unconsciously…

"I hate my head.
Hate my head. Hate my head.
Hate my head. Hate my head.
Hate my head. Hate my head.
Hate my head. Hate my head."
Echoed down every street, avenue, and alley
within my City of Lakes from public
propaganda speakers.

There's no fire escape from my Balcony. So-I kept a rope tied to the railing and tucked away for an emergency. I threw it off the balcony and stepped over the railing when I noticed Joshua's K&B Organics bag hanging off the back of the stool where he was sitting the night before.

When I made it to the bottom of the rope three stories down, I landed in a pizza on the table of the restaurant just below the Loft. The violin at the corner kept playing, as did the pipe organ on the river, but nobody at the table said a word. When I stepped down on the sidewalk, I left on the table all I had in my pocket other than my cell phone… one rolled up dollar bill.

Just as I turned the corner down the street, Joshua called…

"Sup Kind sir?
…You're bag?
Yeah, just found it."

He explained that he was feeling low and that it wasn't his priority to pick it up. He said he was working on a…

"…formula to find the missing
value inside himself."

With that full bag of Molecular Sacraments over my shoulder I wished him well and hung up.

I reached a remote bench by the Mississippi River in Crescent Park. The sun was setting as I opened his sack of goodies. There were enough drugs on my lap to not only forget where I was, but probably who I was, I just popped a couple EASE pills and watched the sunset to turn my racing speculations off. I felt guilty for not further investigating the impressions I got in the past. When the sun fell, I was asked to leave by Crescent Park by security; bag of drugs in hand.

Back at the Loft things where silent when I opened the front door.

"Bella?"
I asked in a loud whisper,
and hesitated to walk in
any further.
"Lenin?"

Before I heard through tears repeating…

"Why my father? Why my father?
Why my father?"
Over and over.

On the way in, I hid Joshua's K&B Branded messenger bag in the Garret closet. When I got to the big room, and found her holding her knees tightly to her chest on the sofa, she never looked smaller. Perhaps I should have just walked in and hugged her. But instead, I just stood there, nervous. I slowly walked in and peeked around into the kitchen to see if he was there, but no.

"Where is he?"
I asked

"My brothers picked him up,"
She said through tears,
"They're contacting
a Lawyer."

I'd never felt such conflict.

"I don't
want my Dad to go jail!"
She screamed.

In his condition, that would be a death sentence.

As I got closer to her, she shook and cried even harder. When I reached the sofa and tried to calm her with a hug, she convulsed out…

"Not My Father! NOT MY FATHER!"
She bellowed, then said,
"It worked for me."

BRIGHTDAWN bit a thumb nail behind my right eye. *M*ES slid on his back down the window he was looking out. Memories of Harry's shocking statements echoed behind them like rolling thunder over my City of Lakes…

"Not that I remember."

"Carol thinks I'm fucking Bella."

*M*ES asked himself,
"It worked for me?"

"What's that supposed to mean?"
BRIGHTDAWN asked himself.

With her right there in my arms my mind kept doing what it does, race. I hate myself when I hate my head… bird life fly's away in a panic from the Lakes shores that they called home during times like these in there. After I got Bella in a hot bath to try and relax her, I ate two dozen pills to get further out of my head and stay in my skin.

Sometime the next day, I could hardly open my eyes in bed. They were crusted shut. When I finally rubbed them clean my vision was out of focus. As things cleared, I glanced at the alarm clock and found that it was nearly 5PM, that shocked me. But I guess I should have been more surprised I woke up at all. When I tried to bring my head off the pillow, my neck was still asleep. It fell back to the pillow again as if my neck were no more than a noodle. The rest of my body was working, but my neck was out of service. I had to jerk my head up with my chest and balance it on my shoulders like a basketball spinning on an index finger. Before grabbing a fist full of hair to hold it up and massage my neck with the other. Bella wasn't home; thank God. I didn't want her to see this kind of hangover. I crawled to the medicine bag in the closet to get right as right again. After chewing a handful of raw Sacraments like Flintstone Vitamins I laid on the floor in The Garret and waited for them to kick in. I took the RED PILLS for power.

What felt like moments but what was more like an hour I woke up in darkness. Confused, I wondered if it were night time, or if I had reached purgatory. I rolled over, crawled around, finally made it to my feet and found the light switch. The air in the Loft tasted stale upon my revival. Either there was a gas leak, or another rat died in the attic. But my neck was back because those RED PILLS work wonders.

"FOCUS is fire."
MES said loving them.

"Let's get some fresh air."
BRIGHTDAWN suggested.

"Got it."
I responded. Then murmured,
"We got-ta call Bells."

Outside, as I walked down French Market Place and bumped up crushed pills from a packed snuff bullet, I noticed a message from her. And played it on speaker…

"Hey…
calling to let you know Dad
turned himself in.
He admitted to everything.
The lawyer hopes his honesty & health will play a
positive role in getting leniency.
The arraignment is Monday.
We're getting ready to post bail for him.
I'm staying at Moms tonight.
I have the car if you're wondering.
Love you."

"Why'd he turn himself in
on a Friday."
Asked *MES*.

"Perhaps he's punishing himself."
BRIGHTDAWN responded.

Depressed, confused, lonely, I went into The Cane & Table on autopilot, and don't recall leaving.

Due to often passing out rather than falling asleep, it had been weeks since I had a very memorable dream. But later that night, drunk in bed, I felt the presence of my brother. And got the impression in the dream that he was a black and red sparrow flying in the sky with a ribbon (or something like that) clutched in his bill. I found myself flying in it too. I chased after him as he dipped and glided through the clouds. When I found where this dream was leading, it became a nightmare. He suddenly perched on a piece of steel in a cloud, before he hopped off and darted straight down from the Crescent City Connection Bridge. As I gave chase, it sounded like I passed the medieval spirit of Hildegard Von Bingen on the edge the bridge along with other feminine spirits raising stretched voices to the heavens as I chased him down, down, down. Experiencing myself what it felt like to fall in his final act; of insanity.

As we descended through the clouds as if we were skydiving higher than the Bridge itself, I wholeheartedly took the opportunity to fall with him. Yet just before hitting the water he straightened out and glided over the River. I followed and tried to catch up, but he was gone. I took notice to my own reflection over the incessant rush of the Mississippi River where I found myself in black, blue, and pink feathers before my subconscious got whitewashed.

The next morning with the taste of that dream still present on my tongue, I was stuck in that rut again. And crawled to Joshua's K&B Organics Bag with my head dangling back and forth as if it were a pendulum ticking me to death. Apparently, I was now suffering with reoccurring Junky-Palsy. When I got to the fucking bag, I stuck my head in it like a dog and ate Sacraments as if they were table scraps. Then I curled up fetal position, spit out some packaging, and waited for them to kick in. I laid there thinking Joshua's going to be pissed when he finally comes back for his bag; but hell-with it. I'd just ask for forgiveness, pay some penance. Extraordinary times call for extreme measures, I'd level out and pay later.

GARRET SCENARIO No.2

After taking an overdue shower I made a puzzling discovery drying myself off in the mirror; new bird tattoos on my left arm.

"Sparrows?"
BRIGHTDAWN speculated looking out
at them.

"We got fresh ink?"
MES asked from
the left.

"Not that I remember."
I said aloud.

And with that, it all came back!

"Not that I remember."
Echoed Harry's voice in a rich
baritone from somewhere.

"It worked for me."
Soon followed.

Then, it appeared as though lips pushed out against the left side of my neck, saying…

"Carol thinks he's
fucking Bella."

"Uaaahh-jezus-what the!"
I screamed slapping the surreal lips
back in with both hands.

Instantly I knew the culprit; *MES!* I wasn't crazy. They had to be his sarcastic lips messing with my insides!

Before I could find the freak-rascal Downtown inside me, he made it to Command Central blowing a siren! In there, he got on the mic. Speakers were installed in my head during an abduction after the Pocono Mountains Rave in the Cave for the alien propaganda. But, I'm not a *True Believer*. From Command Central he broadcast…

"Carol accused Harry of
fucking Bella.
But she didn't realize he was

molesting her own daughter?"

That stopped me in my tracks. *MES* communicates in annoying ways, but he's good for the DL. *BRIGHTDAWN* came around the corner and asked more subtly…

"Is this really our
concern?"

I really didn't know. But I suppose expressing thoughts like these is why Rachelle wasn't happy about my Ethical Audit.

Downtown inside my head where the sky was dry, but yet the gutters were filled and gushing! Water levels in my City of Lakes got critically high from the binge. Selective info seeped into my head and I began to observe evidence that only confirmed my pre-existing assumptions. Such recent hard truths could possibly lead to a collapse of mental infostructure if I didn't find ways to change my mind.

When I gave up on *MES* and them disturbing thoughts of Carol faded, I noticed those unexplainable Birdy tattoos once again on my left arm. Of which, I had absolutely no recollection of acquiring. Two bird tats… a Black & Red on the inside of my left arm. And a Black, Blue, and Pink one on that same shoulder.

"The birds in our dream?"
BRIGHTDAWN pondered.

I could only assume no matter how farfetched that perhaps I functioned during a blackout last night and got inked.

"Plausible."
Said *MES* returning to
the window.

Anybody whose experienced Xanax amnesia can confirm this and that's that. The good news, they're decent tats.

Feeling slightly buzzed-bad-and-tattooed I got dressed before I found some texts that I missed. The first text was from Joshua's. I laughed as soon as I opened it. It appeared as if I were looking at Sacrament propaganda. He had no sense of brevity with the written word. Mimicking how serious he could be, I read it out loud to myself…

"It's with great sadness
that I inform all parishioners of my
fall from grace.
I'm messaging you all from
atop a volcano in Hawaii
where I'm now going to depart the Earth.
May the Divine Creator save my soul
and be the guiding force
in all your lives.
Your Pastor,
Joshua Kerry."

The way things were going, inside and out, I instinctively did the strangest of things… I walked over to my Write-Away Chest to make sure I wasn't there writing this bullshit. After all, I've been getting lost at The Lakes since 1988, but not this time around. After confirming I was actually in my skin and not my head…

"Death by Volcano?
Is there such a thing?"
I asked myself aloud,
"You got-ta be shitting me.
Alexa,
is he shitting me?"

"Hmm…
I don't know that?"
She said.

"Alexa,
Are you shitting me?"

"I'd rather not answer
that."
She responded.

I took a moment to consume this parishioner alert. My first impression; hogwash. Who the hell does this like that? I'd sooner speculate that this was his way of going dark for a minute. I didn't believe that he actually died by suicide, but rather, suddenly was ducking out for whatever reason(s). That's his business. Mine was to keep writing my way forward on the motherload he left behind. To stay calm and on script I directed…

"Alexa,
play Erik Satie *Gymnopedie No.1*"

Inside where this story took shape like sand dunes communicating by way of situational whirlwinds, I had much to observe. High tides of dopamine and serotonin breached levies and overflowed into the City streets where *MES* and *BRIGHTDAWN* where deep in bliss despite the tragedy. The next text was from Bella, her Dad was due in court the next day. Spillways opened for her again and ran down my face.

Harry was arraigned. I went to the court house to meet Bella and do whatever I could. But I felt more like an old friend rather than a part of the family. Bella and Thorsen consulted with the lawyer. The four of us stood waiting for Harry's particular group of defendants to arrive. Bella's brother looked more nervous than her. And I was anxious as well; courthouses don't bring back good memories for me.

By noon her Dad made bail and was later released from the shackles. Apparently, his health declined rapidly over the weekend. He was rolled out to us in a wheel chair.

"When did you get the wheels Dad?"
Bella asked him with
a smile.

"Just now."
He said gasping,
"I had a spell back there a moment ago.
They put me… in… this."

I sensed no anger from Bella or her Brother towards Harry, but rather total support. There was sadness in the air, but that's it. I was the conflicted outsider, and Harry knew it. He said little to me. In fact, only one word…

"Easy."

Easy I was not! What about Kireka? Why did we all have to be so calm about this? Though my anger for all this "understanding" began to boil, I didn't blow; yet. Harry was right. I need some EASY pills so-I jetted…

"Excuse me."

…and went to crush a few in the car ~ I texted Bella from there ~ Drove home. I had to straighten up the Loft for the family meeting.

Immediately after Harry's release on bond the elders in the family came together including Bella's Mom Denise, her older brother Thorsen, and her step Mom Carol. Harry was dropped off with his Mother who came down from up River. Kireka was with her biological father who flew in from Canada.

We gathered to make a decision about where Harry should live now. He certainly, by law, couldn't return home to Carol's place. The steps to the Loft were too much for him. Thorsen lived in a compartment not an apartment. So, we had to think about rooming him somewhere. Now while I was still slow to board the forgiveness wagon with the fam, Harry's new wife, Carol's reaction? Kireka's own Mom I remind you! She was disturbingly understanding too. keep in mind, this is a woman who carried so much anger in her, she believed at one time that teaching Bella Lenin screaming exercises was a good idea to release her anger when she was a teenager. Anger that she herself, CAROL, fueled years ago while jack-booting her way into the Family. When Carol noticed my contempt for her understanding, as I recall, her responses to the act of molestation, of her OWN daughter, was as such…

"In another time, another culture,
it would be acceptable."

I looked over at Bella who, seemed OK with this. I had to get up and walked away! I found myself over at the balcony doors, looking back. And nodded for Bella to meet me outside.

Moments later she did. I asked her…

"You're cool with Carols
response Lenin?"

She responded,
No.
But I'm relived she's being
cooperative at this time.
Not to mention sober.
…Are you?"

That was nearly the last day I attempted to find my place in family affairs, I wasn't big enough.

After Kireka made a video deposition, Carol and her moved to Canada. But my lil-buddy Kireka left me her old Vision Skateboard! Left it behind with a message tagged on it…

Yo Mes!

Skate or Die!

I don't exactly know why she left ME her wheels. Perhaps it was because her step brothers are more chess players than street friendly.

Bella really held it together and was by her father's side all the whole time. I gave them space. But alone, I ruminated in all I had in mind. If Joshua didn't leave those pills who knows what shape I would have been in. There was no trace of him since his death by volcano text. When the family found Harry a little one bedroom on the edge of town by a train yard, Bella was there every day, Bourbon Street every night. She took a hiatus from teaching. Yet not a week passed since we moved him into the dump, before it was time for Hospice care. It appeared his Eternal judgment would come quicker than his Earthly one.

Every time I began to come down, the murmuring in my head got louder, and that made it harder for me to type. But with the assistance of the Sacraments, things were manageable enough to write for about two hours a day. Bella, looking over my shoulder, interrupted me in The Enclave at this time asking…

"Can you let something

like this happen,
WITHOUT,
writing about it?"

"No one should turn a blind
eye to molestation."

"Is it your story to tell?"
She asked me.

"My pages are my voice.
You want me to just shut up?"

She fell silent. I continued…

"Whose story is it?
There are countless people who
could identify with this
suffering."

"Yeah,
No shortage of people getting
high to cope."

…And she walked away. Everybody seems to need somebody to look down on to feel a little better sometimes.

Solo beneath the marquee of Wild Forest I stood outside handing out flyers. It was cold out, but I kept volunteering to stand in the elements where nobody inside knew how I was keeping warm out there. Although I disdained working the entrance, I needed space between I and the jonesing employees/dry-parishioners. The thought of filling Joshua's shoes never came to mind, the pills were all mine. Soon I'd be taking plenty of personal days to keep my habit under the radar.

When I got home after one of these shifts, I found a Pay or Quit notice on the floor at my front door. Dated, and evidently posted, weeks ago. It must have just fell off. I was so disorganized at this time I didn't know if I bounced a check, or just forgot to write them one. When I took a quick look at my bank account, I was just shocked. Either way, I was short.

A few EASE and Tylenol PM's later, I passed out alone in the Loft. At least I think I was sleeping when my 3rd eye opened on my forehead in bed whiles my two other shades were down. Dutch sat up from my skull as if surfacing from an oversized eagles nest, spread his wings, and flew off; nothing unusual. Soaring and gliding pleasantly in circles within the A-frame bringing my awareness with him. I assumed he just need to spread his wings. But from up there, I felt something moving around in my neck. It felt like a rodent! couldn't wake up as it made its way by my jaw, under my cheek, by my left eye, and into my head. Frozen, in a psychosomatic state, the critter emerged from the nest in my forehead. When suddenly yet ANOTHER flying eye surfaced flapping paint from its wings… it woke me; with a pain in my neck. But at least it still worked! When I found a knot in my neck that was causing the pain, I went to the bathroom to get a closer look at it in the mirror.

In my reflection I found a mass that felt like a bone on the left side of my neck causing the discomfort. And, found something else! New tats on my left arm. Just around the bird tattoo's, two new ones appeared out of nowhere. Two Von Dutchy eyeballs! One pleasant, one nasty. I drank some water from the spicket before I took another look. There was now, absolutely no doubt of tat parlor blackouts. But I didn't panic. Whoever was doing them was good. But that bump on my neck, that looked like trouble. I popped some meds and went back to bed that night, alone. Bella practically moved in with her Dad by now.

Much later the next day I woke up when the sun was going down after catching up with about 12 hours rest. Feeling no more than day old bread, I rolled out of bed, put some lotion on the new tats, when, standing in the mirror I found another one! If it was there the night before, I don't know how I missed it. There was no dream foreshadowing this one; on Tylenol I hardly dream at all. I checked the font door to see if the alarm was set… yup.

"We're sleeping walking,
and, turning the alarm on and off
in the process?"
BRIGHTDAWN asked,
"I think not."

And this tat on the side of my neck just over that lump, was a sick one! A photorealistic tat of my skin tearing, and, an eye ball peeking out. Obviously done by another artist because the quality and style of this one far exceeded the work of the others.

Not tripping the alarm last night, I speculated that the "ink" was perhaps a new millennium-stigmata as a result of the Molecular Sacraments or, a silk screen of my dreams on my skin. I took the helm in the Enclave to note this at my Write-Away Chest before I finally remembered to eat. Mostly on a liquid diet to save time these days I blended kale, spinach, and OJ for dinner. I never really enjoyed eating anyway. Still not satisfied after having some after dinner bumps I pined for a higher state of euphoric dessert.

Back in the Garret, I loosened the string on my sweatpants to get comfortable. But after months in the Wild Forest old Cheech Wiz just didn't help me relax. I You Tubed Lola Astanova in concert on my laptop for inspiration. And oh, be-hold… what a smart move. Mixed up on so many sacraments the neurotransmitters in my brain crossed once again to the tune of her genius. My whole body soon became her boy instrument floating on her passionate notes, before I drifted into another personal eclipse.

When I emerged on the other side of the blackout, high as fuck, I found myself in a red Virgin hot air balloon over the ocean with the likeness of Lola herself! A chill was in the air as leaves blew in the wind where we floated through the clouds in the dark blue sky. There was absolutely no chance of me ever, EVER wanting to come down from this one. Nervous, bashful, tongue tied, I was suddenly smacked in the face with a book before I could introduce myself. I shook the blow off and adjusted my eyes in the faint moonlight to find us floating above a gargantuan flock of novels… one million Paperbacks maybe more! They flew by with wings stretched from their spines as I passionately screamed to the loveliest companion of my dreams…

"Their alive,"
I rejoiced in a frenzy,
Look at them
soar!"

By the moonlight glistening on the sea I looked down on paperbacks seagulls with glee, before she said me…

"Your
library of thoughts
are taking flight,
stranger."

The word library in the wind from her lips made me dizzy, but looking into the magic I found in her eyes kept me on my feet. I thought I felt some electricity between us, but no. She didn't even know my name. What I felt, was RADIOHEAD buzzing by in a UFO. And with it, the spell between us disappeared. It wasn't until then that I realized where I was, in my own City of Lakes. In this God complex where I'm more a man than I could ever be, I took the likes of Lola in my arms and asked…

"Please,
Teach me Beethoven's Moonlight
Sonata?"

To which she responded…

"Maybe."

An antique gas lantern floated by at lightning speed as if it were a shooting star. On the Horizon, rolled a hologram of credits for this delusional short fiction.

Sapiosexual Companion

Lola

Book Surgeon

BRIGHTDAWN

Paperback Seagulls

Gondry

With Lola and Michel in my paper mâché mind this lucid dream floated over the City of Lakes and into mornings first light, just, as a door slammed on the whole Scenario…

GARRET SCENARIO No.2

"HEARD DAT! Heard dat."
I said startled,
waking back up in
the Garret.

It was lit with daylight now while Lola was still playing the piano on my laptop. Comics spread out on the floor around me. And Bella stood over me redder than Mars! I sat there with my sweatpants at my ankles (that was awkward) and found my tongue in my cheek before scratching my chin waiting for her to say something, when… smack! Right in the kisser!

"Addict! SOBER UP!"

"Good one."
I responded.

There's no doubt in my mind that I appeared addicted to things at times, but my experience leads me to lean towards a compulsive behavior rather than any physical addiction. I clarified this aloud…

"I wouldn't call me an addict
that easy."

"Oh-no!
What would you say Braze?"

"Regularly… impulsive."

And with that, she took my now late friend Ben Neb's painting on reverse glass off the wall, and smashed it at my feet. I stood up in a shaken state and tried to explain…

"I get bouts
of mania.
And to focus my research I…"

"Research?
Admit the real problem!
You're, an addict."

"Yes.
I'm revisiting a habit."
Is how I rephrased it
before projecting…

"But only because you're dancing
brought me back into
the mix."

"I'm not doing anything behind
your back!
Your sneaking around
getting high."

"I'm the bad guy?
You're father…"

"Don't you dare bring my father
into this!"

"She's right."
Said *BRIGHTDAWN*.

I breathed, and shifted gears,
"We're both hurting here.
I'm… "

"I'm angry!"
She cut me off screaming,
"ANGRY!"

I looked around at the broken glass and could see her anger, clearly. She continued on her tear…

"You're a lazy! Selfish!
Lying, mean, absorbed,
Self-righteous, irresponsible,
Boring, old… "

I found her anger contagious. And feeling more so with every word!
"…insane, pathetic, worthless…"

…making me feel worse than my last visit to an ER! In the middle the shaming the lump in my neck heated up and mushroomed. I bent over and grabbed my neck with both hands trying to stop whatever was going on. But the more she screamed, the more it bulged out. I thought a blood clot was ballooning and was going to burst! When suddenly, those Rolling Stone Lips emerged. Along with the sounds of Kung Fu flutes in my head freaking me out further. Somehow, some way, suddenly, I gave birth to another head!

The explosiveness of the event had me soaring through the Garret ceiling with a roar of Hella-Pain. Bella was knocked back into a wall on my way up. By the time I came down and my ass hit the floor, plaster fell on my head and dusted the room. It looked like a bomb hit in there! A few rats jumped down from the attic and scattered into the Loft. Bella evacuated the scene immediately. Then, I heard it. Heard it cough out some dust to cleared its throat.

Petrified, I looked over from the corner of my eyes to see it, afraid it might, bite! I dared not turn my head! At a glimpse… it was a little younger than me, no glasses, bedhead. Then, it unexpectedly shook some birth tissue off its face and toward the side of mine. With my eyes then shut, I could hear him breathing for the first time. It cleared it's throat! And I could feel it's eyes on me. Then, it spoke…

"I gave you warning.
But all you dids
ignore me."

"MES?"
I asked high-pitched.

The cocky-sucker said
"What?
If-you-da-know.
You better ask some-body."

My junky addict in a panic ass got up and ran straight into the Loft! And he just laughed at my scared ass along the way. With nowhere to go I circled the sofa, as he sung…

"Why
are you running so-fast?
You're trying so-hard to leave me,
but I've come back from
the past."

My fear did nothing but amuse him.

"You can't separate yourself from

what you've done."
He said.

I slowed down. He continued…

"You made your bed Braze."

Still not looking at him straight
in the eyes, I asked…
"What are you?"

"An outing."

I shook my head NO. I didn't understand; any of this! He furthered his description of himself by saying…

"Every writer,
reveals himself."

I finally took a better looked at him. He cracked a smile. This was some personal uncharted territory to which I ventured up in here. I murmured fast…

"I jus-wa write a relevant book.
I's jus-tryin' stay on top wit-duh-pills."

BRIGHTDAWN responded,
"No one fails their way
to the top."

After finally looking at *MES* dead in the eyes, I was horrified. And decided to give up, just like that. I went out to the balcony on an impulse to handle this mental bankruptcy head first, but something big stopped me. As I stood in the winds of my own personal consequences three floor up, I found thousands of people in the light of morning below. From the sidewalk, to the Jazz Museum, they held cellphones videotaping me on the balcony. I asked *MES*…

"What are they doing
here bro?"

He shook his head, shrugged his shoulder. I was not ready for this kind of attention, not now, on video! I looked to the clouds and let out in a raspy tone like Jesus Jones…

"Good-God!
Why have not you forsaken me?"

When no sooner did thunder strike and I got a response ala Stone Roses! *Breaking into Heaven* boomed from clouds above igniting the crowd below. Dancing, their bodies appeared to make ocean size waves of tribal flesh and blood. I went out there to jump, but all I could do now was join in. Thrusting my fists above my heads brought thousands further ape-shit below us! With frankincense, myrrh and music in the air they raged on, and once again, I realized how fucking delusional I am.

After butting heads during my transition Bella raced directly to The Rising Sun following my blow up; she'd said years ago never again, and she meant it. She could live with my drug use, my wandering eyes, but not one more violent outburst from me. When she walked in the club that night with a bump on her head, the hospitality dwarfs wanted blood! And if it were not for the presence of Dutch witnessing their anger, I'd have probably straight walked into them later lookin-for her.

To settle down and get her mind right BLCB drank from a cold bottle of Perrier water and watched her proteges work the program. Her squad may have been rookies but they were selling like hell. That was THE MAYBE moto… SELL like HELL!

"Like football?"
Asked some college kid,
"Come see me QB sometime?"

Miss Blue smiled and responded,
"Oh-football!
Definitely maybe."

She took a deep breath to fill her nearly naked lungs, grinded her ass back and forth on her chair, and shared that…
"I just love balls."

EZ Lap danced scored.

At another table *Miss Blonde* sat with her long hair covering her breast, cleavage in full view, three little gold buttons holding her top on, two-undone, as an Elderly Man in a modest business suit spoke to her chest the whole time…

"You ever been to the
Carousel Bar?"
He asked her
breast.

"The Monteleone is my favorite."
She answered trying to make eye contact
with him.

"Want to meet me there after work?
Go for a spin on it?"

Miss Blonde
had enough of this
guy and dropped a quick,
"Surely Maybe,
Let's get warmed up first.
I'm freezing."

She got up and led the way to a couch, he followed.

Miss Brown was seated at a table with a youngish B-Boy who looked like he'd been endorsed by every brand on the block. He appeared to oozed money, informing her kindly as he could…

"I'm looking for a good stripper
to be my woman.
I got-ta stripper pole at
my front door.
You can keep in shape ever-time
we-comes-home from shoppin.'
No womenz a mindz need-a-work.
You should be minez?"

Miss Brown lowered herself and
responded in character,
"Oh-my baby, Maybe.
Let me show you how good I am
right-cheer right now.
Make it rain
for me."

She table dance his ass.

GARRET SCENARIO No.2

Miss Orange was stripping on stage and leaned down to get some cash from a zealous blue collar customer who screamed up to her…

"When I get my tax returns,
Can I tax that ass?"

"You-crazy! Bu-Maybe."
Orange yelled back in good fun.

"Come on. Come ON!"
He could hardly wait.

Miss White was with a Slick Player that smelled as good as new printed Notes. She was leaning over the cocktail table so much it appeared she was getting in on a secret from E.F. Hutten himself…

"Do you like the fast lane?"
He asked.

"Yes."

"Jet fast?"
He asked.

She nodded YES with her mouth open, and responded…

"Maybe."

"I have a runway for a
driveway."

"Let's jet upstairs
I want to get a feel that
cockpit."

She had him acquire more of her in the privacy of the VIP champagne area.

Not only was THE MAYBE growing but customers who bought in, began reselling it elsewhere! THE MAYBE was clearly destined to sell millions. Consumers knew a good thing when they got it, and they couldn't get enough by design.

Bella remained sitting alone at the bar off the clock watching the scene as the Piano Man was in a jam session with DJ Crowley when she heard a familiar voice from behind…

"Aren't we quite casual tonight."
Said on the On The Job Bob.

"Hello Cuffs.
I just stopped in, because… "
She said taking a deep
uncertain breath.

With no guard up or heels on, and more Bella than Chloe that night, she let out a sigh and admitted…

"…I had nowhere else to
go tonight."

"Buy you a drink?"
He offered.

With nothing else to do, she looked at her bottle of water, before nodding YES. They exited the main floor of the club for the Lobby bar.

The Bartender knew what they wanted…

"A Tanqueray and grapefruit Chloe?"

"Yes please."
She answered.

The Tender asked Bob,
"Club soda?"

"Hell Yes."
Bob said fist bumping
the bartender.

"If it's not a hell yes,
it's a hell no."
Replied the Barkeep.

Since she found out Bob was a cop, she was suspicious of his presence in the club. And, she never heard back from him after voicing her concerns about First Fridays. Finally, she asked about his role here…

"Is it actually legal
for you to just hang out in strip clubs
while at work?"

"It's my job.
Bourbon's my beat."

Perhaps he noticed the bump on her head, but he didn't mention it; yet. Instead, officer Robert Perlinghi continued…

"Cheers to you Chloe."
He said holding up
his soda.

Not feeling good about herself that night, she smirked. It seemed that tonight was the first night she was out of sorts at the club, and he knew it. So, he got to it…

"How'd you get the egg
on your head."

She looked surprised. Perhaps she forgot about it already. But, her troubles at home were public now. That fresh bruise on the forehead from the headbutt put my recklessness on a billboard, A cops a girl's bestie at this time, though, she responded aggravated nonetheless…

"I don't know why I came
here tonight."

He reminded her,
"You said earlier,
you had nowhere else
to go."

She got up to leave. Bob stopped her.

"Wait, I'm concerned.
Now you may think you can take care
of your own domestic disputes.
And we may not be good friends,
but that bump concerns me."

They eyeballed each other. He continued…

"How can I be of service?"

She was frazzled. But she knew, KNEW not to get personal with anyone in there. And told him so…

"I can't get into here."

"Do you have a place
to stay?"

Looking out the front door I guess she said the first thing that came to mind…

"I'm going across the street
tonight."

"The Bourbon Brothel?"
He asked.

"You know about that place?"
She asked surprised.

"Everybody does."

"And,
you're OK with that?"

"It's,
a grey area.
Or, not a priority
is closer to the truth."

"Prostitution's not a priority?"

"To a certain degree,
no."

"When does it become a
priority?"

"There's an operation
assigned to rescuing woman
who've been trafficked."

He eyeballed her. She knew that look from before. He took a breath while checking his peripherals before adding…

"At the end of the day,
I'd rather rescue a person in greater danger,
than arrest hooker."

And with that, Bella Lenin-Chloe Brazil nearly deflated. She was finally in the presence of someone else in this situation who seemed to give a shit. He continued with the business at hand…

"Now,
do you want to tell me
what happened?"

She looked around. Before answering…

"No."

"Would you like to
talk about it somewhere else?"
He asked.

She nodded YES. She was ready to open up. And what I think happened, is that Bob Perlinghi opened up to her too.

While Bella was in a cozy convo with the undercover detective at The Clover Grill and ignoring my texts that night, I now had twice the appetite for chemicals after *M*ES popped up. I could hide my use from Bella, but not him. Yesterday he was inside my City of Lakes, now he was outside and so close he could French kiss my left ear! Tongue in cheek as I chopped rails on a glass coffee table *M*ES commented on the open K&B bag…

"We-so blessed."

When I pulled my head up from the glass *M*ES was right there on que to do the next line. When he came up, he asked as I dipped down again…

"What kind-a tables this
again?"

I dipped down for the 3rd rail off it. And came up saying…

"Noguchi."
My designer imposter ass said to him.

And with that he went down to do the 4th line. With twice the appetite and four nostrils my one heart would be taxed doing such quadruples. After the fourth rail he came up commenting on the table coughing out…

"HIGHLY… functional piece of art."

I couldn't help but notice as HE wiped the residue off the glass with MY left index finger, how often *MES* gets it right, for all the wrong reasons. The more pills came 1st, the more my art, and better living, came 2nd and a distant 3rd. Paying bills to afford the lifestyle I came accustom to completely slipped my mind. And sadly, the natural love I had for Lenin couldn't compete with the enhanced lust I had for the chemicals.

The world may have been on top of me again, but loaded, I didn't feel the load. As *MES* worked on his drip, I stared at him. Another stroke, or going into cardiac arrest made sense under these circumstances. But Two Heads? If I wasn't on the outs with Bella, in the rears with my rent and had a book to finish… I'd have hopped a train to California and try to bum rushing the Chopra Wellness Center after a quick binge in TJ to get my mind right.

"You a Freak-a-Zoid now."
I said looking at him.

"Yeah-you-right."
Said *MES* with a smile before suggesting,
"Let's chop out more pronto."

And with this, I introduce the monkey on one's back. The monkey always wants more, and more. He's both your only friend and your worst enemy in the war with yourself; the monkey's a parasite.

The next morning isolated even further at my Write-Away in the Enclave within my City of Lakes focusing on pages, I tried to block *MES* with my head to get a little privacy. But he was nonchalantly par-oozing my work. Then Bella finally text me back!

Coming over @ noon.
Packing up moving out.
Don't be there @ that time!

GARRET SCENARIO No.2

I called back, but it went straight to voicemail. It was 11am. I looked around, found the place still turned upside down, hole in the ceiling, and started to clean up. While I was in the act of getting it together, *MES* said…

"Why bother?"

"Shut up! SHUT, UP.
This is your fault!
If you so much as whisper when
she gets here…"
…I opened a butterfly knife off a bookshelf…
"I will cut your
throat *MES*."

Rather than take responsibility myself for blowing up the day before when *MES* came out, I just blamed him.

By the time I got the next text at noon, the Loft was straightened up! I was lighting incense, and *MES* was scared quiet. Then I read it…

Here with police
If you're not here
Won't press charges

I looked to the knuckle-head.

"What I do?"
Asked *MES*.

"It got, violent yesterday."
I said staring off,
disgusted with
myself.

She gave me the chance to scram. And by then in this kind of shape, I was easy meat. In no shape for OPP!

I darted to the quarter-moon window over Barracks to find her getting out of an unmarked cruiser. I knew the drop on the back side of the Loft might leave me crippled. So-I grabbed a step ladder from behind the rack system ~ Put it against a wall under the skylight between the Garret and Loft ~ And climbed out to escape the threat police capture.

Just as I made it roof side, the front door opened and Bella Lenin call out…

"Braze? BRAZE?"

…I heard her come in. It sounded like she had a bag and started to throw things in it from the Garret closet. Then she entered the Loft and briefly looked around. I wanted to come out of hiding, climb down, and offer an apology. But with this new super-unnatural development of mine, the fuzz out front, punk I was… nope; not today. She wanted out. It was time to respect that. The Garret door slammed shut during this thought process.

I peeked over the roof and watched her come out downstairs and walk over to that Cop I met at the Orpheum Theater standing there against his cruiser. He opened the door for her to get back in! Jealousy suddenly poured in my City of Lakes. We turned over and laid on the roof looking up at my breath in the cold air. *MES* suggested…

"Let's follow the cops Braze,
steal her back."

A bazar suggestion. But with my broken spirits, not a bad idea. I wasn't giving up on her so easy. Then *MES* looked at me like a hobo in a disco…

"Oh dang!"
She find the pills?"
Asked *MES*.

In an emergency response to that I un-nested Dutch to do a quick recon. *MES* launched his Subway Art eyeball (flapping spray paint on my face) to do the same. Through cascading points of view in mind we found the pills, and breathed once again. I may have wanted her back, but I couldn't live without the Sacraments.

BRIGHTDAWN wanted to get back to the Enclave when the monkey suggested…

"Let's bump up,
get on the same page first."

We all agreed on that.

GARRET SCENARIO No.2

After getting loaded and scripting pages I'd later edit out along with hundreds of others, I showered, before I made a really important discovery afterwards… *M*ES wasn't in the mirror with me! I whipped my head to the left to see if he fell off, but nope, he was there in the room. But not in my reflection. Shocked, I stepped away from the mirror, closed my eyes, and decided he was gone. Then, I stepped back into my reflection, and there I was alone again… for seconds. Before he slowly faded into the mirror's reflection like a thought I couldn't shake.

Frustrated, I shook my head violently trying to shake the thought of him from my head. But trying so hard not to think about him just made him more solid in the mirror. When I reached out cautiously to touch his face, the moment I reached his cheek with my finger, that throbbing pain in my neck abruptly came back stopping the physical investigation against my will. At a closer look I could see my veins coming from my chest and into his neck just under our skin, leaving me more perplexed. I touched one blue vein gently with a finger, and moved up it like a guitar string. It generated the same noise one might hear on that acoustic instrument. And with it, an intense feeling of guilt with the stroke. He was pumping pure shame and made from the same.

I concluded that he could be a multidimensional apparition or, psychogenic stigmata charged by highly dramatized mental health issues. But this still didn't explain the god damn tattoos. I breathed on it, and breathed deep… a real mind fuck was at work on me. There needed to be a more controlled experiment of my out of control nature.

We left the Loft with great caution, and a baseball bat. If we had to beat off a hysterical drunk tourist attacking my alien attribute, it was on. If they wanted to get crazy, *M*ES & I were ready to get Cra-Cra! As we creeped the down stairs *M*ES held the straps of the duffle bag the bat was in. With a covered Aluminum Bomb Bat in my hand, we snuck past the Pizza Kitchen's open back door in the first floor hallway, before we made it to the front door of old 424, when…

I asked um,
"You ready-a do-dis *MES*?"

"I's born ready."

Just to make sure I hyped the beast,
"If you're scared.
Say-ya-scared."

As planned, that agitated him…

"Psh-please.
Do-dis like Brut-ass."

And with no further haste I kicked open the old wooden door and hopped out! Landing on the sidewalk at the head of a full table eating pastas at the Italian Barrel. Everybody froze! Wine glasses stopped tilting in mid-sip, spaghetti dangled from mouths, a lighter held in the hand of a smoker stayed lit just before his cigarette ~ Across the street behind the iron fence of the Jazz Museum Park hardcore readers waited in drum circles on my next book listening to Stone Roses ~ Before the waitress came into the frame with more bread breaking the spell. Apparently, I must have just looked like another weirdo; no biggie.

I closed my front door and walked by the full tables on the sidewalk towards Decatur Street. The table ignored me like I was a street person passing by and got back to their scrumptious dishes. No one could care less if I had Two Heads. But those people across the street got hype. While held back by *Black Steel*, and, the authority of forty or more peelers in riot gear on my side the fence; TRICKY updated my Public Enemy status.

Like another leftover *Duffle Bag Boy* carrying a permanent persona of a reckless youth I made my way to Bourbon Street with *MES* ultra-noid about going public any further. I never thought I'd be just another weirdo in The Quarter, but as cerebral reservoirs continued to breach and flood my skull with antiquated pop culture, The Charlatans played a balcony by the corner of the Nellie Deli confirming the old *Weirdo* I was indeed. Now I may be weird, but the City of Lakes in my head is not the result of wet brain.

My condition isn't specifically the result of drinking too much alcohol, but rather the overproduction of cerebral fluids. If the average brain produces one small plastic water bottle of this organic substance per day, mine produces a gallon jug on drugs. This often resulted in gushing euphoria from the peepers with occasional saccadic dysfunctions as a result. At peak use, my City of Lakes was losing ground faster than the Wetlands. But like the majority, I kept furthering my lifestyle in the face of imminent demise as Me, Myself & I drug our feet down Bourbon Street… Observing youngsters banging on buckets hungry for change in the world ~ Doorway barkers failing in attempts to navigate us into their bars ~ Crackheads greeting us with Mardi Gras beads in an apocalyptic remake of Fantasy Island ~ Well dress middle class peoples parading to restaurants and upper-crust haunts on vacation ~ The smell of cigars, garbage and worse filled the air. And all the while, no one ever took notice of how I perceived myself.

I glanced in the window at everyone socializing inside of Galatoires, being normal, wishing I was. But I'd gone way too far. *M*ES suggested…

"Let's go home and blow some lines."

I shook my head OK. The City of Lakes was now fully dependent on the pills to keep powered. The same thing that kept me going, polluted me. There would be no way of saving the City from bankruptcy. I only hoped I could salvage something worth publishing before the lights went out. But on the way home I couldn't stop laughing about it; all. The overwhelming synthetics in my brain kept overflowing and I must have appeared to be crying happy tears. But the perception of course wasn't the reality. I cried because I felt no escape from my own impending end. I cried because the pills both worked and ruined me simultaneously. I cried because I lost my BEST friend.

With this frame of mind, I passed a dozen or so others in the same condition; Street People you might say. Those without meds, a Loft, or Books to sell. And that was all that separated I from them; for now. Tears fell over raging laughter as I plowed through crowds on the way home like a blind man on autopilot to where I felt safe locked away in the Loft. I only have slight recollections of that dash home. And of some of those memories, well, I'd rather not mention. There was an unfortunate scene I caused at Café du Mode.

By the time I slammed the Garret door behind me, bolted it shut, and set the alarm… I found powdered sugar and glitter all over me; barefoot, scratched up, and bleeding here and there. Knowing my heart might give out before my head drove me to the edge, I still felt compelled to crawl to the finish line of this story before it killed me. It's when I'm in my darkest moments, putting off killing myself is the only thing that saves me. I might be a self-sabotaging goal setter, but finishing chapters buys me time.

While my head consumed me, Chloe Brazil wasn't at work that night, but alone and sitting on the sill of and open window in an empty studio apartment. A neon sign glowed on her face three stories over a busy street below, but I couldn't make out exactly where. Bella Lenin was finally on her own. No family around sleeping on top of each other or self-absorbed guy in the room writing stories about his drama. Though she sat on a sill over a fire escape as if she were a lonely kitten, deep down she was an untamed wildcat breaking loose! Growing up her brothers would sometimes call her "Lion" rather than Lenin when she roamed the woods with them. It was now or never to become that powerful and poised person her family dreamed she'd be. Dealing with her own problems independently, I imagine she reminisced…

Traveling across country in on an old mattress in the back of an older pick-up truck. Dad yelling through a slid open back window at her brothers to kindly move over…

"Let Lenin by the window boys!
Be gentleman!"

Or racing down Old Highway 90 with a van door tied open so she could open her mouth in the wind and catch bugs in her teeth through the bayou…

"Bug are protein Lenin!

Get a mouth full!"
Dad yell out his driver's side
window back at her.

And going to skid row under the overpass on Christmas Eve with him and the family carrying shopping bags filled with cigarettes and beers for the homeless because…

"Give um' what they really want Lenin."
And then he whispered to her,
"Introduce yourself,
and always ask their name.
Humanizing a person can only help."

He spoiled her with love! Then, it came back…

"It worked for me."
BRIGHTDAWN murmured inside.

For months I'd been thinking with feelings. A manic should never do that. Rather than sobering up and being there to save the day in the face of tragedy, I pushed her away. They say hurt people, hurt people. I let my insecurities, judgments, and assumptions rule my head space. There were dire prices to pay for that.

Dutch was perched on the rooftop across the street acquiring this experience as she rocked back and forth on that windowsill with the neon glow on her face. The next thing I had to do was find out where that window was! That while her father was across town trying to figure out what was next for him through the window of the afterlife.

Where did he find messages from a higher power and evidence of traveling souls? Not in the readings of Edgar Casey that he'd been entertained with his entire life. The questions that Christian Mystic answered on such topics of the future and Atlantis were just an entertaining hobby of sorts for him and the fam. His go to for information about the spirit was, as mentioned before, Chico Xavier. Evidently, Chico was a Brazilian medium that wrote on religion, philosophy, science and more. In the Winter of Harry's life, he devoured his collection of 100 or more Chico Xavier books as if cramming for an exam! There was no doubt in Harry's mind that souls moved on once the cells in the body closed for business. So, his obsession became not just to believe it, but to work it. He took those messages he was writing to the family seriously. And while he was finding those words to message, I walked over looking for info on Lenin's whereabouts.

On the edge of the Bi-water where Harry was to live out his days, Bella Lenin's younger Brothers were kicking around a soccer ball out front. Thorsen, who was on the phone with someone, welcomed me in. I went with the flow and *MES* was thoughtful enough to keep his trap shut. Upon my request, a hospice nurse let me have some alone time with Harry. I closed the door behind her for some privacy to see if he could help me out.

Thin as a rail, he was in the fetal position near an oxygen tank by his bed. Even with the extra oxygen pumping in him he still struggled to get air. Maybe I'm wrong, but I got the impression he looked at me as if I were one of his sons, but I wasn't there to play that. Sadly, all *MES* and I could hear was air trickling through mucus in the room. Finding the words was never a challenge for Harry, but now, getting them out was nearly impossible…

"I, need, you."
He struggled to say.

"How so?"
I asked.

Harry coughed and tried to clear his throat, before continuing…

"Be, resourceful.
Get me, to the woods,
to die, please."

"From, a cypress?"

"Yes!"
He got out.

I looked at *MES* to imply that he keeps quit as I continued…

"Perhaps,
you can help me first."

"Ok."
Harry agreed.

"Where's Lenin?"
I asked softly.

Surprised he answered,
"You'd know, better-n-I."

Instead of pressing the dying man any further, I just turned to leave.

"Wait!
What I, do,
to you?"
He asked.

He was right. After all this, I actually had the least to complain about. He continued…

"I just, wan-a-die
n-a-woods."

MES and I looked at the GPS anklet the courts strapped to him, through the walls to the train yard across the street, at all the blighted homes on the block. When he shared…

"Braze,
we're-a-lot-a-like."
He said fighting for
air before
he could continue,
"I's always revolutionary…"

Of what revolution, I don't know. But he continued…

"…and you're always the outlier."

There was a beat between us.

He concluded…
"It's-a lonely life."

He took hit from the oxygen mask, smiled, and asked…

"Am-I going your
new story?"

I nodded YES.

"Ask a favor?"

MES shook his head NO. I listened.

"In your story…
Can-I, die-wit-dignity?
In-a-woods."

I responded gently,
"You're in the woods Harry,"
And exhaled,
"I don't think I have anything to
add to your charades."

Hopeless, he stared off in a haze like Chet Baker blowing a sad note. In that gaze of his I saw the Ponce de Leon Spring, and all his children swimming in it moons ago. Then, from those windows to his soul projected circus tents, many older men, drunken car rides down open highways with his mother laughing up front in the passengers seat, lonely stares from the back of an old Chevy, child births, tire swings, stripper poles, liquor bottles, text books, revolutionary icons cross faded in a hologram between us… before he closed his projectors.

Immediately after MES & I got home from Harry's, we bumped up an outlandish amount of Focus and began looking around the house franticly for clues to where BL might be. She left a lot behind, including a journal she kept. But there were no surprises in it. It seemed she had spoken to me about everything she found noteworthy. But rereading it reminded me of Saint! We dropped that journal and Two-Headed to the Fruit Loop straight to The Socket.

Blocks from the Loft we passed Oz and the Bourbon Pub making a left on Burgundy Street where I was pretty sure The Corner Socket stood. Just before we got there, we ducked in a doorway for a couple bumps. Once all jacked up, we thought we were ready to do this!

Half a block later a dude at the front door checked my ID before he opened it for us…

"Thank you, kind sir."
I said to him as directed

to do so by my late pastor.

Inside, I was disappointed in a heartbeat. I got no sense in there of the debauchery and shenanigans or happenings I'd heard about going down in this corner joint. The mood was dark as a Basketball Diary lost in Needle Park. Dudes in there didn't look gay and happy about it, just dick-desperate.

"Ain't no Yaz up-in-cheer."
*M*ES commented.

Indeed not. Nor any stereotypical anthem trance either. But there was hypnotic noise coming from somewhere. Within this old Midtown Spa atmosphere eyes in the joint probed the meat on my bones when I noticed myself, a rather short old dude in a pair of black leather chaps at the pool table sinking balls with his shirt off. Half his chest was cut off, and he seemed proud of it; dude had one breast. Other than that Dude in chaps and a cage thong, there was no sign of other strippers in here. Thus, no Saint. We could only assume that little cage thong man with the TIM tattoo on his one breast was the only entertainer who showed up that night.

Then, *M*ES spoke,
"His dancer name has to be
Tiny Tim."

*M*ES never matured out of License to Ill.

"Or, One Tit…"

"Dude.""
I said cutting him off.

I took a quick look around at this oh-so-famous gay bar the Corner Socket, but I just didn't get what indeed made it famous. When I sat down and ordered a beer, I noticed what in fact the hypnotic noise was… Ministry!

Ministry brought my attention to a dark, nearly pitch-black room on the other side of the pool table where sweaty men came and went in and out a black hole of industrial music. *Burning Inside* that darkness I assumed must have been The Socket's famous draw. And tonight, a dark Master & Servant party I concluded; they all looked like hardcore bikers over here. I got the bar tenders attention and asked…

"Is Saint in there?"

The Barkeep shrugged his shoulders and said nonchalantly with the only smile in the bar…

"Maybe-baby."

I looked at *MES* like that was a sign! But he just blew a breath like smoke in my face. Without hesitation I went from the bar to that black abyss, certain, I would find Saint. Where else would a guy named Saint be, but rocking out with his cock out to Ministry.

I found the Blackhole humid and smelling like a locker room with *Louder Than Love* music playing in this *Ultramega* Soundgarden. My eyes didn't have time to adjust to the absent lighting before I was gently groped.

"Yo."
MES said me.

A step further… I felts-another gab!

"Whoa!"
I said smacking dudes hand away
quicker than the Pope.

Then it happened again, AND AGAIN! It was like crabs biting at hide tide!

"Natives are raging!"
MES declared.

Everywhere I turned it seemed I was finger-licking good to some dude in the dark! *MES* screamed…

"Beat it bro!"

I turned to find the exit from this sex poltergeist when *MES* encouraged me with a southern female accent…

"Go to the light Braze.
Go into the light!"

Our 3rd eyes un-nested and flew ahead like cock blockers to help us duck, weave, and spin our way through the offense.

Once into the light of the bar I looked back to see if anyone was tailing us and unwittingly ran us smack into One-Tit-Tim! Bounced right off his chest, fell flat on the floor. Eye Balls circling around our heads dazed and confused, Tim was evidently in much, MUCH better health than *MES* and I.

By the time we raced out of the front door I was completely out of breath, when outside the doorman asked…

"Hell's your problem?"

"You need a sign man.
WARNING!
Corner Socket Sex Club."

"Corner Sockets for kids and geezers.
This is the Raw Hides.
Men only."

MES pointed to the Raw Hides sign right next to the door as I scratched my cheek mouth open, and held on to my jizzy-jawn tight.

Much more determined I found The Socket on the next corner, and Saint inside; he stood out as expected. When Saint finally step down off the bar for a break, I was cool, calm and collected… introduced myself, and asked Bella's whereabouts. I could see in his eyes despite what he said that he knew where she was. I persisted…

"OK don't tell me.
But I beg you, call her now Saint.
Tell her I'm here."

He appeased me and gave her a call on the other side of the bar. After a brief convo he returned…

"She said she's on top of The
Pearl on St. Charles."

I must have looked like I needed more.

He continued…
"She said you'd figure
it out."

No one knew me better than her so I nodded YES. Then he poked me in the chest with a finger…

"Get your shit together.
And get off the shit.
DON'T bring my girl down
with you."

Both I and *MES* vehemently nodded OK to Saint before he let us leave. We ran from The Corner Socket like we had a train to catch. Dutch went ahead to scope the scene.

By the time I busted a left on Canal I nearly forgot about my counterpart. I went from the dumps to on top of the World in sixty seconds! These extreme emotional transitions are like playing the piano of emotions with a baseball bat. No matter how hard I've tried at times to quell the intensities of my life, I can't extinguish these overwhelming emotions at crucial moments.

When I got to St. Charles, I found the neon sign of The Perl Oyster Restaurant bright as a Mardi Gras float. Beside it on the 3rd floor, an open window with curtains blowing from it. An obvious way up via the fire escape appeared to my street art eyes ~ As I scaled the first floor facade, then raced up the fire escape, I gathered my thoughts along the way. Every fiber in me craved her forgiveness. Once at the top floor I found her standing in the window when I looked up. I stopped in my tracks (fractured in two) right before her. Then, she put her arms out to come over for a hug. She always accepted my brokenness. I made no mention of *MES*, nor did she. I sobbed and apologized, once again.

"Sorry,
I'm so sorry."

"You should be."

We stared at each other for a beat. I breathed.

"There's that breath of yours."
She commented,

"What do you want?"

"I… don't want us to
end this way."

She didn't say anything, I elaborated with…

"Not on the note we did at
the Loft last week."

"Are you
referring to the end of
our relationship?"
She asked.

I nodded YES. She furthered…

"Or what your writing
about it?"

She not only had me figured out but made it clear before I could answer…

"It really doesn't matter though,
I've made my exit
from both."
She said.

"Well then…
I'd like to talk about your exit from
Bourbon Street."

This got her attention, but she said…

"Don't concern yourself."
She told me.

Yet Like I said I gathered my thoughts on the way up…

"But,
I have an idea.
your Mom, will love!"

"My Mom?"

"I need you to trust me Lenin.
Just one more time.

Then, it's over."

Bella had no idea what I had in mind at first, but once I painted the Mardi Gras finale I had in mind, she was sold wholeheartedly! Inside, we stayed up talking and making plans to surprise her Mom for an hour or so. Then she got a call from Thorsen in the middle of the night; it was brief. When she hung up, she paused, before telling me rather strong and composed…

"Dad died."

Moments later we were in the back of an Uber riding over to his apartment by the train yard. Not having any more Sacraments on me, *MES* got edgy as I began to crash. The last thing I could do was let her see this or worse, fall apart; she wanted me there.

Lenin said her long goodbyes to Dad, and Thorsen made it known to all there, that he forgave Dad for what he did to Kireka. And in doing so, set an example to his younger brothers of what the higher self of Dad taught him so well about unconditional love. I only helped carry Harry from his bedroom to a hearse waiting out front. Upon his request his body would be donated to science. What I too learned from Harry above all else, was a greater awareness of ones higher and lower self.

Whiles the family went somewhere for a couple days of mourning together, I had to go back to work and catch up on a stack of unpaid bills. Not to mention, the way overdue rent! I can't account for where my money went that winter. Months ago, I thought this was just a slip from sobriety and research for this story. But with *MES* around full time and my wife gone now, there was absolutely no kidding myself any longer. Since the sacraments dried up for everyone in the club but me, I'd been calling out so often to hide my highs and write in my cozy Enclave, my bills just stacked and more PAY OR QUIT notices followed. At first, I thought getting behind in the rent and bills was justifiable, because stories like this just don't come cheap. The only reason I didn't get let go at Wild Forest was because it was Mardi Gras season now and they would take whatever they could get and fire me after. My bank account was overdrawn, my safe was empty, and my refrigerator only had Yuengling Lager and Skull Vodka in it. I should have just sold some pills, but I couldn't dare ran out before I finically got back on top of things; that's the catch.

Early one morning or later in an afternoon who knows, I was splashing warm water on my face and found myself in the mirror looking pale with pulsing veins and bleeding gums. *MES* pointed out the obvious…

"Those teeth need
help cuz."

I didn't care to brush. But after a good rinse, I still found blood. As I brushed some blood away with a finger, I noticed a tooth was loose. I wiggled it slightly, and it fell into the sink!

"Dang."
MES said as surprised
as I looked.

I picked it up, looked at it, then smiled in the mirror again. All the fights I'd been in, all the car accidents! And I just loose a tooth out of the blue? I took a deep breath, smiled again and rather than seeing the nice smile I took for granted my whole life, I found the undeniable look of a careless wino. In a panic I tried placing the tooth back in; smiled again. And I looked good! Then of course it fell out and back into the sink. When I looked down this time blood was dripping into the sink. I glanced back up in the mirror, smiled, and found all my teeth in bloody shambles! As I put a hand over my mouth it filled with blood so quickly I had to spit a mouthful out before I put my lips to the faucet to rinse. When it finally stopped bleeding, I leveled out.

Mouth rinsed, cleaned up and good as one could be in this condition, I accidently washed that missing tooth down the sink in my haste. I reached down and tried to find it in the piping with my finger; but no success. I ducked under the sink and haphazardly pulled apart the trap, turned it over, and got my tooth back!

MES asked,
"Why? You believe in the
tooth fairy?"

He was right I had no reason to be happy, I couldn't afford the Mozart of Dentistry. Back on my feet I looked at my new space in the mirror, when I noticed yet another crooked tooth! MES just said…

"Don't look good bro."

And just like before when I checked the first troubled tooth, this second tooth fell out with even a softer touch straight down the drain. Bouncing and rolling around in the cabinet below it. While I looked down, another fell out with no more than a breath behind it. I lost three teeth in two minutes! A tense high-hat symbol reverberated from somewhere creating an even more intense atmosphere. When I looked back up in the mirror and smiled to see where exactly these three holes where in my head, all my teeth fell from my gums like dominoes into the sink leaving me toothless in tears. Then, I woke up in bed, alone, but who's bed I wasn't sure. Not until I noticed that landmark neon Oyster sign by the window.

I had no idea how the hell I got over there. I couldn't even recall reconnecting with her since she left town.

"When'd she get-back?"
I asked MES before I rephrased that,
"Is she back MES?"

"I-don't-know.
We break in?"

"Bell? Bella?"
I called out softly.

But no one answered. I was alone. I checked my pockets for some pills, but nope; I was completely alone. Then I noticed a note on the bed stand under a glass of water…

"Don't come back to the club!
Drink some water when you wake.
Go home and flush
those pills!"

Perhaps I showed up looking for her earlier at the Rising Sun in a blackout? The chutes and ladders of dreams and reality were never so blurred. After giving this situation a little more thought, I realized this wasn't the first time this happened recently.

Whiles she was with family, I did in fact wake up in someone else's bed recently. I woke up in a massage parlor too. I woke up on the sidewalk across the street from the Loft. And, I woke up in the crumby laundromat of Check Point Charlies fetal on the floor under the "folding" countertop. I was experiencing a fractured life that only added up in pieces with no coherent timeline. Apparently, I was functioning enough to get into situations, but not coherent enough to remember how I got there. Now I still had my teeth, but I certainly lost my mind.

Alone in Bella's little place with a somewhat romantic voice of Anthony Kiedis singing from a speaker somewhere, my mind's Eye un-nested and tried to shake the shade of shit I was on, off. I responded graciously…

"Thank You Dutch."

…As he fluttered in front of me like humming bird, before I asked him to…

"Go check on her for me
please."

He saluted me with one wing and flew out the one window she had in her rented room. When around the corner of St. Charles and up Canal my POV soared over trolleys and the evening gridlock before turning onto Bourbon while the soft rock song I woke up to here in Bella's room transitioned into more profound sounds. From where I was four blocks away, I could see Bourbon Street exploding with nightlife as Dutch hovered high above the pulsing action of Carnival Time. With Fat Tuesday coming in a work week everybody let it hang out. And seemingly overnight, masses of people began using THE MAYBE to drive their lovers, followers, and partners crazy. It came out of the Rising Sun like pure underground during my recent nods and apparent blackouts. A new sex-positive infection was spreading fast when THE MAYBE psychology mushroomed like quick-fever. From the lips of Maybe Ladies to the public's ears, this divisive manipulator-boobalator varied in frequency periodically but the results were clearly predetermined by consumer's desires. Dutch made the veils of awareness translucent and connected me to the strings that connect everything. But such connectivity and evolution come at a dire cost. Like the pollutants that got us to the moon, my orbit would never be the same after recklessly burning those sacraments for so long in my City of Lakes.

Dutch hovered over the first block on Bourbon Street by The Hustler Store as masses of new born Maybe Babies gathered in groups below. That while squares and other clueless onlookers gave the infected fanatics room; something was brewing! Each mind in this Maybe Movement that night appeared connected on a higher wavelength apparently reading each other's body language as they warmed up for something. A moment later, showtime! Without exchanging a word but a vibe it was instant flash mob madness for *Block Rockin' Beats*. The pedestrians on the sidewalks roared as The Maybe Mob in street broke it down in sync. Dutch soared over the dangerous dance tribe like a drone with a mind of its own and followed the moves of the Mob for blocks to its source, the Rising Sun of course. By the time my 3rd Eye-Boy got to the club every man and women in sync had their tops off in the Street. And as always, the sky rained beads from balconies for these bare chested revelers! Dutch flew into the club for shelter.

Inside, the club made Moms Ball look like a High School Prom that night. The carnival atmosphere that Gaten created combined with the elements of THE MAYBE LADIES, MOB, and GROUPIES, fused with the explosive energy of Mardi Gras, created a bombastic-scene! DJ Crowley had such pull with his mystic fingers the scene attracted soulsters from around the globe. There was a nuclear cloud of happy mayhem in the air as it rained money on every Stripper in the house. Whiles THE MAYBE LADIES strutted on the stage with stylistic genius only the soul of Alexander McQueen could orchestrate, the spirit of Freddie Mercury gave Rock Hard support drifting in and out of THE LADIES on stage to make them even more irresistible. Under the direction & influences of Saint, Vinnie, McQueen & Mercury THE MAYBE SQUAD were by far the superstars of the bar. It was a perfect convergence of Straight, Gay & Bi, in Gender Fluid times. I burned with desire to get over there and stage dive butt naked. But for all I knew I may have done that earlier.

GARRET SCENARIO No.2

That particular night before Fat Tuesday must have been Gaten's most successful First Friday of all time by design. He foresaw the power of THE MAYBE months ago. There appeared to be more girls imported from around the globe and more jet set in VIP bidding on them than ever. His "Charity" event went platinum that night. I could only image an extra-long weekend for his "International Talent" across the street in the Royal Hotel was to follow. But I highly underestimated his ambitions. Within the MAYBE madness created in the Mardi Gras mayhem he must, MUST have thought he could get away with even MORE in plain sight; there's no cure for chronic entrepreneur. He looked on top of the club world once again standing in the balcony looking over his brain child. But when you reach the top, get ready to drop.

A Day, or days later… shaken & stirred I woke in the Enclave with my head on a few books at the Write-Away Chest. A pillow of books always helps me sort matters. Psychologist William James pointed out *"All around us lay infinite worlds, separated by the thinnest veils."* Within my experiments the veils where getting thinner and thinner, it came with the territory. Occupational hazard one might say.

On that Mardi Gras weekend I recall moments when I found myself in the Gallatin Street Brothel the Loft once was in the 1850's. Back then I made friends with a prostitute who called herself The One, and, her French Bulldog. By delicate handfuls The One gripped my hair in a rocking chair and pulled at my roots just the way I like it. I pet her dog Giovanna on my lap whiles-staring out the quarter-moon window in semi-unconscious bliss where outside hollers, cry's, and laughs were the universal languages. Here inside the brothel more of the same timeless shenanigans, much more. I attribute this and many of these personal experiences directly to my experiments with Molecular Sacraments and not hauntings, or schizophrenia. Like humanity striking oil, those chemicals were both elevating, and disastrous. The evidence that the natural order is forever polluted in my City of Lakes is undeniable, yet in the face of catastrophe I remained on autopilot trashing it further.

Bella finally got in touch with me on Fat Tuesday and asked if we could do coffee first thing. Tonight, was our big night! And I was happy to go over our plan. Though beforehand, I had to crush the proper amounts of Sacraments I was up to at this time to keep me going for an hour meeting at Croissant DE'Or. That being 5 Float, 5 Focus and 5 Ease respectively. Then MES did the same. It was cool though, I wasn't driving; everything's in walking distance round-here.

Three blocks away we found BL sitting in the window of the coffeeshop where she had a latte' and a cinnamon roll waiting for me thank God; I was broke. First thing she said…

"You look horrible."

"Thanks."

"Did you work last night?"
She asked.

"Yeah."

"Are you high?"

"No."

But she wasn't convinced. I doubled down on my lie after washing my face with my dry hands…

"Just coming down from a
writer's hangover."

"Maybe it's time you gave the
whole Brightdawn thing
a rest."

I responded simply,
"Writers write."

She asked,
"Is it worth it?"

"If we surprise your Mom tonight,
I think so."

She almost smiled. I asked…

"How's everybody doing?"

"That's what I wanted
to talk to you about.
Come with us."

"Come where?"

"Brazil."

I suppose that was my life line, and last chance to get out. But at that time, BRAZIL sounded like REHAB spelled backwards. I had a book to finish! Loft to save.

"When?"
I asked.

"Tomorrow."

"What?
You want me to drop everything,
and just…"

"Yes.
Drop everything.
Before it crushes you."

I blew out a big breath out before I put it gently…

"That's impossible."

"I'll buy you a ticket."
She offered.

"It's more complicated
than that."

"Is it? Explain."

"Ask her for the money to pay the rent."
MES said quietly in my ear.

"No."
I responded.

"Why?"
Asked Bella.

"No not…"
I said before I cutting
myself off.

I took another deep breath, then gave her the Readers Digest version of my situation…

"If I drop everything NOW,
I'll come
home to NOTHING later."

"I think you SHOULD move
out of the Loft."
She told me.

"I may have to.
And that's all the more reason
to stick around and do
damage control."

I didn't go into my pending court date that coming Friday due to the pay or quite notices I missed. Or, the resulting withdraws from the pills that would make traveling with me like carting around a weird fish out of water. Instead, I just asked…

"Who's going?"

"Everybody.
The whole family."

"You're taking the whole gang
on vacation?"

"More,
a soul-searching expedition.
Along with Izabelle and The Girls,
we could all need some
healing right now."

And with that… Harry, Chico Xavier, and Mediums surfaced in mind. It sounded interesting, but I'd rather go to Cassadaga and save time sometime. Times not a most precious recourse, it's the only one. But what didn't surface in my City of Lakes was actually how calculated this exit of Chloe's would be tomorrow after the show. All I had in mind, was curtain time.

By noon *MES* and I were home having soup for lunch which was as close to solid food as I could stomach. I really had to get ready for tonight and stop tripping, but that was too much to ask of myself. Nearing the end of this chapter the fabrics of time and space in the Loft were traditionally patchworked to stitch the Soul of my Scenario to a quilt all his own; each uneven square its own translucent hologram with the clarity of an old radioactive color TV. The pastel building blocks of this somewhat-reality appeared to be held together by dental floss. The Loft never felt so warm as it did in the Brothel of my Mind where a log burned in the fire place and a few laughs and sighs couldn't be contained behind their curtains as *MES* and I finished our bowl near the multiracial stew around us licking the bowl clean with both our tongues.

While digesting… we got our hair pulled by the magic fingers of The One in my Great-Great Grandma's rocking chair, Giovanna the bulldog on my lap, as a CD of precious antiquity spun FAR *The Ghost That Kept Haunting* whiles my eyes was closed. Yet still, I found moving pictures on the back of my lids as if projected through a soaked kaleidoscope similar to the appearance of a tin daguerreotype. With eyes shut I found hardcore readers still squatting in the Jazz Museum Park beyond a hyperspectral Aronofsky *MOTHER*-montage fusing Mardi Gras 2020 with that of Carnival mid 1800's on Barracks Street. Page turners camped in a Cardboard City created by Gondry behind the black steel fence where Shaggy types grouped in drum circles singing everything from The Stones, to Stone Roses. Back inside you know where *BRIGHTDAWN* wild-out making these notes at his Write-Away behind my Phillip Glass*ed-eyes* murmuring…

"Here I come, here I come,
I'm coming soon.

There was no escaping my delusions in the Real World, and nowhere to hide in The City behind my eyes. The only off button was a blackout. But I didn't have time to induce an eclipse on this Fattest of Tuesday's. I was still foolish enough to think a Technicolor Sun rises over the Courier Prime herein would be worth this one way journey to Mars in my mind.

We met at Country Flame on Iberville Street before her Mom and Aunty got there. I brought Joey along to escort her party over to the Club whiles I gave her the salon treatment later, per our plan. My face was covered in purple, green, and gold camouflage to try and hide my guilt and stress behind Holiday war paint. Bella was bursting with excitement constantly looking at texts on her phone and appearing to give a number of emojis in responses. Assuming Bella was managing the Maybe Ladies I stayed out of her business and ordered some apps before Denise and Aunt Samantha arrived. I was very thankful that Joey worked the day shift to be my wingman that night. If *MES* & Joey could have ill communicated they'd have got along like MCA and ADROCK. Truth be known, I was more than ready to shed *MES* once the chemicals receded from my streets. It just so happened that I was nearly out of stock by Mardi Gras. I must have easily snorted four, five thousand pills the last three months.

While Joey was having a Margarita, *MES* couldn't help but be jealous of BL texting away and hustling before our eyes. Her apparent event coordination even ruffled the feathers of Dutch nested on my forehead. Outside her Family… I don't think she had much more than I and her friend Izabelle in Brazil months ago. Now, there she was directing a whole Squad and Housing sex trade refugees in Brazil. And, hours away from doing something I tried to do time and time again since I was youngster… get in, and cash out! And the ripple effect: a movement in the world of casual negotiations between the sexes with *THE MAYBE*. I could never do anything like that with such poise or purpose she acquired during this experience of hers on Bourbon Street; most famous strip in the world.

But this thing with Gaten? That was where I thought she'd be tripped up. Know way in Hell's Kitchen he'd let her walk with a hundred grand or more; NOPE. But she had the guts, or gall, to say she wasn't worried about it at all; fucking phone millennials all woke but not awake to see danger comin'. She was so nonchalant about her deal with Gaten that I got the impression she wasn't even going to try and collect at closing time tomorrow. Tonight, was more about Mom. Yet BL kept texting and bobbing her head to some Latin House Music jamming from the kitchen as the door kept swinging open. I tried to mind my business, but finally I had to asked…

"What-duh-hell you got
cooking BL?"

She squinted her eyes just like I remembered seeing her Grandma Ma do many times when she was getting serious about something. And that, was all I got from her.

"She's working a program Braze."
Joey said with a charming
smile.

"Sure is. She's a Wapper!"
MES added.

I looked at *MES* confused, he then explained…

"Working, A, Program."
A Wapper! Idiot."

"Fuck you."
I said softly blowing *MES* off.

Joey was on my left where *MES* was and thought I was talking to him…

"Fuck me? Fuck you."

"No-no. Not… "
I stopped.
How could I explain?

Old school New York Joey took it as bait and retorted…

"You must be talking to me?"
Joey looked around.

"Oh God, here it comes."
MES anticipated.

"I don't see anyone else here."
Joey said
with a heavy New York
Italian accent.

I handed him the stainless steel napkin dispenser from the middle of the table to look at himself. He continued…

"You talking to me?"

Joey said to his reflection as I got back to my concerns before she mentioned…

"Mom'll be here in a minute.
Samantha's gonna-go
crAzy tonight."

Bella was beside herself! I asked…

"Is Sam going to South America with
the family tomorrow?"

Bella shook her head YES with a grin.

"You could have come too."
She added.

Evidently the whole family was in town for Mardi Gras and ready to jet to Brazil tomorrow morning. But tonight, was girls night. Or, so we thought.

Mom walked in the restaurant first. Then Sam with an open beer in each hand who began grooving to the Latin Rascals from the kitchen. Totally unbeknownst to Aunt Sam and Bell's Mom as of yet, was that they'd see their girl all grownz-up and naked starring on Bourbon later that night! The whole night was planned out as a big surprise just for them. But then, trailing Mom and Aunty came in an unexpected guest… Thorsen came yawning his way through the front door!

"Oh look. Hippy-hooray,"
I said shocked looking over at Bella,
"Gangs all here."

She had nothing to say, ZILCH; and froze up! She was so-so proud of herself up till that moment. But I'm a nice guy, I tried to lighten the mood…

"Its-kewl,
jus-imagine your kidz again
skinny dippin' in

the Redneck Rivera."

MES chimed in,
"Come-On!"
How they do.

Joey & I stood up to greet everyone, BL sat there with her mouth opened, *MES* started humming *In the Air Tonight* by Phil Collins and I must say, I enjoyed the juxtaposition of uncomfortableness between her and I. Though our guests were perplexed by our initial silence, Joey stepped in and introduced himself…

"How ya'll doin?
I'm Joey.
Joey G. Beignets."

He regretted that with the quickness when Sam responded hunk hungry and sexy as possible…

"I'm Sam.
Me and you tonight suga-donut.
Come'on."

Joey laughed, a little; very concerned. But this was getting better and better to me and said so…

"Happy Mardi Gras everyone."

After eats at the Mexican Joint we parted ways out front as good old Joey took our guests, Samantha, Thorsen and guest of honor Bell's Mom Denise, up Iberville and over to Bourbon.

"We'll catch up."
I said to the Gang.
"We have to run to The Palace
and grab a friend."

"What club are we meeting at?"
Denise asked.

"Joey knows where."
I said to her pulling BL away,
"Meet you there!"

Bella, *MES* and I cut down an alley to Canal Street to rush over to The Palace Cafe around the corner. My old lowbrow Graf-Art buddy is the Wine Sommelier there and had arranged a space for me to have some privacy. But Halfway down the alley my Partner in Action stopped in her tracks, and waiting for me to do the same. I turned-round urging…

"Let's do this."

"I don't think I want to
do this now."

I think Thorsen showing up made her think twice.

"NO! No. You can!
Think of your Mom.
And if that's not enough,
think of the finale to
our story."

She looked seriously confused when she asked me…

"Our story?
Or, your story?"

I said it like I see it,
"We're all in this together.
Let's do this."

Although the grandest of parades passed in the background at the end of the alley, the party was long over for us in focus; I knew that. But I didn't play such odds not to win! All I had was my way out of this through this Paperback, and she knew it! But she wasn't convinced she wanted to play her part any longer.

"Do you really believe that this, BRIGHTDAWN,
you're trying so hard to be. Can really
have a positive impact?"

"Maybe,"
said *MES*.

"Perhaps."
I hoped aloud.

"How?"
She asked.

"People who've
gone through similar
things should know they can come out
the other side.
And more importantly,
find their own way to say
enough, is ENOUGH.
Before times-up."

I must have sounded like a PSA with TLC before I added quietly…

"I really…
…I'll never get over not
saving my brother."

Pressure on, she continued on, as scripted.

As Joey Beignets escorted the Family through the madness and into the Rising Sun ~ Bella Lenin and I went inside The Palace Café with no time to waste ~ I carved our way through the thick crowd at the entrance and to the hostess stand with a…

"Good evening,
I'm Braze Scanlan,
I think you'll find us down for
something special."

A moment later we were escorted to the elevator.

When the elevator doors opened on the 3rd floor, I tipped our host with some Mardi Gras doubloons before we stepped onto a vacant floor coated with a layer of sawdust. Not, what one would expect in such an elegant establishment. But, that's why we were there! The 3rd floor was under renovations and closed to the public. When the elevator doors closed behind us, we stood in less light, alone in the dark looking at 3000 or more square feet of space lit by only two construction lights hanging by extension cords in the middle of it. I was drawn towards the glow of street lamps on Canal Street and walked to the windows to stand above floats parading through the sea of fanfare & confetti falling from heaven. Nose to the glass, I found a translucent escalator some-what apparent stretching from the clouds to the sidewalk adding to the spirit(s) of Carnival. Bella surfaced from the darkness behind me and put her nose to the glass too. This would be the last view I shared from on top of my world, with the love of my life. But from the corner of my eyes, I looked towards my soon departing friend knowing I could see this again in my illegal grandiose twisted mind anytime.

From the K&B courier bag I was wearing unfortunately empty of Sacraments I retrieved a keepsake; Whale Brand hair buzzers that once belonged to my brother. As Bella looked down on the Parade, I stepped back into the darkness to salvage a wood chair from a dusty stack. Then made my way to one of those work lamps hanging from the ceiling. I put the chair in the spotlight, plugged in the buzzers above to the extension, and tested out the clippers signaling BL it was time. When she got to the hot seat, she said…

"It's so cold up here."

I nonchalantly pulled out a big cotton winter hat I brought for her. But first I held up the clippers…

"Ready-Freddy?"

She nodded YES. I wasted no time and made a quick pass on the side of her skull. She followed it with a big sigh of relief! Before a breath of courage. Perhaps shaving her head represented a fresh start and not just the flashback I envisioned it would be for her Mom. Bella was probably more than ready to leave this battle field of ours behind with her hair on the floor.

I on the other hand began having thoughts of permanently ending the war with myself. As I shaved her head the crowds outside seemed to roar for more! Each pass of the buzzers was met with louder and more pronounced screams from street side. I sensed her getting stronger for the night ahead while I kept getting weaker in it; withdrawing.

As I shaved her head with my right hand, *MES* had to go behind her back with our left hand for the last couple pills we had stashed. Unless there were some at home that I'd forgotten about somewhere, these where the last two to be had. *MES* discreetly fished for them under the keys in my pocket. When he retrieved them, he dropped one! We watched it fall to the floor and bounce off the pile of hair at my feet. *MES* deflated a little bit, I could really careless. After all, what affect would one or even two pills have on what escalated to a 100 pill a day habit this week? No more than a placebo to a nonbeliever. *MES* looked at the last pill in hand and wondered who would get it. This is the same guy who time and time again crawled on kitchen floors looking for dropped pieces of rock at the end of long weekends, so, I knew where it was going; his mouth.

My last memory of that scene was Bella Lenin standing tall in a half-light at the window, silhouetted by the glow of street lamps outside. Tubes of energy flowed from her skull as if she were the love kitten of Jimmy Hendrix and Medusa. And oh, oh-how I burned for her. The fingers on my left hand below the sleeved arm of miraculous tattoo's via Molecular stigmata began to extended for yards. These more than human fingers stretched to inspect the energy tubes coming out of her braincase. Standing at the window with her back to me, where my fingers crept up behind her, these extended tentacles began to snake through the whirlwind of energy twisting from her skull. Outside, crowds continued in pandemonium as beads floated around weightless in the air within the double consciousness of *MES* and I. Nothing is more deceiving and plays greater tricks on my mind than insomnia and withdraw. Other than some blackouts, I probably hadn't slept in a month while *BRIGHTDAWN* made photographic notes like these for you to read.

Exiting the Palace, we raced up Canal Street together and around the corner to Bourbon as we ducked and weaved through the crowd as if we were racing to catch a Cadillac train. Or running from a farmer after disturbing his cows picking mushrooms! Or, at that moment some other thrill we shared moons ago. We were moving so fast on the same wavelength it was as if *MES* was just being dragged along like a tired child. I so desperately wanted to be alone with her… to run, rage, and fulfill this night alone with her and only her. Yet *MES* was not only a psychological handicap by now, but it seemed as if he were a perpetual appendage.

As I carried *MES* on my back like a Sherpa pack he almost brought me down with his pining for more pills by the time we hit Iberville. His tongue was sky blue and visibly flapping in the wind by his cheek. He chewed that last pill moments ago like a sunflower seed. Any of this alcohol around us could have taken the edge off, but the spoiled brat had me jonezin' too. The Lakes inside were no longer tranquilized but going apocalyptic by then. Multiple heated altercations erupted at once in countless locations between him and *BRIGHTDAWN* where 10,000 Manynard Keenan's mislead traffic at every turn! Every random beat on Bourbon Street street sounded like a violent cymbal being hit right next to my heads! I wasn't going to make it through the night unless I found a fix. This scenario was about to kill me prior to curtain time. I prayed there to be some pills in the pockets of dirty laundry back home somewhere! After all, we'd not done wash for weeks.

Once we made it inside the entrance of The Rising Sun the Star of the evening kissed me on the check and said…

"Thanks.
Make sure Mom's ok?"

I nodded OK. She ran up the grand staircase in the Lobby so not to be seen by her Family while coming in.

Then, I noticed a group of five older Russian characters at the Lobby Bar, they must have been Gaten's cronies. Older well-dressed Gents who gave me the impression that perhaps First Friday VIP's were still in town on this longest of weekends. I didn't sense any trouble they were too cool to give that off. But they did look out of place. Way too refined. Helicopter on the roof kind of players. They were in the company of five expensively dressed multiethnic young women with skin made of silk decades away from a first wrinkle. Yet the young ladies lips were so tight they could have been zipped shut. They weren't even talking to each other. At a closer look, these women looked more like girls and were probably too young to drink maybe.

Perhaps in a groove of synchronicity I noticed a business card on the floor and was compelled to pick it up. On one side were Assessment Questions such as: **Are you in control of your ID? If not, who is? Recruited for one job, doing another? Asked to engage in sexual activity in exchange for something? In control of your money? Can you leave if you want?** On the other side of the card: Sex Trafficking & Labor Trafficking hotlines.

I put it in my pocket and made my way back out the front door before I glanced back inside at those girls. They had to be the only five people together completely silent on the block that night.

Once we made it off Bourbon, I looked at my watch to find it just before 11:00pm, Chloe Brazil was scheduled to dance at Midnight. I thought an hour was more than enough time to run home and search for stray Sacraments before show time. There just had to be some; somewhere. I couldn't have done that whole courier bag full of pills without mismanaging a dozen or more. Besides, if I walked in the club without Bella so early the family would be suspicious, they didn't know what they were in for. I called it in…

"Yo Joey.
Relay a message to the fam."

Inside Joey hung up and explained…

"Braze just said she
got carded at the door.
They got-to go home and get
her ID."

Desperate and disoriented I made it home to Barracks in record time through the craziness because when you got-to get high, you go through people. Yet once I neared the centuries old bricks of our building on Barracks, perhaps my inner City of Lakes played more tricks on me once again. I found the pizza place downstairs was cleaned out. And a raging Ballroom was in swing! All present inside taking part in an 1800's costume theme party, and quite a gala it was.

On the way up the steps to my Loft I found a motley crew of antique dressed people of that same era drinking hooch, getting high with old glass syringes, and even sucking each other off in corners. As I climbed the stairs over empty bottle and other trash, I was dumfounded by one particular character. He wore an old handcrafted hat atop his black Typewriter-Head by lunette window at his back. A raincoat over his suit, in black shoes, a young man was licking his keys. Duran Duran *Wild Boys* played from somewhere. Whatever the source of this collage of space and time, it was apparent once again that my own experiment to rise from the heap and script a sensational novel only had me write off the real world again. Then, old Typewriter head started doing at it like a player piano. Once he finished his short note the young man kissing his keys took the fresh page in hand like any poet for hire on Frenchmen Street before handing the fresh ink to me. It read simply…

Hello Son,
Holding any Viagra?
Cordially,
William

Confronted with this manifestation I looked down to scratch my head, before I noticed a limp fountain pen dangling from his open fly. The young man with him spoke to me directly…

"Erectile
dysfunction pills
are dope."

I immediately washed that thought away with excess neurochemicals and continue up the stairs through decades of party people in Old 424 as the multidimensional space fused with my organic fiber and not-so natural wires. Where others would have surly overdosed in their tracks… I glowed as if I were greased and humping a 3rd rail. Reaching the 3rd floor with a burst of euphoria like any other junky nearing the cop-spot, I was alerted by another official post on the front door about my summoned court date that coming Friday.

When I stepped in my apartment, I found a line of translucent dirt-balls in the Garret waiting to get behind the curtains in the Loft. My somewhat pleasant antique hallucinations of the Brothel my Loft ONCE may have been PRIOR to this night felt much more desperate in my condition at this time. The smacking of skin and the volume of screams from the top of men's lungs to the bottom of women's hearts was enough to make me sick! Had I not been ready to kill for a pill I would not have gone further. I covered my ears to move forward. And dashed right through the dirt-balls to the overflowing laundry basket in the bathroom to shake some good shit out of the pockets; when prayers were answered! Almost each and every pair of pants paid off like a hot slot. Pills bounced like superballs when *MES* cry…

"You my hero bro."

Insane in the membrane for the sacraments I gathered the nearly biblical amount in my hands and went straight to the kitchen on autopilot to crush them proper with the mortar & pestle set. But I should have stayed out of the Loft, because I wasn't ready witness what I did. When suddenly the sounds of suffocation, gagging, and annihilation of a woman drowned out all else in the Brothel. Inside that sectioned off space behind me, I found the bare asses of two men standing over a woman, on her knees, being held like a ragdoll by her hair victimized in sickening acts. It was the most graphic, obscene, and a most agonizing sex that I can't bring myself to describe further. I was even further rattled to my core by a bright FLASH from behind the naked three in front of me. A photographer wearing a dark cloak behind an old camera brought everything to light for a brief second before blowing out the scene completely before my eyes. Those five most silent girls on Bourbon Street came to mind in that FLASH. I stood there alone tortured by my story about others getting tortured.

Rapists gone, victim never heard from again, I turned and crushed the foul medicine with the stone pestle to cope and change my mind the only way at hand. After snorting to what then had to be the last, and final, forty or so Molecular Sacraments known to be left on Earth, my highly accurate radio controlled wrist watch read eleven to midnight! I only had ten minutes till showtime to get back across The Quarter. But on the verge of another great rush, highly possible!

At the Rising Sun Bourbon Street's Chloe Brazil was being assisted like a Broadway Diva in a stage mirror by her Squad in the dressing room.

I busted out of my front door on Barracks like felon from a search warrant behind him.

Chloe's face was being extravagantly made up. Her body glittered, nails airbrushed, and hairpiece sculpted to a work of Wig Art.

I raced like a maniac down Decatur Street through crowds in a pair of old pumas with a fedora in hand as my unzipped leather jacket flapped in the wind along with my hair gone Ancient Alien guy. *MES* was calm, cool and in stride in a pair of Gucci shades just above red and green residue rings around each of his nostril. With just minutes to get there I juked tourist in our path with the intensity of a running back on crack. When someone hit me with a Nerf Football in the numbers, I ran with. Nothing would stop me from seeing my Bella Lenin do her grand Chloe Brazil exit off Bourbon Street. I would let no Mardi Gras stop me! As I duck and weaved ordinary peeps *MES* called it…

"Bust left. Roll right.
Bunny hop them. Side aerial binch!"

I followed his every call to get around party people, freaks, drunks and passed out gutter punks who when they tried to look different in their rags, the more they fit right in. *MES* smiled for photos as I steam rolled forward so fast that people began to sense I was coming and got out the way to cheer us on as we dashed by Jackson Square and past St. Louise Cathedral. Drunks sobered. Dummies got smart. Cops copped out. Nobody wanted a piece of Two Heads in the French Quarter nearing Midnight. At a glance of the wrist, it looked like I had five minutes.

In the Rising Sun a dwarf tuned her violin standing on the piano. Dutch as my witness the atmosphere was gala-galactic where our special party enjoyed front row seating as Samantha was being given an exclusive table dance by my boy Joey; what a pal! He answered my call in the act…

"Yo Bro!
Where you at my dude?"

Blocks away
I ran with the celly to my ear,
"Real close Joey B."

Joey's shirt was unbuttoned and he was on Sam's lap when she rubbed her nose in his hairy chest. He checked his back to see if Thorsen would throw him a life line or something, but nope. A *Love Is A Battlefield* remix spun in the background as Sam nibbled on his nipple, Joey responded…

"Yo Bro.
You owe me Biggie."

I turned left off Royal towards Vieux Carré Pizza, but by the time I got to Bourbon my steamroll came to a sudden stiz-op. A river of people gushed from Canal Street down Bourbon with the energy of a mudslide! I glanced at my watch again and found it three to Midnight. And I was still a block away!

Down the street DJ Crowley was making cuts back and forth on antique turntables when he dropped an intro by way of Liken Park: "Folks we have a very special guest tonight, I'd like to introduce… " Then with his old school skills he dropped *"At your Own Risk"* on time before cutting the music off momentarily sobering the mood. Gaten stepped to the railing upstairs, as Crowley announced through a Daft Punk vocoder…

"Attention, Attention,
All hail the Queen of the Scene.
First Lady of The Maybe.
The Soul, Body and Mind, of
Chloe Brazil."

And with that, began the most mythical exit of a Bourbon Street dancer in recent history; truly cosmic indeed.

Tupac and Biggie came down from the clouds friends again and sat together translucent in VIP with Cristal. Chris Cornell and Chester Bennington shared a tall San Pellegrino in the balcony with Andy Wood to see what the Hell this was all about. Hospitably dwarfs stood on the shoulders of giants everywhere. And Lenin's dear Mom, Denise, she was first row stage center!

It would have been silent at this moment if it were not for the sounds of fire truck sirens from outside. Spellbound himself, DJ Crowley puffed an e-cig to chill a second. There was a calmness in that club, at that moment, in middle of Mardi Gras like that only found in the eye of a storm, before her unseen presence created an electricity in the air that woke the hairs on everyone's arm. Church mouses ran for cover when my Bella Lenin, your Chloe Brazil, the Queen of their Scene… gradually became silhouetted on stage by a soft light. Poised like a statue and introduced further by the hairs of a bow on the strings of a violin, she rose to her toes on point shoes, and back down to 5th position. Bending her knees and appearing to extend four arms gracefully as if she were a Hindu Goddess within a yellow and purple video mapped sacred lotus holding on tightly to the groupie awareness in the Rising Sun while *All Eyes On* were on her.

Down the block I had to watch an Old Testament mass of people come one way from Canal Street, and find a way to go against the current of stampeding people! The grand ceremony of clearing the Street by police force was underway and I did not account prior for this tradition. A river of humans not even Moses himself could part were now between my Love and I. There would be no chance of getting there by thinking smart and going the long way-round. I to *MES*, who read my thoughts.

We then jogged back toward Vieux Carre Pizza for a running start. Turned back around towards Bourbon, and took a breath, before *MES* said…

"Make Vedder jelly."

And with that… I booked towards a parked car on the corner ~ Ran up the bumper and hood ~ Leaped over the heads and eyes that started at me to the middle of the street ~ Twisted in midair to get my back facing the ground ~ And landed on the crowds hands, screaming…

"Up stream sheeple!"

The river of humans below passed me up the street as efficiently as a conveyer belt. I had to reach the Rising Sun before the Cops closed that block ahead! In the distance… dozens of New Orleans Police on Horseback were followed by Fire Tucks that were closing in and creating the human tsunami beneath me! An official procedure that was designed to end Mardi Gras with a show of force. And to let the carnival goers know that the party over and Ash Wednesday has arrived with *the whole of the law*! If the officials reached the front door of the Rising Sun before I got there, I'd miss the last dance by the love of my life.

Inside the Club it was Gogol Bordello drunkenness gone Jane's Addiction high-ritual bringing everyone together in love & lust after Midnight watching Chloe Brazil's groove of the heart! A euphoric climax so pure that substances could not alter ones state any further. Everyone appeared on top of the world singing…

"La-la, La-la,
La-la, La-la-la"

…with their arms around each other swaying or dancing, whiles many including Aunt Samantha had their shirts off. Chloe Brazil turned out newbies and made nudists out of squares as she twirled above them all on a silk trapeze. Her arms extended straight out through the fabric, ankles crossed, she stirred the crowd with the impression of a sexual crucifix before their eyes. Below, Body Building Dwarfs bounced like bottle rockets in Speedo's wearing crowns of thorns. And Mom, front row center to see it experienced glimpses of the show through her daughter's eyes; Denise, she was nearly paralyzed by the extravagance of it all. The strength, glamour, and influence that her daughter exuded that night was enough to bring Mom to tears. She didn't see it coming, but this was in every way her doings.

Outside on the street atop the hands stampeding of drunks wrangled by the cops on horseback, *MES* acquired a sorcerer's hat along the way while a cover band was playing *Crazy Train* in bar as we closed in on the Rising Sun. But-so was the gang of city officials marching our way! Sirens roared and lights flashed while horses moved the masses towards me as I continued to crowd surf up stream. The closer I got to the cops, the worse the situation got below me where people got shoved, pushed, and trampled on. When I got to the front line serendipitously at the door of The Rising Sun, I sunk to my feet through the sea of people just yards away from the police on horseback and in just a movie moment's jump cut, we slipped inside the Club.

Inside, at the center of the creative universe, I found Dwarfs clearing the stage of fanatics so Chloe could come down and take her final bow. When she landed back on her feet from the trapeze, she stepped towards her Mom front row and with a flick of the wrist tossed her sky blue wig towards her. At that point the whole world appeared to stop as the wig continued to slowly float towards Denise who got weak as it approached and fell back in her seat. The wig landed right on her lap! Bringing Denise's own experience nearly working in a strip club when she was Bella Lenin's age in a blinding light just before her own eyes that night as her lovely daughter stood there before her completely bald.

Such connections are priceless and can only go down in one's personal history of what it's all about. Bella Lenin Sparks curtseyed for her Mom, before Chloe Brazil took her final topless bow to the crowd bring a roar through the roof not heard since the Saints won the Superbowl. Gaten, he even gave a rare golf clap from above. I made my way towards the front to finally save Joey from Two-Can Sam. Just before Denise and Thorsen noticed me, I made eye contact with Joey and gestured to him that we split. Sticking around would just cramp Chloe Brazil's style, but Denise noticed me and asked through happy tears…

"You had something to do
with this?"

I shrugged my shoulders and responded,
"I may have connected
some dots."

Then I lured Samantha off Joey with a tall drink I found at an empty seat and we jetted out of there.

Outside, the street was trashed ankle deep in beads and other discarded plastic as cleaners began to pick up after tourists with snow shovels and bulldozers ~ Cops looked at their cell phones ~ Zombies headed back to the grave ~ Joey suggested…

"Go to That
Dungeon for a nightcap?"

"Please?"
MES asked me.

I checked my pockets but knew I had nothing, not a dime. Joey read my body language and didn't hesitate…

"I got you."
He said putting his arms around
our necks.

Just blocks away the doorman waved us in with Joey leading the way. To drink in the Good Old Dungeon is to avoid the sun like no other place. There's no telling what time it is in there. In there it's just you, your drink, and your demons; I could see that in every soul at the bar. The composition of everyone in there displayed the life forces everyone hung on to by a drink.

As I became grounded by alcohol it became more apparent how completely unraveled my world had become chasing the dream of completing this book. There were wires in my head that I had no reason to think would ever reconnect. And sitting there with *M*ES it looked as if it were way too late to possibly place my fractured personalities in order ever again. When I got back out of my City of Lakes with those anxious thoughts, I found Joey next to me nearly asleep getting a neck massage from a girl. Rather than busting their groove, I finished my drink and said softly to him…

"Thank-you-my-buddy.
Thanks for everything.I'm out."

"Anytime.
It's automatic."
He said without opening
his eyes.

"You make me homesick man."
I mentioned to him
before jetting.

"Well…"
He said opening his eyes,
"Maybe you should go
home then."

"I think I've gone to far
to go home."

When I met Bella Lenin seven years prior, I had just began creating a life myself in New Orleans and had more friends coast to coast than I could count. But by the time I walked out Le Dungeon that morning from Joey, I felt like there wasn't another person left on Earth for me to even get a cup of coffee with. In the year that passed I wrote the world off to try and write my way to the top of it. Years prior I often reminded myself I was only a hangover away from attempting suicide again. For the past few months I'd been avoiding this morning because of that. Before I caught up with my Brother, I had one more scene to capture a little later.

So, when it was closing time over at the Rising Sun and Bella would presumably be squaring up with Gaten, Dutch un-nested and flew from his spot in my head upon request as *MES* and I made our way back over towards them. I was still a few blocks away when Dutch made it to Gaten's office window above Bourbon Street and hovered outside. Inside, Gaten was sitting at his desk on a laptop when he got a knock on his office door. He opened it with and old school buzzer because his office was forever secure as cash checking. When Bella walked in Gaten closed his laptop and they got to it…

"Morning Chloe.
How was your Carnival?"

"Chaotic,
but fulfilling."
She said exhaling glad
it was over.

They looked at each other for a beat, before Gaten continued…

"I must admit,
by the end of last summer
I was mesmerized by you
Chloe Brazil."

Bella looked completely unmoved. He continued…

"You're not the same old same old.
Nor are the Ladies you trained for me."

Bella confidently put her hands in the air to signal she really didn't care what he thought, and to get on with it. He nodded and took her direction by going to a book self to retrieve a very large leather-bound hardcover. Only to sit back down at his chair and set the big book on his desk. Then, he pushed it her way…

"There we are miss Brazil."

Bella looked a little hesitant, but went over to see what this was all about. The book was so big she had to pick it up with two hands before she could open it and look inside. Inside it, was out of Dutch's view. But it evidently it satisfied BL with just a glance. She closed the book safe and tried to wrap things up by saying…

"Thank you.
Feels heavy enough."

"Heavy enough."
He reiterated with a smirk.

She turned around to leave with the discipline of a soldier before Gaten commented on her way out…

"Heavy as a Glacier?"

She turned her head back at him briefly perplexed by that random comment while reaching for the door knob with the book safe under her other arm only to find the door was locked. She forgot about having to be buzzed out! Her mistake was followed by a breath to quickly suppressed the stress before she said looking at the knob…

"Door please."

"Before you go, tell me…"
Gaten said,
"This… boyfriend?
Husband of yours?"

I didn't see this coming! But she held it together…

"…Ex."
She clarified.

Before she turned around to find Gaten holding up my 1st Novel; Book Safe GLACIER. Damn! I was so shocked Dutch got blood shot!

"Yes,
he's an author."
Bella responded
calmly.

"He mentions a person
by name in this book, me.
Claiming I have ancient
history with his
now deceased brother."

This blindsided her. And he wasn't finished…

"And you… YOU just by chance
walk into this club
for a job last summer?"

This brought her face to a gushing red! But she responded rationally…

"I can't explain the,
scriptedness of our relationship.
He's half writer, half wacko.
But I can sure as fuck tell you I don't
read his work.
Just living with him was
troubling enough."

Gaten sat there silent, not buying it. He grinded his teeth, clinched his lips. But, surprisingly! She was more than ready for this shit and continued to tell him…

"I don't know
what you're getting at Gaten,
but I have two, armed escorts
waiting for me outside."

Gaten smirked. He had thugs looming. Then, she made things more crystal clear…

"Two escorts armed with badges."

Checkmate, she cornered him ~ *MES* gave me five ~ Bella took out her cell phone that was apparently in the middle of a speaker call during all this and said towards it…

"I'm on my way down."

"I'm waiting."
Came from the speaker in the
recognizably heavy voice
of THE Saint.

"Buzz me out,
Mr. Piter Gaten-Thieves."
She demanded with a
sterile smile.

Gaten decided to have a look for himself first and got up to look out the window. Dutch flew a little higher out of sight. Below on the Street sat an unmarked detective's cop car idling, widows cracked. I then noticed myself on the Job Bob was in the driver's seat and the Piano Man in the passenger's. Bad Ass Bella Lenin continued to say…

"If I don't make it down.
They'll come in.
With, the authority to do so."

"You need us up there Chloe?"
Asked Saint on speaker.
"…Chloe?"

Gaten went back to the desk, and buzzed her out.

"I'm good."
Bella said aloud.

"I'll catch-ya later."
Gaten said with utmost seriousness
as she left.

So-he thought!

As if on que and probably so, Bella's whole crew exited the club at once. Her Maybe Ladies and gang of Hospitality Dwarves rolled out like a presidential security detail around her. The dwarves hopped on their pocket rockets parked on the sidewalk and her Ladies jumped on the back of some of them. Bella kept walking across the street as her Fleet sped off. She got into the Unmarked as it peeled off following in the same direction down Bourbon Street and into a Sunrise that blinded me. Unnoticed, I was as important in this getaway as movie extra. But yet no sooner was the coast clear, then a raid swarmed in with sirens blaring! Marked police cars, paddy wagons, motorcycle cops, and horseback sheriffs with cowboy hats! Even a couple of tricked out Blackhawk ghetto birds came flying down the street playing Ride of the Valkyries by Wagner. With my heart in sudden darkness I froze in my tracks as *MES* read my one thought aloud…

"What-duh-hellz?"

A small army in a convoy of official vehicles came racing down Bourbon Street at full speed before some of the posse came to a skidding stop at the Rising Sun. Others proceeded to race down the street and stop in front of other clubs. Law enforcement broke down the front doors of multiple establishments with battering rams as if it were choreographed for the clubs to go down like dominoes. It appeared almost military in scale. Overhead chopper blades stirred me in its winds just as one of the police horses smacked me to the ground with his ass during a spin maneuver. I don't know if it was the rush of it all from the withdraw or a slight concussion from the fall but I blackout momentarily on the sidewalk.

I woke up spread eagle on the pavement as two junkies scurried away after going through my empty pockets. Choppers still circling overhead. I rolled over on my knees and crawled off Bourbon Street with a couple other hungover stragglers from the night before.

When I got home I found the place just the way I left it; in shambles. The smelly Loft made my stomach turn. How could my Shangri-La turn to such shit, me get eviction notices, but still I had electricity? Feeling abandoned up there I turned on 104.9FM as Ludovico Einaudi's *Ascent* was introduced as I went back in the Enclave to finish that last scene and upload it to the public, but of course the fucking I found internet was down. I just gave up. I mean… I'd never be remembered for such a manic, self-indulgent, desperate piece of binge writing anyway and thus, carried on with my own personal epilogue. When I grabbed my car keys, I noticed Kireka's skateboard and decided to skate over to the Mini parked on the other side of Frenchmen.

GARRET SCENARIO No.2

I threw Kireka's board on the passenger's seat ~ Pealed off opening the sunroof ~ Made to the first red light ~ When a guy flying a sign baited me…

"I bet you can't hit me
with a quarter."

His cardboard sign said the same as him. *M*ES couldn't resist. He showered him with a handful of loose change stored in the driver's side door. This being my last joy ride, I just tried to completely ignored *Mr.M*ES the rest of the way.

The road was open till I made the transition towards the Crescent City Connection Bridge where suddenly traffic came to a sudden crawl ~ Before, coming to a complete stop. With the bridge in sight, I decided to put the car in park and skate the rest of the way up ~ As I pushed through gridlock on Kireka's classic Vision I knew she'd have loved the opportunity herself to skate five stories high through traffic over the CBD. To my left and right were rooftops where the graffiti jarred memories of how playing in areas such as those when I was her age meant everything to me. No kid should be cheated out of a beautiful part of their childhood like she was. Why would a grown man want to be that kind of person in any kid's life. And even worse, his own family.

On autopilot I completely forgot about *M*ES and that in itself was a blessing. My goal was to get to where my brother jumped. But as I got above Tchoupitoulas Street I could see why there was a traffic jam on the bridge. The Police had a roadblock and were checking driver's licenses ahead. Probably a sobriety checks to catch drunks on their way to work the day after Mardi Gras. So, I stopped skating. But, not in time.

It appeared that one of the cops ahead noticed me standing in the middle of the highway and started making his way in my direction. Then a few more cops at the DUI checkpoint followed him. I wasn't scared to jump. But terrified to survive. I made it over the guardrail and noticed my soul evacuate my body leaving me a hallow shell five stories high just before I heard her voice scream…

"Braze!"

…Sending chills down my spine that froze me like an ice sculpture. But I didn't look back. I couldn't. What was she doing here? How did she get here? I wasn't shocked, I was embarrassed! Hot tears steamed on my frozen face before they dripped down and made the fall to the ground I couldn't now, when Lenin continued…

"This is not you,"
She cried out.
Then she continued more composed,
"You know what's better,
is brighter, Brightdawn."

I finally turned around, and found the love of my life with a smile on her face; holding up an envelope.

"I was going to mail it later.
But I'm happy to give it
to you now."

How could I refuse? When I reached out for it, she nearly squeezed me to death; and I was more than OK with that.

"How'd you find me?"
I asked

She laughed through some
tears and said,
"You text me Braze."

"Huh?"

Then I remembered we weren't alone. He was right there under them Gucci's acting stupid. I sucker-punched him! MES came back with a left! Anyone who witnessed what followed must have thought it was a most desperate attempt at self-annihilation.

Cops moved in quick to stop my fit ~ Took me to the ground ~ Rolled me over ~ And kneeled on me while taking my wrists in their hands.

"I'm not resisting!
I'm not resisting!"
I screamed.

"Do you have any weapons on you?"

"No."
I screamed.

"Any needles?"

"No."
I yelled.

After being frisked, they stood me up.

"Any drugs on you?"

"No."
I answered.

"Have you been drinking?"

"Last night.
But I'm not drunk."

When I looked behind me Bella was between the Piano Man and on the Job Bob. Whatever was going on they were in on it. I caught my reflection in a passing car, Mardi-Gras make up was smeared all over my face after tangling with *MES*. There was a little on Bella's face too after our embrace moments ago. It was painfully obvious that it wasn't *MES* I should blame, but whom I should thank for not letting my Mother go through Hell again.

Cuffed and in the hands of authorities *MES* & I gazed at our shoes when a compassionate voice in front of us said…

"I'm going to give you
a choice."

I didn't have the guts to look up. But noticed he had my car keys in his hand before he he continued…

"Come back to the station with us and
take a breathalyzer. Or,
let us take you to the hospital
for help."

I knew without a doubt I would fail a sobriety test. Cocky *MES* looked up and asked Bella…

"That ticket to Brazil still good?"

But of course, no one could hear him but me. I said to my shoes in response to the officers ultimatum…

"What's the hospital going
to do with me."

"Ask you a few questions,
check your heart rate,
give you mental health care options,
cut you lose."

It was jail or the ER. I finally looked up at him straight in the face and told him…

"That's very kind Chief."

Nice guy. He knew I was fucked up, and knew where I wanted to go. He even gave me back Bella's letter by sticking it right in my back pocket. Bella suddenly came over and squeezed me tighter than the handcuffs. The cops eventually separated us with what must have appeared like war paint smeared on our face when she asked me one last time…

"Tell me you love me?
Just tell me that you love me."

"I love you."
I said uncertain of everything else,
but not that.
"I love you Bella."

When I was being led back to the cruiser that would take me to the hospital, she yelled with encouragement…

"Uwe-dey-pur! Uwe-dey-pur!"
She cried out with joy and nearly begged,
"Be kind to the mind!"

But we covered this "Uwedeypur" earlier. I Just couldn't make out what she was saying any more than that.

Once in the car
on the job Bob called it in,
"Domestic dispute, male, 38,
Scanlan, Braze, in custody, 10-96. Copy?"

I've been escorted to the ER a number of times on drugs. But this was the first time I'd ever arrived conscious. I guess I should've given myself some credit; this was progress. But that quick turnaround the Chief promised when I reached the ER… bullshit!

At University Hospital I was handcuffed to a chair. Eventually I was asked the usual questions by a nurse. Questions that I vaguely remember being asked on prior trips to the ER over the years when I was more unresponsive. My focus was not to overreact or complain of anything so as to get released ASAP. I still had that court date on Friday and needed to plea for an extension on the rent. After giving healthy lies in response to those questions about my sorry health at present, I was un-hand cuffed from the chair, and led behind some doors that had to be unlocked before we entered.

Once in a cubicle I was given a blue hospital gown to put on. The nurse waited on the other side of the curtain till I changed clothes, she left with mine in her hands. Then, time began to tick slower; much slower. And all I was left alone with Bella's last words haunting my City of Lakes inside…

"Uwe-dey-pur.
Uwe-dey-pur!"

"What was that she said?"
Asked *MES*.

It hurt so-so much not knowing what she said that I found one million Marlon Brando's skipping down the streets of my City of Lakes ~ cartwheeling on rooftops ~ showcased behind every storefront window dancing and singing what fucking *MES* asked me…

"What was that she said?"

And found one Brando that sung better than the rest on top of a *Light House* balcony on a different note…

"Nothing should hurt
this much."
Said this Brando softly looking down over a
coastline above a beached
Statue of Liberty.

"Just keep your mouth shut.
And your thoughts to yourself in here."
MES advised me.

I knew that, I wasn't crazy. Nonetheless I was held till the City Coroner deemed my mental health crisis stabilized. I was told a visit from her could take up to 72 hours from the time I was admitted. And, it would in my case. I'd miss my court date Friday and was certain to become homeless by the time I'd get released.

But it was inside my mental ward stint that not only did I learn the fate of Gaten, but got the impression that Bella Lenin could have played a big part in his take down. When, the Frenchmen Street Pirate walked in the nut house on day three. He came in screaming something French that got everybody's attention.

Then he went into a long story in English about the bust I witnessed myself on Bourbon Street. Everybody listened as he informed the Cuckoo's playing poker…

"The Feds raided eight Strip Clubs
on Bourbon first thing after Mardi Gras!
Got um on lewd acts.
Imagine that in the Quarter."
He laughed and continued,
"Prostitution, drugs.
They'd narcs in every joint for months.
Made a clean sweep
for whoring, drugging AND, get this…
HUMAN TRAFFICING!
Turns out there was a promotional night at
The Rising Sun importing
and exporting girls."
He said shaking his head,
"…Shit.
Next thing you know…
They'll be a GRAND OPENING for a
Chuck E. Cheese on
Bourbon!"

"True dat! TRUE DAT!"
A couple crazy's laughed back.

The Pirate was more coherent than I was at that time. And just when I thought things couldn't get worse, he landed eyes on ME, and screamed…

"Galesburg!
You owe me a lap dance."
He said with his meth mouth smile
pointing a half-amputated
finger my way.

Later that day I was finally out scrubs, back in my jeans, and at the front desk being released from the hospital that Saturday Morning. There I was given back my belongings that included no more than an empty wallet, and of course Bella's letter that baited me from the edge of the bridge last Wednesday. Just I got to the hospital exit, I was asked from afar…

"Is this yours too?"
A nurse asked holding up my skateboard.

A moment later I skated out of University Hospital finally opening up that letter of Bella's.

I came to a stop under steel awning at the back hospital entrance because it was raining. Inside the envelope was one piece of notebook paper and what seemed to be just a little more… and I emptied the contents to find a thin chain with a foreign coin made in to a charm. At a glance it just appeared to be trinket of some sort, but I put it around my neck without further judgement, and read her very short note…

Dear Braze,

Other than Everything that got between us, there are so many amazing things about you that I would never think of changing. But, keep in mind Brightdawn... we all stand in the same sunlight.

LOVE,

Lenin

And that was it. The last I'd ever hear from Bella Lenin Sparks. I pushed her away and let her go damn it. I don't know where my blame starts, or if it will ever end. But I'm certain when sicko's such as I get unhinged, internal chain reactions occur which CAN result in rampages! That is… when we react outrageously, rather than respond appropriately to the overwhelming issues inside us.

This particular morning when the density in the air lifted higher and higher over my City of Lakes, I felt that internal nuclear reaction coming on when *MES* initiated the meltdown commenting…

"Rather than write her off.
Maybe…
we should have just gone
to Brazil."

I crumbled up the note. Her falling out of love with me was all it took for what came next… me going ballistic! I must have forgot about the trinket around my neck when I skated through the downpour from the nuthouse just another junky addict in a panic back on the street.

Like an active killer sparing no soul in our path we skateboarded through the rain in a tantrum and imagined everything in our crosshairs disintegrating into oblivion! With such powers of intentions as mine the Earth started to shake buildings as gusts of wind pushed us to downhill skier speeds on our board! And such winds in my face only brought back memories of riding freight trains with Bella moons ago stirring even more emotions inside me.

BRIGHTDAWN could do nothing but worry and try and calm me with song in attempts to diminish the storm inside like a mystic chanting to howling winds….

"Go awayyyyyy… go away
Go awayyyyy… go away
Go awayyyyy… go away
Go awayyyyy… go away"

But it was too late. Such feeling just don't-go-way during manic episodes such as this; not without know how. My out of control current state of intentions at this time imploded the Hospital behind us that I felt ratified my homelessness. As it sunk into a swamp in the background I leaned into the turn at Canal Street and headed for the Quarter to wreak more havoc.

Crossing below the 10 freeway my powers of intentions obliterated the overpass leaving cars on it skydiving in both directions. As I pushed on, the winds of travel bent palm trees forward that lined both sides of Canal Street only to whip them back to break in half by the increasing momentum of my destructive desires. Every structure I passed fell to the ground and turned back into the dust they came from! Every building ahead on either side of the street looked like Noguchi stacked-stone sculptures on the verge of collapse in my alternate dimension of destructive psychopathy. If I couldn't be happy with her, or my brother again? Nothing else mattered! Within this postal-frenzy everything West of my skateboard as I stabbed Eastward was blown to smithereens in this moving picture inside my toxic heads where I, and only I, could find beauty in such a breakdown.

Out of breath… my out of control but in focus berserk charge of annihilation leveled out when I finally disintegrated Bourbon Street on my roll! I finally took a breather by grabbing the back of a passing trolley car on Canal to skitch a ride and look back on my tear, when during those breaths it appeared once again that I let intangible thoughts and emotions take their best shot at the world that I thought brought me down. Yet at the same time, in those simple breaths, I let go of my destructive thoughts at that moment. Only to find that where I stopped this apocalyptic rage on society, a cliff was created on Canal where a few drivers going West fell to their deaths at Bourbon before others piled up at the edge, then bring an eerie quietness to the surrounding riot.

Letting go of the trolley I slowed my roll and came to a stop just as the Sun finally came out and shed more light on the chaos my head had those around me weather yet once again. Standing there in the middle of Canal Street in the same sunlight as everybody else, a few doomed cars drove West right into the pile up suddenly pushing more into the abyss off the cliff ~ Police ran West right towards the end of the World ~ I soaked up sunshine with mouth open… sipping, from a drizzling cloud. When *BRIGHTDAWN* silently reminded me at this moment looking into the same Sun we all stand under… that it's reactionary measures to this scale, by people in this state of mind, that undeniably gives society today more reason to update our laws. Sadly, crazy hurt people do crazy things to hurt other innocent people.

Alone, troubled, confused and emerging from such an imaginary rampage in mind… I noticed what could be the greatest deity in all city standing just across from me in the Real World! And oh-what a relief it was that I happened to stop my apocalyptic roll just before I took his holiness out too. The Statue I'm referring to is that of one of the greatest characters ever to be inked honoring one of the best New Orleans stories ever published, sadly, eleven years after its author's unfortunate death by suicide. This being, the statue in the likeness of John Kennedy Toole's Ignatius J. Reilly of *A Confederacy of Dunces* on Canal Street.

Being the center of the storm ourselves, we walked calmly over for a closer look while hell broke loose on the Street where tourist screamed for the love of God ~ Locals blamed the levies ~ And homeless danced at home on the edge of the cliff. Once we got nose to nose with the likeness of Ignatius looking down upon us superciliously in front of the Hyatt, serendipitously… *Crown of Thorns* by Mother Love Bone began playing in the Hotel entrance way, when a familiar voice said…

"Mr. Director?"

…before I found a family of ten or so walking towards us out of the Hotel with my co-worker Myra from the French Market.

"Mr. Director
so good to see you!
Why you so flush?
What happen?"

I suppose I was tongue tied and simply gestured behind me for her to take notice to the destruction of my world. But after looking over my shoulder herself, she surprisingly shrugged it off like it happens all the time. And maybe it does these days! I pointed towards the commotion in the street ~ the news coverage on the scene ~ the choppers blowing the wind franticly. But she just smirked and looked at ease as if everyone on the block were simply over reacting. I was bewildered by her calmness. Then, for the first time, I noticed her openly carrying some heat on her side when she casually extended her arm and had the family take a small step behind her, before continuing…

"This is my
family visiting from India!
Family,
meet Mr. Director."

Everyone behind her waved with smiles and we exchanged pleasantries. Then, Myra took notice to that round charm hanging from my neck that I forgot about and asked me…

"Ehw…
what is this?"

She stepped forward and took the coin in her hand for a closer look and upon examination her eyes widen…

"Udaipur!"
She announced with joy.

"Say what?"
MES Asked.

"Uwe-dey-purr?"
I repeated back fast to her.

"Uw-day-pur."
She slowly repeated to me.

"That's what SHE said."
MES confirmed.

"Silly word."
Said one Brando to another inside me.

"What does it mean?
What's it mean!"
I begged Myra.

"I suppose
it has double meaning."

I waited on edge for more before she continued…

"Udaipur is a City
in Western India known as the
City of Lakes."

"WHAT!"
MES screamed.

"What else?"
I pleaded.

"In India… Uday,
in general,
would translate in English…
to, dawn."

"Brightdawn?"
I asked.

"Yes,"
She laughed,
"Oh-yes. Bright dawn.
It's of course better, to be brighter."

And with that, what moments ago I thought was no more than a trinket, I now found as a treasure!

Perhaps finding some color back in my face Myra and her family said their goodbyes to me…

"See you in The Market
Mr. Director."

…and safely went about their day as things carried on under the police choppers circling the aftermath. My arms bristled with goose bumps at what could have been had we hopped trains in India, rather than honeymoon in Amsterdam. The trajectory of our whole relationship was altered by a coin toss. But of course… further gained momentum by the physical pursuit of those sordid dreams of mine last year on Bourbon Street.

"Damn-my-dudes,"
I said to *BRIGHTDAWN* & *MES*,
"I really, really wish I wasn't
such a dreamer."

BRIGHTDAWN appeared to have nothing more to add at this time. Though *MES* on the other shoulder, he looked around slowly. Nodded his head up and down from the sideline of the earthquake, meltdown, loss of God, and massacre that just took place inside our castle in the sky, and simply put…

"Dreams like this are dangerous."

FADE TO WHITE.

GARRET SCENARIO No. 2

THE END

For Those I Loved
And Those I Hurt Exploring The
"business" of *"wildness"*
Herein

THIS HAS BEEN A WORK OF FICTION

The names, characters, businesses, places, events and incidents in this work are products of the author's imagination and used in a fictitious manner. Any resemblance to people living, dead, or actual events are not true or are coincidental.

UNITED STATES HELPLINES

National Sexual Abuse Helpline
1-800-656-4673

Domestic Violence Helpline
1-800-799-7233

Human Trafficking Helpline
(In more than 200 languages.)
1-888-373-7888

Substance Abuse & Mental Health Services Helpline
1-888-662-HELP (4357)

National Suicide Prevention Lifeline
1-800-273-8255

Safe School Hotline
1-877-903-STOP
Is an anonymous telephone hotline students can use to provide info on a crime.

Stay Strong,

BrightDawn

Your Scenarist in The French Market

YOU CAN STREAM

CURE for the CRASH

THE MOVIE LINK

https://vimeo.com/307842353

THE PASSWORD

Booksafe

Other Scenarios By

BRIAN PAUL BRIGHTDAWN

Including:

Garret Scenario **No.1**

BOOK SAFE GLACIER

How The Rails Became My Rehab

Garret Scenario **No.3**

TWO HEADED BRAZE

The Spiritual Tourist Architect